THE MULESKINNER AND THE KING

J. D. PORTER

Historium Press

THE MULESKINNER
AND THE KING

Copyright © 2025 by
J. D. Porter

This is a work of fiction inspired by historical events and family stories. Names, characters, places, and incidents are products of the author's imagination or are used fictitiously, with some names changed to protect privacy. While certain historical elements are based on true events, the narrative has been fictionalized to explore themes creatively and is not a literal account of history.

PAPERBACK ISBN: 978-1-964700-63-2
EBOOK ISBN: 978-1-964700-64-9

HISTORIUM PRESS
U.S.A.

1

ATLANTA, GEORGIA
THURSDAY, OCTOBER 29, 1936

THE SANTORINI BROTHERS Circus parade turned the corner from Peachtree Street and was marching down the rain-slick hill on Atlanta's Ponce de Leon Avenue when a truck came roaring out of the side street at the Sears Roebuck building. For Tembo the elephant, that appeared to be the last straw. He broke out of line and charged at the truck, which made a skidding right turn and roared off past the baseball stadium and up the hill toward the Ford Motorcar plant.

Ignoring his handler's shouts, the angry elephant lunged toward the curb. Buddy Griffith watched helplessly as a young woman in denim pants, cowboy boots, and a red jacket stepped in front of the elephant's impending collision with a nearby baby carriage. She leaned forward, threw her hat at the elephant, and shouted something that sounded like "No!" or "Whoa!".

Tembo veered aside, knocking a young man to the ground with a slap from his trunk and scattering the shrieking spectators like bowling pins. As the truck sped into the distance, Tembo wheeled around in the middle of the road and faced back toward the other elephants. He lowered his head and fanned his ears, ready to charge at anyone else foolish enough to get in his way.

Circus elephants were taught from a young age to walk holding the tail of the elephant in front of them. Reliable old females typically led the procession, and two handlers walked at their left side. For the Santorini Brothers, lead handler Max Winston led the procession while Buddy Griffith, his assistant, had been trying to manage Tembo with calming words of reassurance, gentle tugs on his ear, and the occasional smack with the blunt end of his bullhook. Each man was armed with a stout, three-foot long stick capped with a metal spike for prodding and curved hook for pulling.

Buddy took a step forward, but the elephant backed up and lowered his head again.

Max caught Buddy's arm and said, "Take it easy. He's scared. No telling what he might do."

As he faced Tembo, Buddy heard Max behind him commanding the other elephants to "Come in line!" He couldn't help but glance at the people on the sidewalk, his eye drawn to the lady in the red coat whose hat lay flattened in the road.

This was Tembo's first time in Atlanta, and he had been agitated for most of the route—trumpeting, prancing, and threatening to break out of line. Atlanta's parade was one of the most difficult on the circuit. Not only was it one of the longest, but it had the greatest volume of motorized cars, trucks, and cycles of any parade route they covered, and Atlanta's police department seemed to have little control over the chaos.

A hush settled over the crowded, windswept street corner as Buddy and Tembo faced each other, ten paces apart like a couple of gunslingers. Folks reassembled at the edge of the road with shuffling feet and nervous chatter.

"That was fun," a child exclaimed, as though this was part of the act.

Buddy knew this was no act. He could hear Tembo's warning—a low rumble that reverberated like distant thunder.

The spectators grew still as Buddy eased forward, trying to move with confidence and authority while his heart thumped with apprehension. He heard one of the elephants drop some hay-infused manure onto the pavement behind him, and was oddly calmed by its familiar, tangy aroma.

Tembo swayed from side to side and raised his head slightly but showed no sign of backing down. Buddy had to make the first move despite knowing that an angry elephant could easily crush him.

More than a dozen years ago, when he'd worked with the baggage stock—the horses and mules that pulled the circus wagons—on another circus, he watched an elephant named Rosita go berserk. He never knew what had set her off, but when he heard Rosita trumpeting and the circus hands shouting, he turned in time to see a man running for his life with Rosita hot on his heels. The man dove under a wagon, but Rosita turned it over and stomped him into the mud. Before he died, the man's screams had been pitiful to hear.

Buddy tamped down this terrifying memory as he looked Tembo in the eye. The elephant grew still. Buddy took a deep breath and willed everything around him to fade into the background. A fly landed on Buddy's nose, but he resisted the urge to swat it away. Somewhere in the distance a motor hummed, and the remnants of last night's rain dripped onto a nearby metal drum.

Tembo's large, brown eyes watched Buddy carefully. Buddy kept his hands at his side, his posture erect, and maintained the elephant's gaze.

"Whoa," Buddy crooned—his voice steady, his tone deep and smooth, hoping to calm both himself and the elephant. "Tembo, steady."

He took one step—and when the elephant didn't respond, another step, then another. He walked slowly up to the animal and placed his left hand on Tembo's forehead. Touching the elephant was electrifying. This beast was powerful enough to squash a person like a pinched grape. But in that moment, Buddy could feel Tembo lean into him and relax as if he was relieved to have Buddy tell him what to do. Buddy knew the elephant was ready to follow him back to the line.

Buddy rubbed Tembo's forehead and wheeled around, placed his bullhook behind the elephant's front leg, and gave a firm command, "Move up."

When Tembo responded, the crowd along the sidewalk erupted in applause. Buddy moved him back into line and waited for Max to tell the elephants to tail-up. But before they could move, the woman in the red coat emerged from the edge of the road and retrieved her hat.

She was a beauty—tall and slender with short black hair, dark eyes, and bronze skin.

As she walked toward him, Buddy expected a complaint about the incident, but she just said, "Your elephant lost this." She held out a short piece of chain. It was one of the ankle bracelets Tembo wore on his front legs.

Buddy took the chain from the woman. "You're lucky," he said with a bit of an edge. "That elephant could have killed you."

Before she could reply, the circus master in his white hat and white costume, and atop his white horse rode up from farther back in the line.

"What's going on here?" Jackson "Smokey" Walters demanded. "Why have we stopped?"

"We had a little problem, Boss," Max said. "But we're ready to go now."

Smokey glanced at the woman, who was walking back to the sidewalk, then at Max and Buddy.

"Well get this god-damned show on the road," he growled and wheeled his horse back to take his place at the end of the parade.

Buddy was relieved to see the perpetually angry little man go. With the elephants lined up on-tails and Max in the lead, Buddy moved to Tembo's side.

Max looked over his shoulder and gave the booming command for all of the elephants to "Go on away." As the elephants stepped forward, Buddy glanced at the woman. He felt a flutter of recognition. He had a sister who would be about her age, but it was clearly not her. The woman's face and mannerisms were vaguely familiar, and he had the uneasy feeling that she was somehow connected to his past—a past he had joined the circus to forget.

***

Buddy was worn out after the parade and the two o'clock show. He sipped his coffee and watched Tembo eating hay on the picket line—a long chain to which each elephant was fastened with a short leg chain.

They were tethered in such a way that they could move around and lie down but not run away.

After many years of working with mules and draft horses, Buddy was fascinated by these creatures. In spite of their obvious physical differences, he thought elephants were similar to horses and mules in many ways. They liked physical contact in the form of brushing, rubbing, and patting. They accepted affection and returned it in some measure. They were smart enough to learn commands and seemed to enjoy working with humans when needed. But they could turn on their human companions with sudden unexpected fury, kicking, biting, or—in the case of elephants—stomping a person into oblivion. That was where elephants were unique. They brought a lethal sense of danger to the relationship that helped Buddy forget his troubles.

Tembo wrapped the end of his trunk around a chunk of hay. He then deliberately shook it, folded it, and tapped it on the ground to help roll it into a stalk about the size of a man's arm. In one smooth, graceful motion he curled his trunk inward and up into his mouth, where the hay disappeared. As he chewed, he swayed and looked around for a moment before he repeated the process.

Buddy felt kinship with Tembo. He wondered if the animal had things in his past he would like to forget, too. A light breeze began to flap the canvas overhead. He leaned back on the haybales, placed the coffee cup on the ground, and closed his eyes—reveling in the clear, cool afternoon. He wasn't sure where Max was, but the Highland Avenue circus grounds were relatively quiet, so he might have time for a short nap before they had to get ready for the evening show.

Children's voices caught his attention, and he looked up with one eye open. The circus grounds were not fenced and were never really closed to the public. Four young boys had emerged from between the tents and stood before the picket line. They bore watching, Buddy knew, not because they were Negroes but because they were *boys*. He had seen it before. One of them might pick up a rock, look at his companions, and toss it at one of the elephants.

He eased up into a sitting position, ready to run them off. The boys pointed and grinned but made no moves toward mischief. Buddy was mildly surprised, but he reflected on the differences he had seen in the people he encountered as the circus moved around the country —rural people, city people, whites, blacks. People who attended the circus could be different in appearance, but similar in other ways.

But within the circus, people were generally treated as equals no matter their background. Everybody, it seemed, was running away from their past and nobody felt the need to judge anyone else. So, he had no particular concern for these boys, especially considering the circus ground was located in a colored neighborhood.

He was about to recline back onto the hay when another person emerged from between the tents and joined the boys. The woman from the morning parade had shed her red jacket and her hat, but she was unmistakable in her denim pants and cowboy boots. She ambled up to the boys and placed her hand on the shoulder of the youngest one. Buddy couldn't hear what she was saying but as she pointed, she appeared to be explaining something about the elephants.

He leaned up and studied her. Something about her drew his attention. He could certainly appreciate a beautiful woman and even thought about walking over to introduce himself. But something else intrigued him. As he was considering this, she turned and summoned the boys to follow her. They filed back between the tents, crossed the railroad tracks, and disappeared into the neighborhood.

Buddy lay back again and closed his eyes. Sleep was a reluctant companion, one that often needed coaxing with alcohol. The Great War had left him haunted by images of dead men and dead horses, but the horses were the source of his nightmares and his bouts of depression—horses that died of disease and starvation; horses that were euthanized due to battle wounds, shell shock, and respiratory distress from poison gas; and the horses that were left behind after the war came to an end.

His curiosity about the familiar woman and his desire to learn more about her finally allowed him to relax. But soon after he drifted off to sleep, he was pulled back by the most dreaded word in any circus. Someone was shouting, "Fire!"

The word frightened all experienced circus hands—from performers and roustabouts to ringmasters and owners. Fire could strike at any time and with deadly consequences to people and animals. That's why Buddy bolted upright. Since it was not during a performance or when people were supposed to be on the grounds, his first responsibility was to the animals.

He and Max converged on the elephant picket line with their bullhooks and began to soothe the animals, rubbing their heads and talking to them in calm, reassuring tones. People were running back and forth, and the animals knew something was amiss with the smell of smoke in the air, but they were not especially agitated. If there was a fire, it was not visible to them.

"Look over there," Max said. He was pointing at the plume of smoke blackening the clear, blue sky to the west.

"We don't have anything over there, do we?" Buddy asked anxiously.

Max thought for a moment. "That's the edge of the circus grounds. The only thing over there is houses."

Buddy and Max put fresh hay down for the elephants, and when the animals began to eat, they moved toward the smoke and found a vantage point to see its source. The house was across the street and well away from the circus, but it was a large house with wooden siding, a wide porch, and an air of abandonment about it. The fire department was pulling up and the fire was unlikely to affect the circus, but it stirred Buddy. He wanted to watch it for a while.

"I'm going to check on Amos and the baggage stock," Buddy said.

"Fine," Max replied. "I'll stick around here."

Buddy walked between the tents toward the edge of the circus grounds and found Amos Driesbach standing outside his tent watching the fire.

"How are your animals holding up?" Buddy asked without taking his eyes off the spectacle.

"What do you think?" Amos replied testily. "They can smell the smoke, so they're not too happy."

Amos was a distant cousin of Buddy's ex-wife—a stocky young man who grew up working with performing horses but got himself into some kind of trouble. Buddy wondered if he had angered someone with his short temper or he had hurt someone with his quick fists, but he never asked. He convinced Smokey to hire Amos a few months ago.

The house was fully engulfed, and nobody was going to put the fire out, but firemen had pulled heavy canvas hoses from their red, open-cab pumper truck and were spraying water on the lawn to keep it from spreading. Sparks and embers floated into the cloudless sky above the acrid smell of burning furniture, fabric, and other manmade materials.

The circus hands lost interest and moved back to their duties, but residents of the nearby houses were still arriving. Some of the boys he had seen earlier trotted up the road carrying baseball bats and gloves. He hoped the woman he had seen them leave with might show up as well, but they were surrounded by older boys and young men. They were covered in grass stains, sweat, and red dirt. The smoke must have drawn them from some sandlot baseball game.

"I wonder how it started," Buddy mused. He turned to Amos and asked, "Did you see anything?" But Amos had already gone back into the tent.

Buddy glanced after Amos and returned his attention toward the fire. He should have been relieved that it would have no effect on the circus, but he was remembering another fire. He was just a teenager when the Dotson mansion burned to the ground less than a hundred yards from where he lived with his father and sister. Buddy hadn't thought about that fire in decades, even though it changed the trajectory of his life.

2

TO LOOK AT HIM, one would never know that Buddy Griffith had a splitting headache and felt like throwing up. He studied his breakfast as he pushed it around the plate and didn't look up when Max joined him. Over the years, he had become adept at hiding both being so drunk he could barely walk, and the resulting hangover.

Last night, Tembo acted up on his way into the ring in a repeat of what had happened during yesterday's parade. Smokey was furious, threatening cruel actions on the elephant. Even the threat of such cruelty could set Buddy off. Witnessing the fire didn't help his mood, so he got drunk after the show. He was paying the price this morning.

"What do you think Smokey is going to do today?" Buddy asked as he scratched the stubble on his chin.

Before Max could answer, Amos sat down with a plate of eggs and a cup of coffee. "The police found something in the ashes of that house," he said.

"What was it?" asked Buddy.

"The truck parked out there had *Coroner* written on it."

Someone banged a pot with a large metal spoon, causing Buddy's ears to ring and his head to throb worse than it already was. All eyes turned to the entrance of the cook tent.

"Listen-up here!" Smokey yelled.

The little circus manager was flanked by an equally short, middle-aged, birdlike man in a business suit, and a hulking police officer with close-cropped hair wearing a blue, wool uniform.

When the breakfast crowd grew silent, Smokey continued. "The police have found a body in the house that burned down yesterday, and they want to interview anybody who might have seen anything."

Circus people were, by nature, a suspicious lot. The only sounds in the tent were the clinking of silverware on plates as some people continued to eat. Buddy knew that nobody was likely to raise a hand.

"I'm Detective Ray Stockton," the short man in the suit began. He pointed to the uniformed officer and continued, "This is Sergeant Rocker. We're going to be moving around your grounds today along with some other officers. We're not looking to cause you any problems. We just want to know if you saw anyone coming or going yesterday or if you might know if anyone is missing."

The detective was from the North. Buddy couldn't place the accent. It was subtle, maybe Boston or New York. The officer in uniform didn't speak. Buddy didn't like the way he looked around the room with his round, freckled face, and his small close-set eyes. He gripped his nightstick like he couldn't wait to use it on someone.

Smokey left and the two policemen moved to the table nearest the door.

"The body must be someone from town," Max said as they watched Amos duck out of the back of the tent. "If it was one of us, we'd have noticed somebody missing."

"Maybe," said Buddy. "Unless one of us has something to hide."

"Who has something to hide?" Smokey said from behind them. He must have circled around the outside of the tent.

"Jesus, Smokey," said Max. "You scared the shit out of me."

"Have you two sorted out that elephant yet?" Smokey was standing with someone Buddy had not seen before, and he made no effort to introduce his companion. The stranger was middle aged and balding. His pudgy build and pasty complexion gave him the look of someone who had spent much of his life in clown makeup.

"Tembo's fine," said Buddy. "He's just nervous in these new surroundings."

"He's not fine," said Smokey. "And if you don't sort him out, I will. I'm not a bull-man but I've been around the circus all my life. Real elephant men would have already taken a stick to that animal. Teach him who's boss or he'll keep pulling that shit and somebody will get hurt—or worse."

"Now Smokey," his companion said. "I'm sure these gentlemen have it under control. I'm Wayne Kasinski," he continued, extending his hand. "Folks call me Kaz. Smokey and I go way back."

Smokey ignored his smarmy companion and turned to leave.

As the two men walked away, Buddy asked, "Does he really expect us to beat Tembo with a stick?"

Max got up and grabbed his tray. Buddy caught up and as they dumped their trays and walked back to the elephant yard he asked again, "What does he expect us to do?"

"How long were you with that other show? You must have seen them break down a rogue bull or a raw punk," Max said.

"I got picked up by the Mason and Barnes Circus right after I mustered out of the army in May of nineteen," Buddy said. "But I only ever worked with the horses and mules. The only elephants I ever saw with them were ones that did what they were told." He didn't mention the one he saw go berserk.

Max sighed and glanced at Buddy as they kept walking. Max was a broad-chested bear of a man, probably in his mid-fifties, but Buddy had to step lively to keep up.

"When elephants are brought in from the wild, they're orphans that don't know anything," Max explained. "They're 'punks' that have to be broken and taught to mind us. Trainers have different methods, but the most common is to tie their legs to four stakes so they can't go anywhere and teach them commands. When they respond they get rewarded. When they don't, they get punished."

"Punished how?" Buddy asked.

"Beaten," Max replied. "For most of 'em, they figure it out pretty quick. But the stubborn ones are a bit slower and need more persuasion."

Buddy thought for a moment and said, "I guess that's why they're afraid of the bullhook."

"That's right. That bullhook we carry and smack them with doesn't hurt them. See that man over there?" Max was pointing to a man who was walking across the circus grounds with a little boy. "If that kid acts up, chances are dad just has to swat the kid on the behind and he'll straighten up."

"And if he doesn't listen, the belt comes off," said Buddy.

"Right," said Max. "The belt comes off."

Buddy and Max stopped as they entered the elephant yard. Buddy walked up to Tembo, patted him on the forehead and asked, "How do you take a belt to an 8,000-pound animal?"

Max moved to join them and said, "Getting his attention won't be easy. Smokey will probably treat him like he was a punk—chain his legs and beat the shit out of him with an iron pipe or a metal tent stake. Some guys enjoy hurting big creatures like this." Max was holding Tembo's ear.

"We can't let him do that," Buddy said.

"We don't have any choice," Max said. "He's the boss. He can do what he likes."

As Buddy recalled the cruelty to animals he had witnessed during the war, a profound sadness enveloped him. He could feel it in his chest, and he was powerless to stop its advance. A feeling of emptiness, of death, and of failure. He knew he would work his way through it, but it would be like pushing through a muddy battlefield, stepping over bodies and bombs as he went. But maybe this time would be different. Maybe this time he could fight back. It wouldn't be the first time he had resorted to extreme measures to save an animal.

***

"Do you know who it was?" Buddy asked.

"It's probably a woman," the detective said. "We found some fabric from a dress. That's all we know at the moment. We don't know if she was young or old, black or white."

The two policemen arrived at the elephant area after lunch. Max and Buddy were getting the animals washed for the two o'clock show but paused to answer questions.

"So," Detective Stockton continued. "Did either of you see anything yesterday?"

"I barely saw the fire," said Max. "I walked over with Buddy but only watched it for a minute."

Buddy's imagination conjured the woman in the red jacket, who was not in the crowd at the fire. "I stayed over there for a while," Buddy said. "I watched it with Amos Driesbach, the man who manages the horses."

"Did he—"

The detective's question was cut short by a grunt and a thud. The three men turned to see Sergeant Rocker lying on the ground in front of Tembo. As they rushed to him, the sergeant pushed up on his elbows with a grin.

"That son of a bitch packs quite a punch," he said as he got up.

They helped him to his feet and Max said, "What are you doing over here? That elephant could have killed you."

"He just smacked me with his trunk," the sergeant laughed. "I've been hit harder than that in the ring."

"Rocker," said Stockton. "We're supposed to be questioning witnesses, not messing with the animals."

As the big sergeant got up and brushed himself off, the detective turned back to Buddy and Max. "Sorry about that," he said. "Have there been any unusual happenings around here? Any fights or disagreements? Any strange people hanging around?"

Buddy thought about the young boys and their lovely companion but decided not to say anything. They had been nowhere near the fire until well after it had started.

"We're a tight-knit community, here," Max said. "Everybody knows everybody. We have our disagreements from time to time, but we'd know if anybody was missing."

"It must be someone from the city," Buddy said, continuing the thought.

"That doesn't mean you lot weren't involved," said Sergeant Rocker.

Buddy sensed that the sergeant liked to provoke trouble. Detective Stockton gave the sergeant a disapproving glance and asked, "Where can we find the horse guy?" He consulted his notes and continued, "Amos Driesbach?"

"I'll take you over there," said Buddy.

As they emerged into the open field opposite the fire and approached Amos's tent, Sergeant Rocker observed, "He sure had a good view of the fire."

"Amos," Buddy called from outside the tent. "The police are here to ask you some questions." He ducked inside and looked around. The horses and mules were in a corral at the far end of the large tent. Amos's cot was just inside the opening of the tent to the right and his worktable was to the left. Buddy glanced around the empty space and when he emerged from the tent, he saw that Smokey had arrived.

"This circus isn't going anywhere," Stockton told Smokey.

"How long do you expect us to sit here?" Smokey asked.

"Until we figure out who killed the woman in the house."

"How do you know she was even murdered?" asked Smokey.

"That's none of your business," said the sergeant from the sideline.

Stockton and Smokey stood toe to toe like two boys in a schoolyard, their fists balled, and voices raised. Buddy wondered how Smokey thought he could pull up stakes and leave town under the circumstances. The fire had occurred across the street from the circus grounds and circus hands were no less likely to be involved than people from the neighborhood.

Max pulled Buddy aside and said quietly, "We need to get back and feed the animals before the show."

"I don't know who killed the girl," Smokey said to the detective, "But I have an idea who might have set that fire. Why don't you start with the kids who have been hanging around the yard since we pulled into town. I knew they were trouble the minute I saw 'em."

"We'll need a description," Stockton said.

"How can I describe 'em?" Smokey complained. "They all look alike to me."

Buddy and Max walked back to the elephant area, but as he began his chores of hauling hay and shoveling manure, Buddy recalled watching the fire with Amos and seeing the young boys show up to watch. They were carrying baseball gloves and surrounded by other players.

He jammed his pitchfork into the pile of hay and said, "Max, those boys had nothing to do with that fire."

Max parked his wheelbarrow full of elephant dung and looked at Buddy expectantly.

"I need to go warn their parents that Smokey is sending the police in their direction."

"Warn their parents," Max said, "Or warn that brunette who looks after them?"

When Buddy hesitated, Max continued. "I may be old," he said with a laugh, "But I'm not blind."

Buddy laughed back. "Look at me," he leaned on his pitchfork and patted his stomach. "She's not likely to be interested in the likes of me."

"I won't argue with that. So, why are you so interested?"

"I'm not sure. I just can't put her out of my mind. There's something familiar about her." Buddy loaded the last fork-full of manure into Max's wheelbarrow and said, "I'm going to skip dinner this evening and see if I can find them."

"Fine," said Max. As Buddy turned to go, Max said to his back, "Better be careful out there. They might not welcome you into their neighborhood."

Buddy waved his acknowledgement. He had spent time in Atlanta years ago playing baseball for the Atlanta Crackers, so it was not unfamiliar territory. But he would carry his bullhook just in case.

***

Buddy pulled his flat cap low to block the setting sun from his eyes as he crossed the railroad tracks and walked south and west. He turned right at Edgewood Avenue, walked a few blocks dodging heavy traffic, and turned right again into a quiet neighborhood. The area, he knew from the people who watched the parade, was predominantly colored. He figured there must be a field nearby where people played baseball. But as he walked, he realized he must look lost as he wandered down the street, looking down side streets. He was about to give up and turn back when he found what he was looking for. A bunch of men were playing baseball in an empty lot across the street at the intersection of Auburn Avenue and a street named simply, "Boulevard."

He leaned against the wall of the two-story red brick fire station on the corner and wondered about his next move. The dirt ballfield had been worn into the grassy lot from years of play. The three bases were half-filled feed sacks, home plate was a rusty metal plate nailed into the ground, and the pitcher's mound wasn't a mound at all.

The players were of various ages—teenagers, young men, and a few in the outfield who looked like they might be too old to chase down a fly ball. And on the sidelines—too young to play in this game —were the boys he had seen looking at his elephants. They wore their gloves and were tossing a baseball. He sat on the curb across from the fire station to watch.

His baseball career began on a sandlot just like this one. He wondered how many of these boys dreamed of making it to the Negro

League. He had run away from home to play professional baseball but look where he was now—shoveling elephant manure in a travelling circus.

The young pitcher went into his wind-up and delivered what looked like a pretty good curve ball, but the batter wasn't fooled. Buddy watched the ball sail over the outfielder as the pitcher dropped his head, and the batter began his jog around the bases. Twenty years ago, Buddy was that young pitcher.

3

THE CRACK OF THE BAT sounded like a rifle-shot in the nearly empty stadium. Buddy turned, looked over his right shoulder, and watched the ball sail out of the park. It was a grand slam—hit by the opposing pitcher, no less. As the runners loped around the bases, Buddy looked toward the dugout where, sure enough, his manager was ambling out to the mound.

"What wrong with you, Griffith? Spangler's the worst hitter on their team, maybe the worst hitter in the league." The manager of the Reds, or "skipper" as the players called him, was Christy Mathewson. He had recently retired as a player and had only been with the Reds for a few weeks, but he'd had a legendary career with the New York Giants. He made Buddy uncomfortable because, while Buddy served up a home run to one of the worst hitters on the opposing team, Mathewson was also a pitcher who had won nearly four-hundred games for the Giants and had helped them win the World Series a decade ago.

"I don't know, Skip." Buddy raised his pitching arm. "I guess my shoulder is a little sore."

Mathewson just held out his hand. Buddy carefully avoided looking his manager in the eye as he handed him the game ball and shuffled toward the dugout.

Redland Field was only a few years old, one of several steel and concrete parks around the league. The boomerang-shaped, red brick structure featured a covered double-decked grandstand that wrapped around home plate and extended about thirty feet past both first base and third base. With so few people in attendance that afternoon, the person Buddy was looking for should have been easy to spot in the first few rows. He didn't know whether to be disappointed or relieved that the man wasn't there.

***

"You in, Kid?"

"What? Yeah." Buddy stubbed out his cigarette, finished his last swallow of bourbon, and pushed all his chips to the center of the table. "Call," he said.

Murphy's Restaurant and Pool Hall was across Findlay Street and up Western Avenue, a few blocks east of the ballpark. It was a favorite haunt of the players who did not have other jobs or families to go home to after home games.

Big Bill Leonard, the only other player left in the game, slowly laid down a full house and said, "Kings over threes," with a grin.

"Screw you, Bill." Buddy threw his cards face down on the table and pushed his chair back.

He weaved his way to the bar, where a couple of outfielders stood watching the card game. He turned his back to the bar and looked around the quiet room as the alcohol in his system dredged up memories of how he had come to be here.

Buddy had spent a year in the minors with the Atlanta Crackers before being called up and having two good years as a major league pitcher; but now in his fourth year of professional baseball he was, at best, a mediocre pitcher. Playing pro ball with the Cincinnati Reds had given him quite a ride. His short career had taken him to play against teams in New York and Philadelphia in the East, Chicago and St. Louis in the West. It had meant overnight train rides, cheap hotels, and poker games to kill the long hours between games. He'd had his first hooker in Brooklyn—a dark-eyed, dishwater blond with small breasts and wide hips who could ride a man all night. With a young Buddy, it had been a quick erection and even quicker climax.

He had started chewing tobacco and smoking cigarettes as soon as he left home. The chew kept him going during the games and the smokes filled the time in between. The veteran players in Atlanta taught him how to fill the little papers from a tobacco pouch and carefully roll them into a cylinder. Now he preferred the ease of pre-packaged cigarettes. He liked Camels because they tasted milder. Cigarettes calmed his nerves and made him feel grown up at the beginning of his career, which was important when everybody was calling him "Kid." He got along well with most of his teammates because he didn't take shit from any of them.

When he finally learned how to throw an off-speed pitch and a curveball to go with his blazing fast ball, he was called up to Cincinnati and encountered his last vice, bourbon, that elixir from across the river in Kentucky. It fueled the late-night poker games and the gambling habit that cost him every penny he earned.

"Hank," whispered Buddy, trying not to sound as drunk as he was. "Loan me a few bucks, so I can get back in."

"Sorry, Kid. Tapped out."

"Jimmy," Buddy pleaded.

But Jimmy just shook his head.

"Looks like your luck's run out," said Hank. "Why don't you go on home?"

Buddy looked at his so-called friends. He looked around the room and thought about saying something, something like "screw all of you." but he didn't. He just staggered to the door and slammed it on his way out.

***

The night air felt warm and thick, but it helped Buddy sober up as he weaved his way home. It was just after ten at the end of a rotten day, but at least Lucy would still be up. He didn't want her to know how drunk he was. He drank too much, gambled too much, and forgot his troubles by having too much sex. And now, worst of all, he was making money to fuel his gambling by deliberately losing baseball games. It was as though he had fallen into a well and couldn't seem to claw his way out.

As he approached his door, he took a deep breath, smoothed back his thick dark hair, and put on his most charming smile. He was not, he knew, handsome. But, for some reason, Lucy found him irresistible.

"Where have you been?" she said with a hint of anger when he walked in.

He had his work cut out for him. He put his hands on her hips, but she pulled away.

"Come on, baby," he crooned. "I was out with the guys. They're still at Murphy's, but I came home early to be with you." He reached out again and firmly pulled her in this time. When his lips touched hers, he felt her melt in his arms.

Lucy Bello was one of the few women he had been with who had never, as far as he knew, been a prostitute. Buddy had met her when he'd been invited to a dinner at the Italian American Club. She worked there as a waitress. She wasn't pretty, at least not in the classic sense. Her nose was a bit too large for her face. But she made up for it in personality—and in other ways.

Buddy lowered his hands to her back and tried to pull her against him, but she placed both hands on his chest.

"Don't," she said weakly. "I'm tired." She did not pull away completely, but she did turn her head. "What's going on with you? You stay out all hours. I never know when you're coming home."

"Nothing's going on," he lied. "I'm just going through a rough patch. I'm going to get it together when I pitch in St. Louis, I swear."

He continued to hold her, unsure of what to say next. He was in serious trouble, and she sensed it. He almost let her go, when she moved back in and kissed him.

"I love you," she said. She took a step back, but this time she was pulling him toward the bedroom.

***

Running on the pavement made his headache worse, but he was late for the train to Chicago. The Reds had a three-game series with the Cubs and Buddy was meeting Cyril Dotson in Chicago to get paid. He had made up his mind to tell Dotson he was out. He wasn't going to throw any more games. He would take the money for what he had already done, since he needed the cash, but it was over. Throwing a game, then facing his skipper—especially a legendary pitcher like Christy Mathewson—on the mound was more than his conscience could stand.

His relief at seeing the train still in the station faded when he saw the skipper pacing the platform with a watch in his hand and a concerned look on his face. He made for Buddy as soon as he saw him, but Buddy ducked into the last car on the train, tossed his suitcase in the overhead rack, and found an empty seat next to an elderly lady in a gray dress with matching bonnet.

"Beautiful day, isn't it?" he said with his most charming smile.

She gave him a grumpy, side-long glance and returned to the book in her lap. Buddy kept his smile as the skipper made his way down the aisle. When he saw the old lady, he just glared at Buddy for a second and kept walking.

Buddy had hoped to catch up on his sleep during the train ride, but when he pulled his cap over his eyes his mind raced. Cyril Dotson would not be pleased when Buddy told him he was backing out. And Lucy—what was he going to do about her? He had feelings for her, but love wasn't one of them. He wasn't ready for that kind of commitment. When the train pulled into Chicago, Buddy was out of his seat before it stopped, snatching his suitcase from the overhead rack and knocking down a man's brown fedora in the process. He picked it up, attempted to straighten the crease he had caused, and handed it to the man two seats behind him with a mumbled apology.

Buddy had to move quickly—off the train, across the platform, and down the steps. He wanted to avoid any of his teammates, and especially the skipper. He didn't want to try to explain why he wasn't going to the hotel with the team. He would join them, he hoped, before anyone knew he was missing.

Fortunately, the Fred Harvey Restaurant was tucked inside the Dearborn Street train station and Buddy spotted Dotson sitting alone at a table in a back corner of the room.

"Buddy," said Dotson with a smile but without getting up. "How was your trip?"

Cyril Dotson had grown a little thick around the middle, but he was still in very good shape for a man his age, which Buddy guessed to be mid-forties. He had recruited Buddy as a teenager, enticing him to run away from home to play professional baseball. He had paid for Buddy's travel, accompanied him to try-outs, and managed Buddy's career.

But somewhere along the way, Dotson had become involved with a gambling syndicate. He had asked Buddy to go easy during some of his pitching assignments until Buddy was too far into the activity to back out. Dotson had long been a successful businessman, but he had developed the look of a man who would not like to be crossed. Behind polite manners lurked hard eyes and a firm mouth. Then there was Dotson's bodyguard, Luca, who stood at the bar sipping a coffee and seeing everything.

"Trip was fine," said Buddy.

"Can I offer you a drink?" asked Dotson. "Maybe you'd prefer some coffee?"

"I need to get to the hotel," Buddy said. "You have my money?"

"Of course. That was quite a performance yesterday." Dotson slid an envelope across the table. Buddy opened it and looked at the money without taking it out. He glanced around the room as he put the envelope in his coat pocket and froze when he saw a man at the table by the door. The man appeared to be reading a newspaper, but the creased brown fedora caught Buddy's eye. Buddy's alarm must have registered on his face because Luca followed his gaze. When the man wearing the hat leaned back in his chair dropped the pretense of reading the paper, Luca moved quickly to whisper to his boss.

Dotson rose casually, picked up the coat he had draped over the seat next to him. "Good luck, Kid," was all he said as he left.

***

The Reds lost all three games at Wrigley Field. It appeared they had a last-place finish all sewn up, even without Buddy's help. As Buddy and his roommate, first baseman Hal Chase, appeared in the hotel lobby to join the team for the trip to St. Louis, Christy Mathewson approached them. "Give us a minute, Hal."

"What's up, Skip?" asked Buddy, as Hal walked away.

"Claude wants to see you."

"Now?" asked Buddy. "We're getting ready to leave."

"Now," said the skipper, pointing back at the way Buddy had come. "He's down the hall, room one hundred."

Buddy's stomach tightened and beads of sweat appeared on his upper lip. The team's owner, Mr. Herrmann, used Claude Erskine as his representative. Claude was all business. If he wanted to see Buddy, it wasn't to offer him a raise, especially after his last performance. It could only be bad news. He was probably being sent back down to the minors—most likely back to Atlanta.

When Buddy knocked on the door of room one hundred and entered, the news got worse. At a table in the center of the room, alongside Mr. Erskine, was the man in the brown fedora. He must have been an investigator for the owner's association. Buddy knew at that moment that his baseball career was over.

***

As Buddy walked the streets of Chicago, he didn't know whether to be ashamed or relieved. In truth, he was both. He would need to return to Lucy in Cincinnati, but what would he tell her? He tried to imagine putting on that smile and convincing her everything was all right when, in fact, it had all turned to shit. He tried to imagine going home and explaining to his father that the old man had been right all along. He had been too young to run off and live the life of an itinerant baseball player. And his sister—God, what would he say to her? He had thought about writing to them from time to time but never did. How could he start now?

At least he had Cyril Dotson's money in his pocket. He waited until the team left town before he returned to the train station, bought his ticket, and found a spot on a bench near the platform—a spot across from the brightly colored red, white, and blue poster. A pair of hooded dark eyes and a crooked finger pointed accusingly at him. *I Want You for the U.S. Army* and in smaller print, *nearest recruiting station*—seemed to be an omen. He was out of options with no idea where he was headed, and here was Uncle Sam pointing out an opportunity.

"What the hell," he said to himself. He wondered where the nearest recruiting station might be. He would write to Lucy from there.

The station master had been helpful, pointing him up Dearborn Street, but not before reminding him that there was a war going on in the trenches of France. "We aren't in the war," Buddy had countered, and now out in the sunshine with a purpose other than baseball ahead of him, Buddy's spirits had brightened.

The Army Recruiting Office wasn't much of a space, tucked between a Chinese restaurant and a drug store. As he drew near, he saw a big, ginger-haired man in his olive-colored uniform standing on the sidewalk handing out flyers. He couldn't believe his eyes.

"O'Malley?" Buddy exclaimed as he approached.

The big sergeant looked at Buddy for a moment, then brightened. "Well, well," he said. "If it isn't the wild-throwing kid who ran away from home! What brings you to Chicago? Still learning how to throw a baseball?"

"Not anymore," said Buddy. "I'm looking for a new line of work."

"Well, step inside and let's have a catch-up," said the big Irishman.

Buddy and Sean O'Malley had played minor league ball in Atlanta, rooming together on road trips. O'Malley had been a promising outfielder until he ran into a fence chasing a fly ball and hurt his shoulder. He never came back from that, and he and Buddy had lost track of each other.

"So," O'Malley began. "Are you thinking about joining up?"

"As long as you're not going to send me to war."

"That's not likely," O'Malley replied. "Not with the president we have. We're strictly neutral. That war will be over soon, anyway. So, what did you have in mind—infantry, artillery?"

"I don't know," said Buddy. "I haven't really thought about it."

O'Malley thought for a moment, and then he brightened. "I've just the thing for you," he said. "The army is mechanizing. The newest thing is all the motor cars, transport trucks, and the like. But there will always be a need for horses and mules. They go where those vehicles can't. They pull cannons and ambulances. Why, even the generals have their own horses. That's the ticket for you, my boy, especially with your background."

Buddy was taken aback. Sure, he had some experience with animals, but when his father had taken over the local zoo, he hated the idea. He'd even had a run-in with a bear that had almost killed him. But horses and mules were a lot different from bears.

Buddy was suddenly tired after the most miserable couple of days of his life. He had lost his career and was too ashamed to face his girlfriend. As the big, smiling Irishman pushed the paperwork across the table, enlisting seemed like the most logical decision in the world.

4

"ARE YOU LOST, MISTER?"

Buddy had moved in for a better view of the sandlot baseball game. He had been smoking a cigarette, lost in his memories. He had moved to a bench behind home plate and hadn't noticed that the game was breaking up.

"Not really." He stood up. "I was just watching the game. I played in the big leagues a long time ago."

"Who did you play for?" asked one of the outfielders. He clutched a tattered cap in one hand and a baseball in the other.

"I played here for the Crackers when I first started out. Then I pitched for the Reds."

Buddy could see the doubt creeping into their faces, as the players glanced at each other and rolled their eyes. He thought about challenging one of them to hit his fastball but quickly reconsidered. He didn't really have a fastball anymore. He also began to feel vaguely uncomfortable being the only white face in this sea of Negroes.

"I'm with the circus," he said. He held up his bullhook, both to verify his claim and to show he could defend himself. They did not appear to be impressed.

He glanced nervously at the scene beyond the players, back the way he had come, and wondered if barging in had been a mistake. The Friday evening sidewalk bustled with activity and, except for the firemen lounging in rickety chairs outside the station, there was not a white face in sight. Women pushed baby carriages. Businessmen stood in conversation. A man carefully locked the door of the church across the street before turning in their direction.

"You're a long way from the circus grounds," one of the players said.

Actually, it wasn't that far, but Buddy wasn't sure how to respond. He didn't think it would help his case to tell them there had been a fire near the circus yard, and the police were going to be coming to their neighborhood to question some of the children in this very group.

"Is there a problem here?" said the well-dressed man who had been locking the church.

He was of medium height and sturdily built. He had the appearance of someone who could take care of himself in a fight, but Buddy didn't think these men were yielding to him because of that. He carried a briefcase, and although he appeared to be about Buddy's age, the few words he had spoken suggested that he was a leader in the community. And, most importantly, two of the young boys Buddy had come to see now clung to the man's side. One was five or six years old and the other a year or two older.

"We were just talking baseball," Buddy said.

"You look a little out of place here," the man said. "If you don't mind my saying."

"Do you live around here?" Buddy asked the man.

"I do."

Buddy inflated his cheeks and blew out a puff of air. He was stalling for time trying to decide how much to reveal. "May I walk with you to your home and explain why I'm here, so I can get back to the circus grounds?"

The man hesitated briefly, then took a step. He looked at Buddy and said, "You'd better talk fast because I live across the street." He pointed to the third house beyond the fire station.

Before they moved away from the small group of men, Buddy turned to the young pitcher and asked, "What's your name?"

"William Greason."

"You've got good stuff, William, but you need to work on your release point. Make your curve, your fastball, and your change-up look like the same pitch to the batter."

Buddy waited for a sign of recognition, which came in the form of a smile and a nod.

As they left the playground with two little boys in their wake, Buddy said quietly to his companion, "There was a fire near the circus grounds yesterday, and a body was found in the ashes. The police are crawling all over the place looking for someone to blame."

"Let me guess," the man interrupted. "The police suspect us."

"Somebody is trying to point them your way, at least for starting the fire." They stopped in front of the man's house, and he sent the boys inside. Buddy nodded toward the boys. "Somebody mentioned some young boys that were seen around the grounds yesterday, suggesting they may have had a hand in setting the fire."

"We spoke of the circus at dinner last night," the man said. He was clearly annoyed. "But I can assure you those boys had nothing to do with that fire."

"I saw your boys looking at my elephants.," Buddy said. "Later, I saw them come to watch the fire. They were with a bunch of older boys. They had obviously just come from this sandlot," Buddy nodded over his shoulder, "and couldn't have set the fire. I'll tell the police."

"Why would you do that?" the man asked.

Buddy didn't want to tell the man that he had been attracted to the beautiful woman he had seen them with, so he said, "I'm not from the South, but I know how things work here. White people are quick to point the finger at the Negro. I know these kids didn't do it, and I want the police to find out who did, so we can get back on the road."

The man looked at Buddy for a long moment as if sizing him up. Finally, he said, "I'm Martin Luther King, Senior. That's my church down the street." He turned toward the door to the house and continued, "I appreciate your warning us. We'll be ready."

Buddy smelled bacon cooking and felt the eyes of people across the street on his back. He glanced absently back toward the ball field, where play had resumed, then said what he had really come for. "The boys were in the company of a woman."

"That would be Naomi," Reverend King said thoughtfully. "Naomi Webster—a member of my congregation."

Buddy nodded and waited to see if the man might give him more information on the woman. When he did not, Buddy turned to leave but hesitated when Reverend King spoke again. "It was kind of you to help young Greason. You seem to know a lot about baseball."

"I played professionally a long time ago."

"And now you're with the circus."

"And now I'm with the circus," Buddy repeated as he turned to walk away.

***

It was just getting dark when Buddy strolled back onto the circus grounds. The atmosphere was unlike any he had seen. At this time on a Friday evening, he expected to see everyone preparing for the evening show. Tonight, the crew was subdued. When he got to the elephant area, Max told him why. There would be no more shows for a while as the police conducted their investigation.

"What else?" Buddy asked. "I can see something's bothering you."

"Smokey came by with his friend, Kaz," Max said. "He wanted to know if we had taught Tembo his lesson. I lied and told him we had. But he was showing off for his friend and grabbed a bullhook. The minute Smokey raised the bullhook, Tembo knocked him on his ass."

"Shit" said Buddy. "Was he hurt?"

"Knocked him out cold."

"Shit," Buddy said again. "Shit, shit."

"We got him up and sat him in a chair till he got his wits about him. Smokey was furious but tried to be casual about it. I think he was embarrassed to be knocked down in front of Kaz."

"What do you think he'll do?" Buddy asked.

"I don't know for sure," Max said. "But what do you suppose he'd do if some Negro man walked in here and punched him in the mouth —put him on his ass in front of his friends?"

Buddy thought for a moment and said quietly, "He'd get even. Maybe not then and there, but he'd sure go after him."

Buddy had worked with some stubborn animals. He'd been kicked, bitten, and head-butted. He had even been knocked around by Tembo. But never had he ever felt the need for revenge on an animal. Revenge was a special kind of hatred that should be reserved for humans.

"Doesn't this bother you?" Buddy asked as he sat on a box and leaned forward, placing his elbows on his knees.

Max was sitting in an old canvas chair with his feet up on a box and his hands behind his head. He stared into a small fire that crackled in a metal drum.

"I grew up an orphan out in Iowa," Max said. "My old man was an Indian who married a white woman and got them both shot for it. I think I was about eight or nine. I knocked around in orphan homes for a few years until a man from Illinois took me and a few other boys to work on his farm near Peoria."

Max poked at the fire with a stick.

"Old man Weatherby had cows and horses, mules, pigs, and chickens. And he had me and Andy and Sam and little Horace to do all his work for him. He was the meanest man I ever knew. He would beat us for screwing up, for disobeying him and—sometimes—just for the pleasure of it. One day, when Horace forgot to feed the chickens, Weatherby beat him so bad he ended up dying. He fed Horace to the pigs." Max paused for a long moment. "Luckily for me, the circus was leaving town. I was about fourteen."

Max stopped poking the fire and looked at Buddy. "That was about forty years ago. This has been my home ever since. Nobody has beaten me here. I've never gone hungry or had anyone creep into my room in the night. So as bad as I feel for that elephant, I'm not going to risk being put out on the street for him."

"I get it," Buddy said as his mind churned through solutions to this problem. To allow Smokey Walters to go after Tembo for simply being an elephant was more than he could stand, but the only way he could think to stop Smokey would land him in jail—or on the electric chair.

"I'm not sure you do," said Max. "I think you've got some demons chasing you—demons you chase away with the bottle." When Buddy didn't reply, he continued. "And I've seen you fingering that pistol you keep in your bedroll."

Buddy looked up sharply, but Max raised his hands. "I'm not spying on you. I just saw it in passing one day and worried that you might do something to yourself."

Max waited, but when Buddy remained silent, he asked, "Were you beaten as a kid, too?"

"No," Buddy said as he lit a cigarette. "My mother died when I was young, and my old man raised me and my sister. But he was honest and hard-working. Never raised a hand to us. He ran the local zoo, and his only fault was wanting me to work there."

"That must be why you're so good with elephants."

"Maybe," Buddy said. "Maybe, I absorbed some of what he was trying to teach me. But at the time, I hated animals—and I despised him. I only wanted to play baseball. I was good at it. I loved having people watch me pitch and cheer for me. A local man offered me some money to play ball, so I ran away like you did, but it was to chase a dream."

"Did you catch it?"

"I did for a while. But I let it slip away." Buddy said. "When I washed out of baseball, I should have gone home. The old man would have been thrilled to have me work with him and my sister," Buddy choked up. "My sister." He couldn't finish the thought.

"So," Max said quietly, "You joined the circus instead."

Buddy laughed. "No. That would have been too sensible. I joined the army."

5

Paris, France
July 1917

In spite of what he had been told when he signed up, Buddy was sent to war. On July 4, 1917, while General John J. Pershing paraded through the streets of Paris signaling the entry of the United States of America into the Great War, Sergeant Buddy Griffith's horses were pulling an overloaded wagon from the French port of Saint Nazaire to a new American encampment outside the french capital. He had been promoted twice in his first year in Uncle Sam's Army and now found himself bivouacked in the shadow of an honest-to-God fourteenth century castle.

Buddy worked out of that base on the outskirts of Paris, helping haul supplies to and from the coast in a never-ending line of horse-drawn wagons and motorized vehicles. The 300-mile march took nearly two weeks round-trip, which was about the same amount of time he and his horses had been on a transport ship dodging German U-boats in the North Atlantic. His unit was in constant motion, and this day would be no different. He had to get his horses hitched to the wagon and get into the line heading back toward Saint Nazaire.

"Excuse me," Buddy said to the stranger standing in the shadow of the tent as he approached the horse corral. "Can I help you?"

He had been warned about German spies and was told to report any suspicious activities.

The woman turned toward Buddy and said, "I was just admiring your horses."

"And you are?" Buddy asked.

"Gabrielle," said the woman with a hand extended. "Gabrielle Saint-Simon."

Buddy shook her hand and wondered how she came to be in a military compound. She was French, judging by her accent, with dark hair and dark eyes. She was wearing khaki slacks with a loose-fitting white shirt. She was attractive enough, but on the slender side. He preferred more voluptuous women.

"You speak English?" he said, both a question and a statement.

"I spent time at boarding school in England before the war," she said.

"Where do you live?" Buddy asked.

The woman turned and gestured toward the castle on the hill that loomed over the area then turned back to the horses.

"They are beautiful," the woman continued when Buddy was too surprised to reply. "I love the Percheron. It is a French breed, you know."

"Yes."

"Do they have names?"

Before Buddy could reply, he was interrupted by a British officer rushing toward the corral. "Ah, there you are," he said. He whisked the lady away—but not before she gave Buddy an appreciative smile and an apologetic shrug of her shoulders.

An hour later, Buddy was standing in the officers' tent. "You wanted to see me, sir?"

"At ease, sergeant." Major Stephen Miller was a West Point graduate with a short fuse and little tolerance for incompetence. Buddy Griffith got along with him just fine, for the most part. Major Miller had been Buddy's commanding officer since he signed up and had taught Buddy much of what he knew about the military and the horses that kept it moving. The major seemed to like Buddy's work ethic and his ability to take care of the horses, under sometimes adverse conditions.

"We're not going back to Saint Nazaire. Some of our horses are being loaned to the British," the major stood and began to pace, "…

for a big battle that is underway up in Belgium—a place called Ypres. Mud's so deep their damned trucks are bogged down. Only thing that can get through is horses."

"How many, sir?"

"A dozen, all told. I'll need two of yours."

Buddy exhaled sharply, which was as close as he dared come to complaining.

"I know, sergeant—but orders are orders. I'll leave it to you to choose." After a brief pause, the major continued, "And sergeant, I saw you talking to Mrs. Saint-Simon. You need to stay away from her." The request caught Buddy off guard, and it must have registered on his face. "Her castle is British headquarters, and they don't want us Americans bothering her."

"But sir, she's the one who approached me. She wanted to see the horses."

"That's an order, sergeant."

"Yes, sir. Anything else, sir?"

"Have the horses ready to go tomorrow at first light. Somebody from the Expeditionary Force will be by to pick them up."

Buddy saluted, turned on his heels, and left. He was already thinking about which horses to send. After dinner, he went back to the corral. They had no barn or stalls, so the horses were either loose in the corral or tied to hitching posts. Buddy hated the set-up for them and hoped it was temporary.

He walked down the line and was greeted by each animal as he drew near. Queenie and Raven were his favorites, and he gravitated to them first. They were an unusual pair, in his experience, because they worked as a true team. When he asked them to pull, they both worked together. The other teams had one animal that let the other horse do the work. He stood between the girls and allowed them to push their noses against him, sniffing for treats. He would not send either of them.

Next in line was Joker. He would be an easy choice because he was an idiot.

"Maybe you'll take a bite out of one of those Limeys," Buddy said out loud, "like you've done to everyone else you've come in contact with."

The second choice would be more difficult. Jack, Ace, or Diamond. It was a toss-up.

He moved up to Diamond, the big roan male. He hadn't tolerated life aboard the ship very well. He was seasick more often than the other horses and even seemed depressed. At the time, Buddy wasn't sure he would make it to the end of the voyage. But once they were on dry land, he perked back up. He was a good, hard worker with a pleasant disposition.

Blackjack was also a hard worker, but he was more skittish. The sound of the shelling put him on edge, but when there was work to be done, no animal worked harder than Jack.

He decided on Ace, a good horse, but a little less dependable than the others.

The next morning, Buddy handed the lead ropes of Joker and Ace to two British soldiers who hadn't even bothered to dismount from their horses.

"Anything we should know about these two?" asked one of the soldiers.

"No," Buddy lied. "They should work out just fine."

Even though they were not his favorites, he felt a loss as he watched them led away. They were part of his family, and he had singled them out to go to war—a war he had not yet seen for himself.

***

"Good morning, *monsieur*," said Mrs. Saint-Simon.

"Good morning, ma'am," said Buddy.

"Please," she said, "Call me Gabrielle."

Buddy was uncomfortable having her at the corral after just being told yesterday to avoid her. She was a striking woman, now that he had a good look at her. She appeared to be about ten years older than he was but with the regal bearing of one who is much older and a warm smile that could not conceal the sadness in her eyes.

"I still want to meet your horses," she said. The horses had been tied outside, and Buddy was mucking out their manure under the canvas. "You appear to be two horses less, this morning," she continued.

"Had to send two away."

"Ah."

"Ma'am," Buddy began awkwardly. "I've been ordered…"

"Not to speak to me," she interrupted.

"Well," he stammered, "yes."

"*Mon Dieu*," she scowled. "Those British officers are so uptight and self-righteous. I cannot stand them. Who is your commander?"

"No," Buddy said. "Don't go to him. He'll think I put you up to it, and I'll be in even more trouble."

She looked at him for a moment and stomped off. Fifteen minutes later, she was back with her hair pushed up under a broad-brimmed hat, eyeglasses altering her face, and her figure concealed by a man's clothes.

"Now," she said, "You can introduce your horses."

Buddy laughed, looked her up and down, and began the introductions.

"This one is called Blackjack, after General Pershing. He has white stockings that make him look like a general. Diamond here…"

"Has the white diamond blaze on his forehead," Gabrielle interrupted.

"Correct," Buddy smiled. "And we have two mares. Queenie is the gray and Raven, the black one."

Gabrielle grabbed Queenie's halter and said, "The Percheron is a marvelous animal—well muscled, intelligent, and willing to work all day."

Buddy smiled.

"You clearly love these animals," she said.

Buddy was taken aback. He thought about his father and sister who had loved animals back home. He had always been the selfish one who cared not one bit for the animals he was forced to work with as a kid. But now…

"I admire them because of their power and ruggedness," he said as he leaned into Raven and allowed her to push at him with her muzzle. "They can pull just about anything and will do it without complaint—smart, easy going, good disposition—all except the one we call Joker. He's a nasty piece of work. That's why he's no longer here."

"You light up when you talk about them," she said. "You seem to be talking about your children, not just some animals that pull your wagons."

She was right, of course. When he'd first reported for duty at Fort Riley, Kansas, he was convinced that joining the army had been a mistake. The strict routines of army life did not suit him. The only happy times were spent in the stables, and the best of those days were after he had bonded with his horses. They had spent so many hours enduring harsh conditions together that he had developed a certain fondness for them, and, he was sure, they returned the feeling.

Gabrielle rubbed Queenie's forehead. "Most people like the black ones. I prefer the grays."

"How do you know so much about horses?" Buddy asked.

"I have been around horses all my life. And growing up on this estate had me in contact with many animals." She motioned up the hill toward the chateau. "Horses, cattle, pigs, chickens, but that was before the war. They are all gone now, either conscripted for service —or long ago eaten."

Buddy was taken aback at the thought of eating Queenie. He moved in, leaned on her flank, and asked Gabrielle, "Do you have a barn?"

"*Oui*, but of course."

Buddy looked at his horses and back at Gabrielle. It took a moment, but she finally smiled. The next day, after she had made the offer to Major Miller, Buddy's horses were in stalls for the first time since they had left the States.

The stable on Gabrielle's estate was unlike any he had seen before. The gray, stone building was built into the side of a hill. It featured eight horse stalls—four on each side—and a two-story hay barn and wagon shed along the back, enclosing a central, cobblestoned courtyard on three sides. Buddy was especially impressed with the hay delivery system. Instead of hoisting hay up to the loft of the barn, hay was delivered by driving up the hill on the backside of the barn and straight into the loft.

A dead tree stood watch In the middle of the courtyard and the wood-shingled roof had fallen in on one section of stalls. Years of war and neglect had taken their toll. Gabrielle apologized profusely for the stable's condition. But the horses didn't care, and Buddy was happy to have them enclosed in sturdy, stone walls with doors that latched.

***

As the days turned into weeks and summer cooled to fall, Buddy returned to his routine of hauling supplies from the coast. He knew the road to Saint Nazaire intimately—every crossroad, every feed depot, and even a few lonely French women. Between trips, he and Gabrielle spent hours riding the horses around the countryside and became fast friends. He learned that her husband had been killed early in the war and that she had no children. He came to appreciate her strong sense of adventure. She had proven to be a resourceful ally, helping Buddy find small amounts of fodder for the horses, although much of it was barely edible. The constant rumble of the guns in the distance put the horses off their feed, which may have been a blessing. But when they were called to action, they would need their strength.

"I may have a barn for us to look at tomorrow," she said one afternoon. "I hear there may be some hay that was put up last spring."

Before Buddy could reply, Major Miller and Lieutenant Williams strolled into the courtyard. Buddy snapped to attention and saluted. The officers glanced at Gabrielle—now a familiar figure to them in her own stable—and addressed Buddy.

"We're shipping out in the morning," said the lieutenant. "Have the wagons hitched up by 0500 hours."

"Yes sir," said Buddy. "Where are we headed?"

"That's classified," replied the major glancing at Gabrielle. And they walked out.

Buddy looked directly at Gabrielle for a long moment. "Looks like I have work to do."

6

BELLEAU WOOD, FRANCE
JULY 1918

"YOU MUST HAVE really pissed someone off, sergeant."

Buddy wasn't sure how to respond. He had, indeed, fallen out of favor with Major Miller for continuing to see Gabrielle, even though they had tried to be discreet. But, he figured his punishment could have been a lot worse than being temporarily assigned to a colored regiment.

"Yes sir, I probably did."

"You gonna have problems taking orders from me?"

"No, sir." Buddy looked the man before him in the eye. According to the insignia and name tag, he was Major Glover, and according to the patch on his sleeve, he was with the 92nd Infantry Division—the "Buffalo Soldiers." He was tall, had a commanding voice, and was wearing what looked to be a brand-new uniform. This was Buddy's first experience with a Negro officer. Judging by the crisp uniform, his unit had just landed in France. This was likely their first posting.

"What's our assignment, sir?" Buddy asked.

"More than a thousand Americans are lying dead in those woods out there," he pointed over Buddy's shoulder. "Our job is to bring them in and see that they get a proper burial."

"What about the injured?"

"Shouldn't be any injured," Major Glover replied. "They've already been tended to and taken out."

"What about injured animals?"

"Help them if you can. If not, use your sidearm."

"I don't have a sidearm."

The major looked surprised, then went to a footlocker and retrieved a battered Colt 1911 pistol, a box of .45 caliber ammunition, and a form for Buddy to sign. Fifteen minutes later, Buddy was driving Queenie and Raven down a dusty road with two soldiers riding on the back of the wagon. They had been assigned to load his wagon with bodies as he drove through the fields. He had just reached the first anniversary of his arrival in France. He had hauled supplies, moved cannons, and served as an ambulance for casualties, all the while working across difficult terrain where motorized vehicles couldn't go. But this assignment was the worst one yet.

He wondered about the men who rode with him. Had these men pissed off someone, as well? Or was picking up the bodies of dead soldiers—and what was left of them—just their lot in life?

They had been assigned a sector and shown the location on a map. As they rounded a bend, they came to a crossroad with a burned-out vehicle blocking traffic in both directions. Buddy steered the horses off the road and into what was left of the forest ahead. He stopped, so his companions could hop down and begin their work.

The woods ahead of him were nothing like anything he had seen. The landscape had been decimated. Amid the charred stumps lay the bodies of men, horses, and mules as far as the eye could see. He had passed plenty of battlefields and seen his share of dead bodies, but this was different. He would not be passing them by and putting them out of his mind. These men's lives had come to an abrupt and horrible end a few days ago, and he was going to drive through their resting places and stir up their ghosts, along with clouds of flies and the stench of rotting flesh. The smell was familiar to him but always as a fleeting unpleasantness. At the Belleau Wood, he was about to jump into the deep end of the pond and was inclined to hold his nose to protect his senses.

"Jesus," Buddy muttered to himself as he took it all in. He then turned back to his companions and asked, "You got anything to cover your mouths?"

The men stood next to the wagon with eyes wide and mouths agape.

Welcome to the war, Buddy thought.

"What're your names?" Buddy asked as he tied a bandanna around his face.

"I'm Corporal Herman Dixon. Folks call me Dix. This here is Private William Carter."

Dix was a handsome, slender, light skinned Negro. He moved with the fluid motion of an athlete. Carter was quite the opposite— short, heavy set, and dark-skinned. He also appeared to be a man of few words.

"Where you from, Dix?"

"Georgia," Dix replied. "Willie here is from Georgia, too. In fact, our whole unit was signed up in Atlanta. How about you, Sarge," Dix continued. "Where you from?"

Before Buddy could answer, they were shocked by the sound of a horrible scream. Buddy instinctively ducked, but this was no incoming artillery. And it didn't sound like a man. It was animal in origin, and it was coming from a shell crater ahead of them.

Buddy climbed down and tied the horses to a stump. The three men crept forward and peered into the pit but jumped back as another squeal pierced the air. Below them, at the bottom of the crater, a mule lay on its side. When it saw the men, it brayed and thrashed around trying to get up.

"Looks like its leg is stuck under that rock," said Dix.

"It's probably broken," Buddy said. He felt the weight of the pistol on his belt but couldn't bear to pull it out.

After a long pause, Dix said. "Let me try and get it unstuck, Sarge."

"We've got work to do out here, corporal. We can't be wasting our time on an animal that we're likely going to put down anyway."

"Sarge," Dixon pleaded. "What if it was one of your horses?" He nodded back at the wagon. "You'd at least want to try."

In the few years he had been working with his animals, he had never had to put one down. He looked around the battlefield. A fine mist hovered over the dead soldiers he needed to retrieve and the dead horses that would be left to rot. This living mule, and Herman Dixon's attitude toward it, stirred a rare glimmer of hope.

"All right," he said finally. "But let's make it quick."

He sent Carter back to the wagon for a shovel and a rope, and joined Dixon, who was already at the bottom of the crater kneeling at the head of the mule. As Dixon touched the animal, it began to bray and thrash, but he pressed its head down to the ground with one hand, stroked its neck with the other, and crooned, "Whoa. Easy girl."

Carter slid down the bank with the shovel and rope, and Dixon got up and took the shovel.

"Sarge," he said, "If you'll hold her head down, I'll see if I can dig her out."

As Buddy knelt at the head of the wide-eyed mule, he had the uneasy feeling that his authority as the senior member of the team was being stripped. He should have been directing the action, not this corporal that he had only just met. But, for some reason, he didn't mind. He knew that everything Corporal Dixon was doing was the right thing to do.

Buddy held the mule's head down and stroked its neck while Corporal Dixon carefully dug under the animal's leg. Carter stood nearby, making no effort to help.

"Just about got it," Dixon panted. "Y'all gonna have to pull her back a little bit."

"This thing weighs a thousand pounds," said Buddy.

"If you start pulling her head, and I pull her leg, she'll do the rest when she realizes her leg's free," Dixon said.

"Private," Buddy said sharply to Carter. "Get your ass down here and help me."

When Buddy looked back at Dixon to see if he was ready for them to begin, their eyes locked, and a connection passed between them.

These two men from widely different backgrounds were united in a common cause—saving the life of one mule.

Buddy fished the rope around the mule's chest and handed one end to Private Carter. On a count of three the men pulled, and the mule was freed from its trap. They helped it stand, but it was not putting weight on its leg. Dixon felt the leg and Buddy followed suit, running his hand down the leg feeling for broken bones. It was a big female—a blond with a white mane—and so tall that Buddy couldn't see over her back.

"Seems to be fine," Buddy said to Dixon.

"Yep," Dixon replied proudly. "I reckon she just needs to get the blood flowing in it."

"Well," Buddy said. "Let's get her out of this hole and tie her to a tree. We can take her back to headquarters when we take our first load."

***

It was midday before they had the wagon loaded. They had been told to work deliberately and respectfully so the bodies were wrapped in various types of cloth—sheets, feed sacks, and the like—and stacked neatly. The body parts were placed in a large box. His wagon and two-horse hitch could haul up to four thousand pounds of cargo. If each body weighed about one-hundred-eighty pounds, Buddy figured twenty bodies was probably their limit.

Dixon and Carter argued constantly. First it was about how to lift the bodies. Then whose turn it was to retrieve a foot or an arm. Buddy listened without comment until the men almost came to blows. After he told them to knock it off, they worked in sullen silence while Buddy tried to understand the dynamics.

He had once worked with a Negro man back home. He had also encountered them in the South when he briefly lived there, but this was the first time he had been in close association with them. He had no animosity, but he did assume certain racial stereotypes which neither man fit.

"This will be the last one," Buddy said. "The horses can't pull any more."

The uniformed man Dixon and Carter approached was sitting with his back against a boulder. His helmet was on his head and his rifle in his lap. He had no visible wounds, so they approached him cautiously. As Buddy watched from the wagon seat, he wondered if the man was really dead. Carter settled the question with a shove. The body slumped to the side without any reaction.

"What'd you do that for?" exclaimed Dixon.

"Just seeing if he was really dead." Carter said.

"Course he's dead. Everybody out here's dead 'cept you and me and the Sarge."

"Just get him loaded up," Buddy said. "We need to collect that mule and get back to camp."

After the body was wrapped and loaded, the men hopped on the back of the wagon.

Buddy turned back toward where they had tied the mule and stopped. "I've got room up here if you want to ride on the seat."

Dixon hopped down from the bed of the wagon, came around front, and climbed the wheel spokes to the seat. Buddy glanced back to where Carter remained and looked questioningly at Dixon. He just shrugged his shoulders and shook his head. Buddy shook the reins. "Get up," he said to the horses.

"So," Buddy said after a few moments, "You say you're from Georgia?"

"Yep."

"I spent some time in Georgia. I played baseball for the Crackers."

"I never was much of a baseball fan."

"What did you do back home?" Buddy asked.

"My father owns a business hauling stuff and selling horses and mules—Dixon's Livery. My sister and I work with him."

"That's why you wanted to save that mule." Buddy said, almost to himself. He was developing a quiet admiration for the man sitting next to him. Corporal Herman Dixon had taken charge of a situation without offending Buddy, who was senior in rank. Since Buddy had begun observing the man, he had concluded that Dixon was smart, personable, and compassionate. He especially appreciated the man's positive attitude in these miserable conditions.

"You must be from somewhere up North," Dixon said. "White men from where I come from wouldn't be riding on no wagon seat with the likes of me."

Buddy glanced at Dixon. He wasn't sure how to respond.

"There's a dog following us," Carter hollered from the back of the wagon.

"What's it look like?" Buddy asked Dixon, who had turned and kneeled on the seat.

"It's a big black and brown one," Dixon said. "Looks like a wolf."

"Probably speaks German," said Buddy. "They use those big Alsatian shepherds as guard dogs."

"Maybe you should keep him to ride the wagon with you," Dixon said. "He could guard your horses."

Buddy looked at the man to see if he was joking. Dixon was smiling, but he was serious.

"He wouldn't understand a word I say," Buddy said.

"He's a dog," Dixon countered. "How hard can it be to teach him English?"

Buddy was pondering the idea of having a dog when he realized something was wrong ahead.

Dixon saw it too and said, "The mule's gone."

"Shit," said Buddy. He pulled on the reins to stop the wagon and looked around. The branch Dixon had tied the mule to was broken. Something may have spooked the animal, but she was nowhere to be seen, and in the ruined landscape, they could see for a considerable distance in most directions. Where they were headed was over a rise, so unless the mule was headed in their direction, Buddy figured they might as well proceed.

"You want me to see if I can get that dog for you?" Dixon asked.

Buddy turned around for the first time. The dog was only about thirty yards behind the wagon. He was a scrawny male whose downcast demeanor indicated that he was probably desperate for company.

"I don't have anything to feed him," Buddy said.

"Carter's probably got something," said Dixon. "He's always got some kind of food squirreled away in his pockets."

Buddy pulled up and handed Dixon the reins.

"What are their names?" Dixon asked.

"The gray is Queenie, and the Black one is Raven," Buddy explained.

Buddy coaxed a piece of biscuit and bacon from Carter and squatted next to the back of the wagon. The dog approached and took the food immediately, but when Buddy tried to grab him and put him on the wagon, the dog slunk away. He was looking suspiciously at the cargo on the back of the wagon and decided he wasn't going to join the party.

Buddy climbed back onto the wagon seat. "He'll probably follow us back to camp," he said as he took the reins.

They came across the injured mule grazing beside the road and tied her to the wagon. As they trundled back to camp with the mule and the dog following the wagon, and Private Carter dozing on the back, a loud thump caused both of them to turn back.

"What was that?" Dixon asked.

Buddy saw the growing crimson stain on the back of Private Carter's uniform. He stopped the horses and jumped to the ground as he held the reins.

"Get down," he shouted to Dix.

When Dixon moved slowly, Buddy reached up to grab his pant leg, but the man suddenly lurched forward and fell on Buddy's shoulder. They both tumbled to the ground. As Buddy struggled to get up, he saw the blood on his hands and realized that Dixon had been shot, as well. He sat Dixon next to the wagon wheel.

When the horses jumped, he tied the reins to one of the wheel spokes and began to check Dixon over.

"What's happening?" Dixon asked as he gripped his blood-stained side.

"German sniper," Buddy said. "Looks like he got Carter."

"What do we do?"

"How bad are you hit?" Buddy followed Dixon's hand to his side where the bloodstain on his uniform was growing.

"I don't know," Dixon gasped—near panic. "I ain't never been shot before."

Buddy thought for a moment. The bullet hit Carter on his left side. There was high ground to the west, so that's where the sniper had to be. Buddy had known instinctively that they would be safe on the east side of the wagon. But they had to move quickly, or the shooter might decide to target the horses.

He reached up and grabbed the first aid bag from under the seat as a third shot splintered the side of the wagon just above his head.

"Can you walk? He asked Dixon.

"I'm not sure," Dixon grunted as he held his side. "You're not going to leave me, are you?"

Buddy opened the supply box under the wagon bed and started pulling stuff out, placing most of it under the wagon seat above his head. Two more shots splintered the wagon. When the box was empty, he grabbed Dixon in his arms and helped stuff him into the coffin-sized box. He then untied the reins, shook them, and hollered at the horses to move up. He remained on the ground as they trotted ahead about a hundred yards until a grove of trees gave them enough cover that he could help Dixon out of his box and tend to his wounds.

"How bad is it?" Dixon asked.

"I don't know," Buddy said. "It looks like the bullet went clean through your side. If it didn't hit anything important, you should be okay. Can you climb back up to the seat?"

"I think I'd rather stay in there," he nodded at the supply box, "If it's all the same to you."

"Suit yourself. Let's get the hell out of here."

7

ATLANTA

SATURDAY, OCTOBER 31, 1936

FOR SUCH A large animal, an elephant can move with surprising speed and stealth, especially with his handler trotting along beside him. Buddy's biggest challenge had been silently unfastening Tembo's chains and placing the hobbles on his front legs.

After his fireside chat with Max, Buddy had gone to his cot and his bottle. That's when things usually began to unravel for him. When sleep finally came, it was haunted by the screams of bullet-riddled men on their way to a hospital in the back of his wagon, images of horses and mules ravaged by war, and—on this night—men with torches and guns coming for his elephant.

He woke with a start and grabbed his pistol, but all was quiet. He sat for a moment to gather his thoughts. His dreams were more than some abstract haunting. They were real to him. He could smell the smoke and the rotting flesh of France. His dreams of the war were not new, but having the elephant in them was.

Max had assured him that Smokey's rage would pass. Smokey couldn't do more than rough the animal up or he would answer to the circus owners. Buddy just needed to buy some time. He slipped on his boots and coat and crept out into the darkness.

He could hear Max snoring a few yards away as he unchained Tembo. The elephant rumbled quietly as Buddy tossed a length of chain over the animal's neck and whispered the command, "Move up."

He kept well-away from the street and the houses in the distance but would have been visible in the moonlight if anyone happened by. He had seen several empty warehouses near the railroad tracks on his walk back from the house on Auburn Avenue. Most were rickety, wooden buildings, but one was a solid brick structure with pipes set in concrete that were perfect for tethering an elephant.

Tembo had balked at the entrance to the building, but Buddy persuaded him with a gentle prod and a firm command. Fortunately, much of the roof had rotted away, so Buddy was able to secure Tembo by the dim light of a full moon. He found an old pail and filled it with water from the spigot in the backyard of a nearby house. He then stripped branches from trees and shrubs around the warehouse. Tembo was happily munching on them when Buddy stole back to his bed just before dawn.

***

"Buddy! Wake up!"

Buddy hadn't thought it possible, but he had, in fact, fallen asleep —only twenty minutes ago.

"What?" he asked, hoping he sounded surprised. "What's going on?"

"Tembo's gone," Max said. "Get out here."

Buddy stumbled out of the tent feeling legitimately sleepy. "What do you mean he's gone? How does an elephant disappear?"

"It looks like he broke his chain," Max said. He held up a broken link. "Come on, let's find him before Smokey gets here."

Buddy held back and let Max take the lead. Max followed Tembo's tracks to the west across the field toward the burned-out house, but when they reached the railroad tracks and the paved road beyond, the trail disappeared.

"He could be anywhere by now," Max said as they paused to look around.

Max scratched his beard, stared into the distance across the tracks, and turned slowly to squint at Buddy. "You wouldn't know anything about this, would you?"

"What do you mean?"

"You were awfully worried about that elephant," Max said.

"So?"

"So," Max responded, "If Tembo ran away, he wouldn't go far." Max waved his arm around the circus grounds and continued. "This is his home. We're his herd."

Buddy did not reply.

"He doesn't know he's in danger," Max was getting exasperated. "But you do."

Buddy's heart sank. "I'm not going to stand by and watch Smokey beat that elephant," he said.

"Look," said Max. "I care about Tembo as much as you do. But this is crazy. You can't do this on your own."

Max was right, of course. Buddy wasn't stupid. Irrational, maybe. Desperate, certainly. But not stupid. He knew that when he and Max returned to the circus yard to tell Smokey that the elephant was missing, a full-scale search would be launched. The police would probably be involved, and it wouldn't take the community long to discover his nearby hiding place.

Buddy thought for a moment, looked around to make sure nobody was around, and said, "Come on."

They walked down the tracks and ducked into the warehouse where Tembo was munching on the last of the branches Buddy had left for him. Both men patted the elephant and sat on a concrete curb to think.

"The thought of an animal getting hurt intentionally makes me lose my mind. I get angry. I get depressed. I get drunk." Buddy's hands began to shake. "I saw men during the war who were shell-shocked from the horrors they had seen on the battlefield. I'm haunted by the things I saw, too."

They sat in silence for a while and watched Tembo eat—oblivious to the drama unfolding around him.

"There's only one way I can see this working out," Max said, finally. "You need to disappear with him."

"What do you mean?" Buddy asked.

"I mean nobody is going to believe Tembo just ran off on his own. The search won't need to be as urgent if people think you're with him. It'll buy you more time." Max let that sink in for a moment and continued, "Are you willing to do that?"

Buddy nodded slowly and said, "Yes, I am."

"I'll stall as long as I can, but I don't get it," said Max. "You're willing to throw your job away for this animal? They're going to find you eventually."

"I can get another job," Buddy said.

Buddy tapped his bullhook on the concrete floor at his feet and drew circles in the dust. He had seen too many animals killed for no reason. The memory of thousands of them—horses, mules, livestock, and dogs—haunted his dreams. After living through that, he could no longer look the other way.

***

After gathering some supplies back at the circus grounds Buddy returned to the warehouse, fortified by the stiff drink from the bottle in his bedroll. He was heading south along the railroad tracks when he saw her. Max promised to stall for time and lead searchers for the missing elephant in the wrong direction as long as he could, but Buddy knew his prospects for success were not good. Now, with the appearance of the woman from the parade walking in his direction, the game might be over before it had begun. At least she was alone this time. Maybe he could talk his way out of a problem.

"Good morning," he said as they drew together. The sun was climbing over the circus grounds behind him, but it was still cold enough to see his breath as he spoke—a gorgeous day that would have been worthy of comment in other circumstances.

"Good morning," she replied.

He had some hay, a bundle of supplies, and his bullhook stuffed into a wheelbarrow. He also sported the disheveled look of someone who had been up all night—which he had. She, on the other hand, looked fresh and clean in her boots, denim pants, and the same red jacket he had seen her wearing at the parade. Her black hair glistened, and her dark eyes were warm and inviting. Despite his exhaustion and the stress of what he was up to, he couldn't help being drawn to her.

"Reverend King told me what you were doing for his boys," she began as she eyed his load. "I was just coming to thank you."

"Look," he began, "I…"

But he was cut off by Tembo trumpeting for his breakfast from inside the building.

She looked at the warehouse and looked at his wheelbarrow. Her gaze turned to him with eyebrows raised in amusement.

"Shit," he said. "Pardon my French. Look, I hate to be rude. But I need to go."

As he turned to leave, she said to his back, "It looks like you could use some help."

He paused but then continued walking, hoping she would get the message. She didn't.

"Let me guess," she said as she entered the warehouse behind him. "He acted up again like he did in the parade, and the man on the white horse wants to do him harm."

Buddy sat the wheelbarrow down and turned to her. "What makes you think that?"

"Let's just say I've known men like him. He had a mean look about him at the parade. He's probably arrogant and cruel. Now, you and the elephant are holed-up in a warehouse away from the circus."

Buddy was growing frustrated and wanted to warn her away. "But you don't know me," he said. "I might be arrogant and cruel, too."

"Don't be ridiculous," she laughed. "I've seen the way you handled that elephant. *He* trusts you."

Not only beautiful, Buddy thought, but smart. How should he reply? It was bad enough to bring trouble on himself. He did not want to involve her, too.

"You're right," he said finally. "And I'm going to be in a lot of trouble if they find me."

"Well, it won't take them long to find you here," she said, looking at their surroundings. "These warehouses along the tracks would be the first place I'd look." She walked over to Tembo and asked, "Can I pet him?"

"He doesn't like strangers. That's why he's here."

She grabbed an armload of hay out of the wheelbarrow and dropped it in front of the elephant. He began eating, so she shoved the pile closer with her foot and cautiously moved in to rub him on the forehead. He rumbled contentedly.

Buddy sat down on the same concrete curb he and Max had occupied an hour ago and watched this woman rub the forehead of an elephant that likes very few people. He fished his lighter and cigarettes out of his coat and lit up without taking his eyes off her.

"I don't even know your name," she said as she patted the elephant.

"Tembo," Buddy said as he blew smoke at the ceiling.

"Actually," she laughed and looked over her shoulder at him, "I meant your name."

"Buddy," he said with a smile. "Buddy Griffith."

"I'm Naomi Webster."

"Well, Naomi Webster, you certainly have a way with animals."

"I've been around animals all my life. I was raised with horses and mules, and we always had dogs and cats around the barn." She leaned into the elephant. "How long have you been with the circus?"

"I've been knocking around with circuses since after the war, mostly with the horses that pull the wagons and such."

She stopped rubbing the elephant and came to join Buddy on the curb.

"I may have a better place to hide him, if you're interested," she said.

"Why would you do that?" he asked.

"Maybe because I like animals. Maybe in return for your kindness in helping the boys." She turned to look at him with a twinkle in her eye, "Maybe, I just like lost causes."

He laughed. "Are you referring to the elephant or to me?"

"I don't know you well enough yet—although, judging by the smell of alcohol on your breath..." She didn't finish the thought.

"Where do you propose we move him?" he asked, changing the subject. "An elephant is not an easy thing to hide."

"There's an old trolley barn not far from here. It was built years ago for an electric trolley car line that ran from here to downtown. When the trolley company went bust it became a Baptist church for a while, but it's been vacant for several years now."

Buddy went quiet as he thought things over. He had gone out of his way to warn the young boys, mainly to find out more about the woman in their company. Now that she was here, he wasn't sure what to do with her. He was attracted to her, but not in his usual physical manner. There was something familiar about her that was putting him off—something at the edge of his memories. Besides, trusting someone he barely knew made no sense, but trust her he did. His main concern now was the risk for her to be drawn into his plans.

"We'll need to wait till tonight," he said finally. "Can you do me a favor while we're waiting?" She nodded and he continued, "Go to the elephant area and find Max. He's the lead handler. You saw him in the parade. He knows what I'm up to. Tell him what we're going to do, so he can find me when he needs to."

"You look exhausted," she said. "Do you want to sleep awhile while I keep watch?"

"Don't you have someplace you need to be?"

"I run my own business," she said. "My people can manage without me just fine."

"What's the business?"

"We buy and sell horses and mules and haul some freight. I inherited it from my father."

"I worked with horses during the war," Buddy said wistfully.

"Do you prefer horses or elephants?"

He laughed. "Not sure. Horses got into my blood in the war, and they're what got me into the circus." He paused. "Horses have pretty well defined my life."

***

The squeak of rusty hinges woke him. Someone had opened a door at the far end of the building out of sight. Tembo began to rumble and sway as Buddy sat up and grabbed his bullhook. Judging by the shadows on the walls, Buddy figured it was late afternoon; he felt pretty good after a few hours of sleep. He heard footsteps in the distance, and the door squeaked closed. Silence settled back in.

He stood to walk down to the end of the building to see where the sound of the door had come from when he heard another sound. It was a booming voice that had only one volume—loud. Max was outside the building, and Buddy hoped he was being led by Naomi.

"I brought you some things," said Naomi as they approached. She was wearing the same boots and denim pants but had changed into a brown oil-skin work coat and was wearing a dark fedora.

Buddy opened the large sack and pulled out a blanket, a book, and a separate paper bag with a tinfoil wrapped plate of food.

"It's chicken and biscuits," she said with a nod toward the food.

As he began to eat, he picked up the book. "*National Velvet*?" he asked.

"It's a new book about a horse. It might give you something to do while you're on the run." He glimpsed a mischievous smile as she turned away.

"I thought *you* might bring me something to eat," Buddy said to Max's back, as he rubbed Tembo's side. "Or at least some hay for him."

Max turned and said hotly, "I could hardly waltz out of the yard pushing a load of hay for the elephant that is supposed to have disappeared."

As tempers began to flare, Naomi stepped between them and said, "I took care of that, too. I had one of my men bring some hay."

Buddy sat and began stuffing food into his mouth as Max went for the hay at the end of the building where the door had squeaked. Naomi brought Buddy a cup of water and sat beside him.

"Thanks for all of this," Buddy said, holding up a biscuit.

"You're welcome."

They sat in comfortable silence and watched Max return with a bale of hay and drop it at Tembo's feet. The elephant rumbled his gratitude and began to eat, as Max joined Buddy and Naomi on the curb.

"Smokey came back shortly after you and Tembo left," Max began. "He brought four men, some extra chains, and an iron pipe. He was so angry when I told him you were out looking for the elephant, I thought he was going to have a heart attack. He mumbled something about killing both of you."

"Did he tell that policeman?" Buddy asked.

"No. I don't think he wants the police involved yet. I led a search party up the tracks and then to the west. Tomorrow, we're coming down here."

"We won't be here," said Naomi.

"We?" asked Max. There was an awkward silence until he turned to Buddy and asked, "What are you doing getting her involved in this?"

Buddy had his mouth full but held up his hands.

"It's my choice," Naomi said defiantly. "I'll get involved where I want to."

***

"Is everything ready?" Buddy asked when Naomi returned. It was after midnight, and he had built a small fire to light the inside of the warehouse. Tembo was swaying and rumbling, and Buddy was nervous.

She sat next to him and said, "The barn is ready."

"Did you eat?"

"I went home, ate, and went to bed," she replied. "I crept out about an hour ago and checked out the trolley barn. But there's a problem. It's Saturday night, and it's Halloween. A few people are still out on the streets."

"Where is this barn?"

"Your circus parades start down on Edgewood and head toward the city, right?"

Buddy nodded.

"The trolley barn is the other way up Edgewood, away from the city. But with all the people on the street, we're going to cross Krog Street," she pointed to the east. "We'll go through some neighborhoods and down Springvale Park."

As Buddy mulled over the possible problems that awaited them sneaking through people's yards in the middle of the night, the unseen door at the far end of the warehouse opened with a loud squeal and voices entered the room.

"What is this place?" a woman asked.

"Someplace we won't be bothered," said a man. "Come here," he crooned.

Buddy and Naomi exchanged a glance. They sat in the shadows at the edge of the flickering fire, but Tembo was in the middle of the cavernous space and would be unmistakable to the lovers if they entered the room. As they spoke to each other in hushed tones, Tembo became nervous and began to sway and rumble quietly. When one of them kicked a metal can against the wall, the sudden noise caused

Tembo to let out a terrifying trumpet that reverberated throughout the building.

The woman screamed. "What was that?"

"Let's get out of here," the man shouted.

They didn't close the squeaky door when they left.

Tembo calmed down in the silence that followed, and Buddy looked at Naomi. She was grinning, so he began to laugh which caused her to break out in laughter.

After a few moments, the realization of their situation hit them. They had been discovered.

"We need to move," Naomi said.

They both stood. She began loading the wheelbarrow as Buddy grabbed his bullhook and unchained Tembo from the post. He attached a short length of chain to both of the elephant's front ankles.

"What is that for?" she asked, as she moved up beside him with the wheelbarrow.

"It's called a hobble. It allows him to walk but not run."

"Ready?" she said finally.

"We'll follow you." And they marched out into the night.

They walked in silence down moon-lit city streets and through a deserted park. Tembo's chain rattled quietly, and every step rustled the fall-leaves that covered the ground. If he was uncomfortable following this stranger through the darkness, he didn't show it.

Naomi's confident gait calmed Buddy, too. He wasn't sure what to make of this woman. In some ways, she reminded him of Gabrielle. She was beautiful and confident in her own skin. But Naomi was more down to earth. He couldn't imagine Gabrielle pushing a wheelbarrow through a sleeping city with an elephant following her. His admiration was growing into something more substantial.

As she crested a small rise, she stopped at the edge of a wide street. "Here we are."

The long, wooden, window-lined building before them had seen better days. It sported a round cupola in the roofline and corbels supported the rafter-ends along the side, but the windows were boarded up, and the siding was unpainted and hanging loose in places. The tall, arched door at the end of the building could easily accommodate an elephant and the space appeared to be large enough for them to stay at least a few days.

"What do you think?" Naomi asked.

"Let's have a look."

A woman's laughter in the distance reminded them that not everyone was asleep. They paused, then crossed the street and approached the door of the barn. Naomi pushed the door open, but they could not see in the gloom. She stepped inside and lit a lamp that she must have left earlier. As the space lit up a door slammed at the other end of the building.

Buddy looked at her in question and she said, "Probably vagrants."

Buddy's heart sank when he took a good look at the space.

"We can't use this," he said.

"Why not?" Her eyes spoke to her disappointment—perhaps even hurt.

"The wooden floor," he said. "It's broken in places." He took a few steps inside and jumped up and down. "And it's spongy. He might fall through even if he would come in here—which I am pretty sure he wouldn't."

"I'm so sorry," she said. "I only wanted to help."

Buddy wrapped an arm around her and said, "It's not your fault. You couldn't have known."

She pulled away slightly and faced him.

"I have another idea," she said, "If you'll let me."

8

SUNDAY, NOVEMBER 1, 1936

THE FIRST PEOPLE Buddy saw as he walked Tembo from the trolley barn were gathered at the railroad tracks near the circus grounds. Max was addressing Amos and some of the other men with his back toward Buddy and Tembo. It was the search party, and they were astonished to see the object of their search marching up the tracks in their direction.

Max turned as Buddy approached but, before he could say anything, Smokey came rushing across the yard with his friend, Kaz, in tow.

"Where in the hell have you been?" Smokey yelled as he approached.

"I've been out looking for Tembo," Buddy said. "He must have wandered off."

"Bullshit. You took him because you didn't want to discipline him properly."

Buddy was getting nervous. He was badly outnumbered. His story was pretty thin, and Smokey wasn't buying it. Tembo was beginning to sway, probably agitated by Smokey's aggressive demeanor, and Buddy was beginning to feel sick to his stomach.

"What are they doing here?" Amos asked.

Buddy turned and was relieved to see Naomi with a small crowd of about a dozen people approaching.

Smokey glanced at them but turned to Max and said, "Get that animal back to the picket line. And as for you," he said to Buddy. But he was interrupted by Naomi.

"We came to thank you for sending this man to get that beast out of our neighborhood," she said to Smokey.

"You all need to get back to minding your own business," he said.

"Did he cause you any harm?" asked Kaz, speaking for the first time.

"No," she replied. "But he sure did cause us a fright. We just don't want any harm to come to the animal from his escapade." She was addressing Smokey again. Her implication was clear. The community would be watching.

"I don't need you people coming in here and telling me how to handle my show." Smokey looked around. The search party Max had assembled was made up of circus hands. They were answerable to Smokey. Naomi had brought an equal number of citizens from the nearby community.

"Smokey," Kaz said quietly as he tugged on Smokey's arm. "These are your customers. If they decide not to show up for our shows, Mrs. Santorini isn't going to be happy."

Kaz approached Naomi and said loud enough for all to hear, "I'm sure nobody's going to harm this elephant. Right, Smokey?" He gazed at Naomi for a moment, said something to her nobody could hear, and turned to Smokey who was glaring at Buddy. A hush fell as the assembly waited to see how the angry little man would respond.

"Of course not," Smokey replied finally. "Let's just get him back to his herd, so we can all get back to our business."

Smokey nodded at Max to take Tembo, looked around, and stomped away with Kaz in his wake.

Buddy chanced a look at Naomi. She gave him a sly smile before turning with her neighbors to leave. He then caught up with Max and Tembo on their march back to the elephant yard.

"That was some trick you pulled," Max said, with a sidelong glance.

"It wasn't my idea."

"I figured as much," Max said. "You look like you could use some sleep. I'll get the elephants taken care of. Get some rest. I need you for the two o'clock show."

"We're going to open?"

"Yep. The police said we can open the show. We just can't leave town."

"Speaking of the police," Buddy said, as a police car pulled up next to the elephant yard. Detective Stockton and Sergeant Rocker emerged, and Max stopped Tembo as they approached.

"I see you found your elephant," Stockton said to Max.

"How did you know he was missing?" Max asked.

"Word gets around," said Rocker. "You should have called us."

"Was he?" asked Stockton.

"Was he what?" asked Max.

"Was he missing?" Rocker replied.

Buddy and Max exchanged a look. A horn honked in the street behind them as the circus grounds around them came to life. Preparation had begun for the two o'clock show.

"He was just wandering the neighborhood," said Buddy.

"Wandering the neighborhood," said Rocker. "Where, exactly?"

"Well," Buddy stammered, "I don't know the area very well. He was just out there." Buddy waved an arm in the direction of the warehouse and the Edgewood Avenue area.

Stockton and Rocker exchanged a look. Stockton then looked at Max and said, "You can go."

As Max and Tembo walked away, Stockton and Rocker faced Buddy.

"Care to tell us where you really were?" asked Stockton.

"What do you mean?"

"We mean," said Rocker, "We found elephant droppings outside the trolley barn down on Edgewood. One of our men managed to track the animal back to a warehouse down the railroad tracks not far from here."

Buddy hesitated for a moment as he weighed his options. He finally decided telling the truth might work in his favor. "Okay," he began. "I took the elephant because they were going to torture him for acting up. I stayed at the warehouse for a night then tried to use the trolley barn to hide out, but I couldn't get inside."

"Why couldn't you get inside?"

"The floor is rotten. It wouldn't hold his weight."

"Can anyone corroborate that?" asked Rocker.

"Uh, no." Buddy lied.

The three men stood in silence for a moment.

"What's this all about?" Buddy asked.

"We found another body this morning," said Detective Stockton. "A young woman was strangled and dumped in the trolley barn."

Buddy stared past the two policemen as he processed this information.

"The thing is," Detective Stockton said, "You were not only at the murder scene, but you were also seen in the presence of a young woman."

"Seen by who?" Buddy said, surprised, and stalling for time to think.

"Doesn't matter," replied Sergeant Rocker. "We can place you at the scene of a murder."

"I had nothing to do with it." The officers remained silent, so he continued. "Look, I was in the presence of a woman, but she is very much alive."

"Why didn't you say so?" asked Stockton.

"I didn't want to get her involved." He hesitated. "I'll bring her to your station this afternoon and we can clear this up."

"Not good enough," said Stockton. "You'll either come with us to the station or you can take Sergeant Rocker to this woman to corroborate your claim."

Buddy sighed and looked at the sergeant. It didn't take a genius to figure that the big, white man in the police uniform wasn't going to be welcome where they were headed. It was also just dawning on him that he had no idea how to find Naomi. His search would need to begin where he had first learned her name.

***

"What's he doing here?" Reverend King said from the top step of his front porch. Buddy was taken aback by his early morning dress—shined black shoes, creased pants, crisp white shirt—until he remembered it was Sunday.

"He's escorting me to find Miss. Webster," Buddy explained. "There has been a body found at the trolley barn and they think I had something to do with it. Miss. Webster can vouch for me."

King hesitated and watched Rocker, who remained in the street holding his night stick in his right hand and tapping it in the palm of his left hand. "I don't like her getting mixed up in your mess," he said. "Especially with him involved."

Buddy glanced back at Rocker who was watching Buddy and Reverend King intently. "You know him?"

"Oh yes."

Buddy waited for King to elaborate. When he didn't, Buddy asked, "Can you reach her by telephone?"

King sighed, clearly wanting to be done with this. The front door squeaked open, and a woman joined the conversation. "What's he doing here?" she asked, looking at the policeman standing in the street.

"I'm sorry for the intrusion, ma'am," Buddy said. "I'm looking for Naomi Webster."

"With him?" she replied, still looking at Sergeant Rocker.

"Yes, ma'am, with him."

"Well, we're not sending him to Naomi's place." She turned to her husband and asked, "Is this the man from the circus?"

"Yes." He explained the situation to her, then said, "Go inside and call Naomi. See if she wants to come over here and get in the middle of this." Reverend King then turned his attention to Buddy, who remained at the bottom of his porch steps. "I appreciate what you offered to do for my boys, but..." King hesitated and glared at the policeman, "Let's just say, we have history. This is his regular beat. We prefer to steer clear of him."

"I don't have much choice," Buddy said under his breath.

"I can see that." King shifted his gaze from the policeman to a point up Auburn Avenue to the east. "Ah," he said. "Here comes Naomi."

***

Buddy wanted to punch Rocker for the way he treated Naomi. He not only leered at her with obvious relish, but he also questioned what she was doing out at that hour with a white man and suggested going to her home for further questioning.

"You got what you came for," Reverend King said. He walked down the steps from his porch and folded his arms.

Rocker locked eyes with Buddy for a moment then turned on his heels and left.

"I got the feeling there was more to that exchange than just my situation," Buddy said as he and Naomi walked up Auburn Avenue.

"That sergeant is well known around here. He likes to use that night stick on colored men when the police break up our demonstrations."

They turned right onto Howell Street and stopped. "This is my place," she said. "For now, at least."

About halfway down the block toward Edgewood Avenue stood a stable and some surrounding paddocks. Buddy might have seen Dixon's Livery when the parade passed it on Edgewood, but he wouldn't have known where to look. It was modest in size and simple in design but a building of substance and character, about half the size of the trolley barn he had seen the previous night.

Two medium-sized, long-haired, black and white dogs rushed out from inside the barn to greet them. They ran circles around Naomi and greeted her as though she had been gone for ages and, when Buddy dropped to one knee, they jumped on him as well, tongues licking and tails wagging.

"Who is this?" Buddy asked.

"I'm afraid they aren't very good watchdogs," Naomi began. "The girl with the black face is Inola. It means 'black fox.' The other one is Yona—'the bear.' They're Cherokee names."

As they entered the barn, they passed an open door. A cot and nightstand surprised Buddy and he asked, "Do you live here?"

"No." She laughed. "I live with my Aunt Thelma. That's my cousin Thornell's room. He stays here and looks after the place."

They took a few steps and, as Buddy's eyes adjusted to the dim light, he took in the modest space. It was neat, clean, and lovingly cared for. That was, he suspected, because of someone named Thornell. A central entrance large enough to drive a wagon through was flanked by five stalls on each side. Exercise paddocks surrounded the building and Buddy counted four mules, several draft horses, and other assorted horses and ponies.

"Why is this called Dixon's Livery?" Buddy asked. "Your name is Webster."

"Dixon was my maiden name. My father started the business."

Buddy plopped himself on a bench in the hallway as he processed this information and studied her face. He had been a fool not to recognize her. She was the spitting image of her brother, Herman.

"What?" she asked. She grew concerned and said, "You look as though you've seen a ghost."

BUDDY HAD JUST delivered two seriously injured soldiers to the emergency entrance and had begun his journey back to camp when he pulled up short. The army had set up the hospital in an old school for girls and built dozens of outbuildings to house the sick and injured. The shaded courtyard of the main stone and brick building was a peaceful setting where people scurried about, most in uniforms, some in white hospital coats, and all seemingly indifferent to the men in hospital gowns parked in wheelchairs around the grounds. But it was the man ahead of him who had caught his attention.

"I thought I recognized that ugly mule," Buddy said.

The man who was sitting on the back of his wagon turned an angry face toward Buddy, then broke into a grin. "What're you doing here, Sarge?"

"I could ask you the same thing, Dixon. I figured the army would have patched you up and sent you home by now."

"Well," Dixon replied. "They patched me up all right, but they gave me that mule we rescued and a job driving an ambulance hauling injured soldiers." He raised a soiled cloth to his mouth and broke into a deep, rattling cough, then continued, "You still picking up dead bodies on the battlefield?"

"No," Buddy replied as his dog raised a leg on the wagon wheel and plopped down in the grass. "I'm stationed a couple of miles south of here, but I'm hauling live ones now, same as you."

"I see that dog is still following you."

"I named him Hound," Buddy said. He leaned against the back of the wagon and pulled out his cigarettes, offering one to Dixon. His friend just shook his head.

"I never got to thank you for saving my life," Dixon said.

"I'm just sorry we couldn't save Private Carter."

"Yea," said Dixon, "me too."

He paused for another fit of coughing and Buddy saw red spittle as Dixon lowered the cloth.

"This an ugly business they've put us in," Dixon continued as he tried to hide the blood by lowering his hand.

The two soldiers sat for a moment and looked at the chaos that surrounded them.

"Why did you enlist, Dix?" Buddy asked his tired looking friend.

"Democracy," Dixon cleared his throat and said, "Seems like if America's willing to put all this effort into fighting for democracy in France, maybe we'll be willing to have democracy at home—for us, I mean."

Buddy wondered if his friend still believed that after being forced to serve in a segregated unit that picked up dead bodies. He decided not to pursue it, so he said, "You remind me of a guy I worked with back home."

"Colored?"

"Yep. A guy named Rondell Boyd. He was smart, like you. We worked at my old man's zoo."

"That wouldn't happen where I come from," said Dixon. "White men and coloreds don't work together in Georgia. Doesn't happen much in the army either, come to think of it."

"How big is your father's freight hauling business?" Buddy asked.

"He has three wagons and a stable full of mules and horses," Dixon replied. "He served in Cuba with Teddy Roosevelt. So, when you asked why I joined up, I suppose it's a family tradition." He coughed, blew his nose, and continued. "Anyway, my mom is a full-blooded Cherokee, and I got a little sister. She's seventeen."

"I have a sister, too," said Buddy. "Her name is Raven. But I ran away a few years ago to play baseball and haven't seen her since."

"Baseball," said Dixon. "You ran away to play baseball? Most kids run away to join the circus."

They both had a laugh—something Buddy realized he had not done in a long time—but the laughter brought on the worst fit of coughing yet. They sat in comfortable silence for a few minutes until Dixon had another fit of coughing that brought him down from his seat on the back of the wagon. He doubled over and coughed into this cloth until Buddy caught the attention of a passing nurse.

***

"You look like hell," Buddy said.

"I feel like hell, too." Said Dix. He coughed and winced in pain. After he gathered himself, he eyed his surroundings continued, "What happened?"

"You know damn well what happened. How long have you been sick?"

Dixon glanced at the man in the next bed, and then around the crowded hospital ward. Buddy could see that every bed was taken, and doctors and nurses scurried around like mice working their way through a maze. It was a colored ward, so the only other white faces were a few nurses who were most likely French.

He knew from his time on the wagon that the last few months had been a busy time for hospitals. He had seen hundreds of casualties from the Meuse-Argonne offensive, and he knew of a growing number of Spanish flu patients. Buddy guessed that's what Dixon was fighting. Dixon's normally dark complexion had lightened and his bright eyes dulled.

They sat in silence for a moment before Dixon continued. "Can I get you to look in on Thelma, my mule?"

"Thelma? You named your mule Thelma?"

"After my dad's sister, Aunt Thelma." Buddy was glad to see his friend smile. "Aunt Thelma is the smartest, sassiest, most opinionated woman I know."

"So," Buddy said with a touch of sarcasm. "Are you telling me your mule is smart?"

"Way smarter than your horses," Dixon smiled. "People call them stubborn, but I say mules are just opinionated—like Aunt Thelma. If a mule comes across something new, it will likely stop and study the situation. A mule won't run away like a horse. My father says if you wanted your cargo to be safe, then the best one to haul your wagon is a mule."

"That may be," countered Buddy. "But I've seen a few men in my unit get sent to the infirmary after being kicked by a mule."

"They just didn't know what they were doing. You have to handle them with patience and trust. Thelma trusts me. That's why I intend to buy her from the army when we get home."

"Buy her?" said Buddy. "I didn't know we could do that."

"Well," Dixon said. "I'm not sure we can, but I intend to try."

Dixon coughed again then closed his eyes, took a shuddering breath, and appeared to drift off to sleep. Buddy gazed around the ward without really seeing anything. There was talk around the mess hall about the war coming to an end. People were making plans— plans to go home to families, plans to go into business, and plans, for a few, to remain in France with a new-found sweetheart. He'd never heard any of the wagon drivers mention purchasing their animals after the war. But what was the Army going to do with all these horses and mules?

Buddy stood to leave and glanced back at Dixon. His friend appeared to be asleep, but something was off. It took a moment for it to sink in.

"Nurse!" He shouted.

A tall, thin Negro woman in a white smock with a red cross on the chest approached looking closely at Dixon with a knowing eye. She placed her fingers on his neck, looked back at Buddy, and gave an almost imperceptible shake of her head. Dixon was gone.

Buddy stared at the man with wide eyes. For a moment, he thought about telling her to do something, but his panic jumped past sadness and directly to anger. To go from such hope for a life after the war to nothing was so unfair. Why Dixon, of all people?

Buddy stumbled out of the ward and across the hospital grounds in a daze. He had seen enough death to last a lifetime, but it looked different up close. He walked up to his wagon and stood between the horses' heads, hugging both animals at the same time. They leaned into him, as if sensing his distress.

He stood for a while lost in thought as his tear-stained eyes took in the scene. Damaged men rolled themselves in wheelchairs or hobbled around on crutches. Some sat helplessly on benches with their eyes covered in bandages. They would go home broken—but, at least, they would go home.

10

AS SHE LISTENED to Buddy's story, Naomi leaned into him. By the time he finished, she was crying quietly. "This the first time I knew how it ended for him," she said.

Buddy leaned back on the bench, placed an arm around her, and said, "I only knew him for a few months, but Dix was a good man and a true friend."

A man emerged from the end stall to Buddy's left pushing a wheelbarrow full of manure and straw, stopped when he saw Naomi crying, and eyed Buddy with suspicion.

"Thornell," Naomi said wiping her eyes after Buddy's shocking revelation. "This is Buddy. He was a friend of Herman's in the war." She turned to Buddy and continued the introduction. "This is my cousin, Thornell Dixon."

Thornell looked Buddy in the eye, stuck out his hand and said, "Pleased to meet you."

He appeared to be a good bit older than Buddy with his close-cropped gray hair and the stubble of a gray beard. His handshake was firm, and his voice was deep but quiet. Probing intelligent eyes peered out from behind wire rimmed glasses.

"Thornell," she said to his back. When he turned, she continued. "I need you to go to the trolley barn and pick up that hay you left there."

"Trolley barn," Buddy said. "He was at the trolley barn?"

She looked at Buddy for a second, then toward Thornell. "Oh, my goodness. Surely you don't think he had anything to do with that girl. Why, he wouldn't hurt a fly."

"It doesn't matter what I think," Buddy said, letting his implication float in the air.

She thought for a moment, then said, "Thornell, just leave the hay."

He went back to work, and they walked out the back door and sat on the back of one of the wagons parked there.

"This is quite an operation you have here."

"It's not what it used to be," she said. "When my father was alive, and Herman and I worked for him, we had a dozen wagons working from dawn to dusk, six days a week. Today I'm lucky to keep half that number working."

"You don't work on Sunday?"

"This is the Lord's Day. We take care of the animals and let them rest."

"It looks like you use horses *and* mules."

She pointed to the paddock to her left and said, "We run two pairs of mules, Mike and Ike and Thelma and Bunch."

"Dixon named his mule Thelma," Buddy said with a smile. "Your Aunt Thelma must be quite a woman."

"You could say that." Naomi laughed. "She and Reverend King's wife—he calls her Bunch—are two strong women."

"Bunch?"

"I don't know where the name comes from. Nobody calls her that but him, and it might be best if you don't mention I've named one of my mules after her."

"What kind of horses do you use? I don't recognize the breed."

"That's because most of them aren't a particular breed. If they were dogs, you'd call them mutts. The only purebreds we have are those two chestnut Belgians, Herman and Martin."

"So, Herman has a namesake here," said Buddy. "I suppose he'd like that."

"I like to think so."

"Earlier you said this is your place *for now*," Buddy said. "What did you mean by that?"

She hung her head slightly and looked around. "When my father started this business just before the war, the city was booming, and he couldn't keep up with all the business. By the time the war was over, things changed. Horses were being replaced by motorized vehicles and electric streetcars. Those big, stinking gasoline powered trucks were faster than our horse powered drays and wagons, they took less room to store, and they eliminated the problem of manure all over the streets. Even the traditional horse-drawn hearse eventually gave way to machines."

"We've seen the same thing in the circus," Buddy said. "When I joined the circus after the war, everything revolved around horses. We announced the arrival of the circus with a parade like the one we did here a few days ago, but it featured those beautiful dappled gray Percheron horses pulling ornate, painted wagons. These days, most circuses are using trucks. Those beautiful two-horse teams have practically disappeared."

"I may be running a dying business," she said. "There is a growing market for draft horses with the farmers who can't afford to buy gasoline, but here in the city…" Her voice trailed off.

"Maybe you could find some use that motor vehicles can't provide," Buddy said. "During the war there was no shortage of vehicles, but they always called for the horses when the vehicles couldn't get through."

"Maybe I just need to buy a few trucks," she said. "But, I love these horses and mules."

Thornell walked past them pushing a wheelbarrow full of hay for the mules. They watched in silence as he tossed it into the paddock and came back toward them. After he had passed them, Naomi suddenly turned and called him back. "Thornell, I need you to saddle up that roan and take those horses in the inside stalls down to Cabbagetown." When he nodded and turned away, she continued.

"And stay down there for a few days." He turned back and looked at her, but when she did not explain further, he continued on his way.

"What's Cabbagetown?" Buddy asked.

"An area south of here across the railroad tracks. It's a mill town and the people who own the mill are Jewish. They are sympathetic to our people. If the police come looking for him, they won't find him down there."

They sat in silence for a moment, and she placed her hand on Buddy's.

"I'm glad he had a friend like you," she said.

Buddy just hung his head. "We dodged some bullets and bombs over there. It broke my heart to see how it ended for him."

As he felt the warmth of her hand on his, a wave of shame crept over him. He felt himself becoming drawn to her, so he hopped down from the wagon bed and pulled away—confused by his sudden attraction.

"I'm not someone you want to get mixed up with," he said, without looking at her.

She got up and moved beside him. "Why is that?"

"I'm sorry you lost your brother in the war, but some of us who came home from the war haven't done so well either."

"At least you made it home," she said. She wiped her eyes on her sleeve and continued. "Daddy was proud when Herman joined up, but it broke my heart when he went away. I was afraid I would never see him again—and I never did." Her voice shook. "We never even got a body to bury. Without a grave to visit, it's like he's still out there somewhere."

"Are your folks still around?"

"No," she said. "Daddy passed a few years back. *Agitsi*—my mother—moved back west after he died. It's just me now."

They watched in silence leaning on the back of the wagon as Thornell placed leads on the horses and tied them to the back of a one-horse dogcart. He set off on his trip to Cabbagetown without a backward glance.

She wiped her eyes one last time and announced, "I need to get ready for church."

"I need to get back to the circus, anyway."

He followed her inside, watched her open a can of dog food, and lock the barn door with a padlock on a chain. They walked in thoughtful silence the two blocks to Aunt Thelma's, and he turned back toward the circus grounds.

His recollection of the war opened old wounds for both of them. His dark, brooding memories contrasted with the families walking in the other direction clutching their Bibles, dressed in their suits and dresses, hats and coats, and spit-shined shoes. Herman Dixon should have been among them. These were his people.

They eyed Buddy warily as they passed him and whispered to each other when they thought he didn't see. This was their world. He, with his white skin, was an intruder.

He pressed on with his head down and recalled his time in France with Dixon. Their skin color didn't seem to matter much in the midst of the death and danger that engulfed them. Dixon had his mule Thelma and Buddy had Queenie, Raven, and the big Alsatian dog. And, the two men had each other.

He wondered if it was just the animals that brought them together like some common language. Or was there something more, something shared between two men. He found himself wishing that skin color didn't matter so much—wishing that the children passing him on these sidewalks didn't view him with such suspicion and distrust.

He knew that if he had Tembo with him, these same people would be smiling at him as they approached and asked questions. He had seen it a thousand times. But animals weren't what was drawing him to Naomi. He was drawn to her as a person. He was attracted to her caring nature, her poise and grace, and to her love of animals. But, as he looked around, he realized he was a foreigner in her world. Nothing would change that.

11

SUNDAY, NOVEMBER 1, 1936

"WHERE HAVE YOU been?" said Max with a hint of annoyance.

"Trying to prove I didn't murder anyone," Buddy replied.

"And?" Max paused his work and looked at Buddy with a smirk.

"They seem to be satisfied, for now."

Max did not respond. He returned to shoveling elephant manure into the wagon and said without looking up, "You don't look very happy, considering your new lady friend rescued you from getting tossed out of the show."

"I can't imagine that went over well with Smokey."

"He plans to fire you as soon as he sees you."

"Great," Buddy said as he sat and lit a cigarette. "You don't seem too broke up about the whole thing," Buddy continued as he eyed his friend.

"Well," Max said, "I think things are working out pretty well."

"How do you figure that?"

"These murders have Smokey on the hot seat. He's lost interest in Tembo. He's mad at you, but he needs you to help me with the elephants. The owners must be breathing down his neck."

"So," said Buddy hotly, "Tembo's a winner, and I'm a loser."

"Just tell him you're sorry. Let him jump up and down for a while and call you some names."

"I'll not say sorry to that son of a bitch," said Buddy.

"Who's a son of a bitch?" Smokey said, as he emerged from between the tents.

Max and Buddy exchanged a look.

"I suppose you think you're pretty hot shit right now," Smokey said to Buddy. "Why don't I just kick you out of here on your ass?"

"Smokey," Buddy began.

"Shut up, you ungrateful bastard. I gave you a chance, and you stabbed me in the back."

"Smokey, I'm sorry," Buddy shouted. "I screwed up."

"Let him stay," said Max. "We need him, Smokey. I need him to help me with the animals."

Smokey walked over to the elephants and said, "There might not be any animals to manage."

"What?" they asked in unison.

He appeared deflated when he continued, "The owners want cutbacks and layoffs. They're planning to purchase two trucks and a tractor to replace half of the Percherons."

"That's crazy," Buddy said with panic creeping into his voice. "The Percherons are part of the show. Nobody's going to pay to see a tractor pull a cat wagon or a calliope."

This was the very reason he was happy to be with the Santorini Brothers show and working with elephants. He had been in charge of the baggage horses at his previous circus, and when they had decided to mechanize, it had fallen to him to dispose of the horses. It had reminded him of the end of the war and all the horses and mules they had left behind.

"And that's not all," Smokey continued. "They want me to get rid of the elephant."

"Tembo?" asked Buddy. "That elephant is the star of the show."

"Save your breath," Smokey said.

"So, what are you going to do?" Max asked.

"People are shipping horses and mules all the way from Texas to be auctioned off here in Atlanta—a thousand at a time." Smokey looked sadly at the horses across the way. "Those Percherons ought to bring top dollar against a bunch of nags from Texas."

They sat in silence for a moment. Buddy began to feel sorry for Smokey. The bombastic and animated little man looked tired and defeated.

"Well," said Smokey, "I guess Tembo can be the star attraction at the local zoo. You," he pointed at Max, "find out if they'll take him. And you," he said to Buddy, "get me a good price for a team of Percherons, and maybe I'll let you stick around."

After Smokey left, they did not speak for a while. Buddy was grateful for a second chance, and he had an idea about where he might sell some horses, but he felt bad for Tembo. Getting locked up in some zoo for the rest of his life seemed crueler than an occasional beating. With the circus, at least, he had a life of travel and work.

"What are we going to do?" Buddy asked, finally.

"First," Max said, "let me tell you what we're *not* going to do. We're not going to try to hide an elephant again."

Buddy smiled but didn't say anything.

"Let's get these animals fed so you can go talk to your lady friend," Max said. "See if you can find out if this town even has a zoo."

***

"You've got to be kidding!" Naomi exclaimed. "How can I buy your horses when I can barely take care of the animals I have?"

"Sorry," Buddy said. "I just thought maybe they could help revive your business. People love those Percherons. Maybe you could use them for tours, or weddings, or funerals."

"Most undertakers don't use horses anymore and, if they do, they are always black not white."

She was clearly annoyed with the conversation, so Buddy held his tongue and sat on a haybale. They were in the hallway of her barn, and she was leaning against the door of one of the stalls. Since she had sent Thornell away, it looked as though she was forced to do her own cleaning.

"Look." She said, finally. "There is someone who may be able to help you. He's one of the richest men in town, and he likes animals. He had his own zoo until his neighbors threatened to sue him. He sold all of his animals to the city zoo last year."

"What kind of animals?"

"I don't know," Naomi replied. "Monkeys, big cats, elephants."

"Elephants?" Buddy said. "Where can I find this man?"

"I have no idea." As she turned to go back into the stall, she said, "Since you're here, how about helping me clean this barn?"

Buddy stared at the empty door. "What happened to your husband?" he asked without thinking. "Mr. Webster."

She stuck her head out the door, replied, "That's none of your business." And went back to work.

He smiled to himself. He liked this woman. He moved down the hall to the stalls that had been vacated by Thornell and the horses he took to Cabbagetown. He found an empty manure cart and some tools and began cleaning. He assumed these stalls would be empty for a while since the horses had been taken away, so he shoveled the hay and bedding along with the manure and wheeled it up the ramp and onto the manure wagon parked by the road.

He and Naomi worked in silence at each end of the barn. When she had finished, he heard her in the feed room opening bins and filling bowls. He had one stall left to clean. It held a small, black horse that, judging by the gray about its muzzle and its gaunt frame, was past his working days.

"Whoa," Buddy said as he entered the stall. "What's your name?"

The horse answered by pinning his ears back, baring his teeth, and letting out a loud whinny. He lowered his head and ran at Buddy, who stumbled as he pulled the door shut and fell into the hallway.

"I see you've met Eddie," said Naomi from down the hallway.

She invited him into the feed room where they removed their coats and washed up. Naomi busied herself brewing a pot of coffee and opening a tin of blueberry muffins.

"Do you have any other murderous animals I need to know about?" Buddy asked as she handed him a cup of coffee.

"No," she said as she took a seat across the small room. "Eddie is one of a kind. Thornell rescued him from an abusive teamster." She sipped her coffee and took a bite of her muffin. "He doesn't like strangers—especially men."

They sat in silence for a while, each lost in thought.

"Eddie reminds me of my late husband," she said finally.

"Where is he now?"

"Killed in a bar fight. Can't say I miss him much."

Buddy paused then said, "I'm surprised you haven't found someone to take his place."

"Who says I need someone to take his place?" she said bitterly. "The minute I bring a man in here he'll be telling me how to run this business. He'll be wanting me to wear a dress while I fix his dinner and iron his shirts. He won't want to crawl in bed at night with a woman whose hair smells of horse manure."

Buddy took a bite of his muffin and said as he chewed, "I kind of like the smell of horse manure."

He glanced in her direction but, if she caught his meaning, she showed no sign. So, he continued.

"I'm surprised you still keep mules," he said. "What do you use them for?

"Mostly for hauling big, heavy loads. There's an old quarry west of town at Bellwood Prison Camp. Chain gangs break up the granite and it gets used all over the city. We used to take the mule wagons out there a few times a week when they needed us."

"Used to?"

"We got cut out by another hauler last week. Bellwood Quarry uses convict labor—chain gangs. Since the gangs are almost all colored, they don't trust colored haulers. Another hauler raised a fuss, and they stopped calling me out there."

"Do you see that a lot? I mean white businesses cutting you out of work?"

"Of course, I see it a lot. Almost all my business is in our own part of town. But the funny thing is, the man who took away my quarry job is colored, not white. Sam Bennett owns Bennett's Feed and Livery. He's as black as Thornell, but he uses white workers to cover that fact. I don't have any white drivers."

"Why don't you expose him?"

"That would be vindictive," she said. "That's not my way. Besides, Sam and I have some history."

Buddy waited to hear what that history might be, but she did not elaborate. He wondered if Sam Bennett was one of those men who would be happy to run this business while she cooked his dinner and ironed his shirts. As he watched her move about the room in her rough clothes and messy hair, he could see she was in her rightful place. She was beautiful in her own way but would be nobody's housewife.

"Let me take one of your wagons out there," Buddy said. "Maybe I can get you back in business."

Naomi laughed.

"I'm serious," he said.

She looked at him closely, then said, "Let me think about it."

He stood and handed her his coffee cup. "I'd better be getting back."

"Thanks for your help," she said. Their fingers touched as he handed her the cup and they lingered a few seconds. "I'll come over to the circus after church if that's okay and have a look at those horses. Maybe I can help you find a buyer for them." As Buddy turned to go, she said, "I'll ask Reverend King if he knows how you can get in touch with the man who had the zoo animals."

***

"It looks like I've come at a bad time," Naomi said.

86

Buddy turned and paused. He had Tembo's headpiece raised and the elephant had lowered his head to receive it. "I'm afraid so. We begin the two o'clock show in thirty minutes."

He proceeded to throw on Tembo's headpiece and buckle the strap under his chin. He then turned his attention to his guest. "I'm glad you came, though."

"I can come back later."

"No," he said a little too quickly, "Stay. Amos will be using the Percherons to pull the cat wagons during the opening procession. You can see them then."

"I'd like that," she said.

He continued to harness the elephant as he watched her out of the corner of his eye. She seemed fascinated with the process, and he liked having her there.

"I wonder if you'd care to join us for dinner this evening," she said, finally.

He stopped and looked at her. "Who is us?"

"Well," she said, "It's at the church. We have a potluck dinner on the first Sunday of the month."

"I don't know," he said, trying to be polite. In fact, he wanted to give her a flat "No." He hated crowds, especially crowds where he knew nobody.

She moved closer and placed a hand on his arm. "Look," she said. "I know it might be uncomfortable for you. There won't be many white faces in the crowd. But you're something of a hero to some of us."

"What," he said. "Why?"

"Because you were a friend of Herman's. Because you were with him when he died. And," she gave his arm a squeeze, "because you're a friend of mine."

He couldn't say no to that.

***

Ebenezer Baptist Church was an imposing stone and brick building with twin bell towers that stood across the street from the park where Buddy had watched the boys playing baseball. As he pulled open the heavy wooden door to enter, this man who'd dodged whizzing German bullets and faced off with angry elephants, was sick to his stomach with fear. He wasn't accustomed to being inside a building, and he couldn't remember the last time he had set foot inside a church. And, this wasn't just any church. It was in the heart of a southern, Negro community. He didn't belong here.

As he walked down the stairs and into the banquet hall, all eyes turned his way. He was wondering why he had ever agreed to this, when an imposing woman stepped to his side.

"You must be Naomi's friend," she said extending her hand. "I'm Thelma Dixon."

"Pleased to meet you Mrs. Dixon," he feigned a smile and hoped she could not hear his heart thumping. "I'm Buddy Griffith."

Thelma was a short, buxom woman with a round face and a permanent smile. He scanned the room and was immediately struck by two things: First, he wasn't the only white person in attendance and second, Naomi was nowhere to be seen.

Thelma must have sensed his concern. "She'll be along soon. Let's get you a cup of coffee."

As they stood along the wall with cups in hand, Buddy asked, "Do all of these people belong to your church?"

"On, no dear," she laughed. "This is part of our mission work. Once a month, we open our church to the needy. We'll feed our neighbors a hot meal and, after an evening service, we will provide some clothing. At this time of year, it will be mostly coats, hats, and socks."

"Is Reverend King here?"

"He'll be here in a few minutes to bless the food, so we can eat at six o'clock," she said. "Then he'll get the sanctuary ready for the service."

"Naomi said some of Herman's family and friends would be here."

"They will be. We'll gather in the conference room to remember him, since you're here."

"She also said Reverend King might know how I can get in touch with the man who had a private zoo," Buddy said.

"That would be Asa Candler, Junior," she said. "Everyone's heard of him. His father owned the Coca Cola Company. He's one of the richest men in town."

"He must like animals," Buddy said.

"Oh, I don't know about that," Thelma said. "I expect he just likes having things that get him noticed."

A hush fell over the room as all eyes turned toward the door. Reverend King and his family had just entered. He began shaking hands with people as he worked his way through the crowd, making his way in Buddy's direction followed by his wife and three children. Behind him, standing in the doorway and shedding her red jacket, Naomi made eye contact with Buddy. Her smile hypnotized him, and he was stunned by her beauty. Her short, black hair was combed into a stylish bob. Her white sweater and blue dress hugged her curves in a way that was attractive but not out of place in a church.

"Mr. Circus Man," Reverend King said as he extended his hand. "I'm surprised to see you here. You're not here to warn us about some trouble, I hope."

"He's here at Naomi's invitation," Thelma said.

"His name is Buddy Griffith," said Naomi as she joined them. "He's going to drive one of my mule wagons out to the quarry tomorrow."

Buddy's mouth fell open in surprise as Reverend King said with a smile, "So, you're a muleskinner as well as an elephant man."

"Elephant man!" exclaimed King's daughter.

"Pardon my manners," King said. "This is my daughter, Christine and my wife, Alberta. I believe you already know these two rascals," he continued, pointing to the boys. "Martin and Alfred Daniel—A. D."

"Can we go now?" asked A. D.

King and his wife exchanged a glance, and she dismissed the boys with a nod.

A.D. barreled into the crowd. Buddy thought he looked like he was bent on mischief. Martin, on the other hand, stayed next to his father eyeing Buddy with curiosity—or was it suspicion?

"What's an elephant man?" asked Christine. She appeared to be the oldest of the children—about ten or eleven, Buddy guessed.

"I work at the circus," Buddy told her.

But before the girl could respond, Alberta said, "We have work to do young lady." And she began to make her way toward the kitchen with her daughter in tow.

Naomi grabbed Buddy's arm and addressed King, "Buddy served with my brother Herman during the war, and I invited some of my family to meet him. I hope that's all right."

"During the war?" Reverend King questioned. "I thought our troops were segregated."

"We were," said Buddy. "I drove a wagon. Herman and another fellow were assigned to me on a work detail. Herman and I became friends."

Reverend King gazed at Buddy for along moment before he turned to the room and said, "Ladies and gentlemen, let's bless the food so we can eat."

Buddy heard little of the prayer itself, but he would long remember the surprising comfort of being welcomed into this roomful of strangers.

Naomi guided him through the food line where kind ladies loaded his plate. He followed her into a separate room where Thelma and a half dozen people had set up a long table. She placed him at the head of the table and sat to Buddy's right. Thelma was already on Buddy's left.

Someone brought him a glass of tea and a plate of peach pie as he whispered to Naomi, "I don't know what I'm supposed to say."

"Don't worry," she said. "I'll do most of the talking. You've already told me all we need to know."

He felt like the air had gone out of his balloon. His relief was instant, and his appetite returned. The fried chicken was too hot to eat, so he began with the bacon-infused green beans and cornbread.

He pointed to something on his plate and asked Naomi, "What is this?"

"That's okra," Thelma replied.

He poked it with his fork and looked at it uncertainly.

Naomi and Thelma exchanged a laugh.

Buddy put butter on his cornbread, hunched over his plate, and began to eat. As people filtered in, the volume of the laughter and conversation swelled. It was nothing like the somber, businesslike meals he experienced at the circus where people kept mostly to themselves.

Naomi's church family had made him feel welcome, but as he stole a glance at the people sharing the table, he felt out of place—partly because of his complexion and partly because he was an outsider. This was an extended family. Their lives were linked like trees in a forest. He was like a tendril of ivy that had insinuated itself into the landscape.

As he imagined his own family back home and wondered what it would be like to be seated among them, he was startled out of his reverie by the clanging of a fork on a glass. Naomi had risen to her feet. "Can I have your attention, please?"

12

Monday, November 2, 1936

Naomi had the mules hitched to the wagon when he arrived and he left the barn before sun-up, clear-eyed and sober for a change. This task was important to her, and he wanted to do it right. He was also pleased to be back on the seat of a wagon.

Traffic had been light, but the route to Bellwood Quarry took him through the heart of downtown. He had to stop at traffic signals and wait for delivery trucks to unload. And there was no making up lost time with these mules. The quarry was northwest of town, five or six miles from Naomi's barn. Naomi had written out directions for him, but once he had seen them and got his bearings, Buddy's sense of direction took over. The Percherons he had driven in France could have covered the distance in a little more than an hour. He had been on the road nearly two hours and wasn't sure how much farther he had to go.

As he left the traffic congestion of the city, he decided it was time to test the buggy whip Naomi had placed under the seat. She had said to use it sparingly. But she also warned him that Ike, the mule on his left, would likely test Buddy by letting Mike do all the work. Mike was, indeed, straining in his harness so Buddy gathered the reins in his left hand and fished the buggy whip from under the seat.

He planted his feet on the floor of the wagon, gripped the reins tightly, and tapped Ike's muscular rump with the whip. At the same time, he shook the reins and shouted, "Ha! Get up, mules!"

Buddy rocked back on his seat as both mules shot forward. The buggy whip bounced at his feet as he grabbed the reins in both hands and let the mules trot on. He steered them around a stalled car, enjoying the exhilaration of the open road with a couple of animals at his command. He smiled at the recollection of the preacher's comment from last night—Buddy Griffith, muleskinner.

They covered a mile or so at a brisk trot until traffic forced him to pull them up as he fell in line with the other trucks, carts, and wagons that were headed in the same direction. When the column came to a halt, he knew they must be close. As he thought about what lay ahead, he began to observe the enormous truck ahead of him. It was large enough to haul a small locomotive. Suddenly, Naomi's big mules didn't look so big.

Their proximity to the quarry became clear when an enormous explosion caught him off guard. Rocks and dust rose into the air above the trees in front of him and he tugged on the reins as Mike and Ike jumped forward. A team of horses ahead of the truck he followed bolted and careened off the road to their right, pulling their wagon into a ditch.

As pebbles rained into the litter leaf around Buddy's wagon and dust drifted over the convoy, people rush to the aid of the overturned wagon. Buddy's memories of French battlefields caused a moment of panic in him, as well.

"Whoa," he said to Mike and Ike as he kept light pressure on the reins. After their initial fright, the mules stood perfectly still. His command was more to calm himself. It also helped prepare them for the two blasts that followed. The panic he felt was irrational and deep-seated. He had to fight the urge to jump from the wagon and run back down the road. But he put his head down and waited for his heartbeat to slow down and his hands to stop shaking. Within a few minutes, the convoy began to move. The quarry was open for business.

They entered through a narrow cut on a slight downhill grade. It was just wide enough to accommodate vehicles entering and exiting. A man with a clipboard checked the truck ahead of him while a similar man sat on a boulder across the road awaiting the first vehicle to exit with its load. Buddy counted four men with shotguns, one with each of the clipboard-men, and one on each side of the bluff above the road.

"Name," the man with the clipboard said when Buddy finally got to the gate.

"Dixon's Livery."

The man sized-up Buddy's wagon thought a moment and wrote something. He handed Buddy a slip of paper and said, "Keep to the right. Follow the signs to curb stones."

The morning sun reflected off the dampness of a sheer granite wall that loomed to his left as Mike and Ike pulled Buddy farther down into the pit. Buddy shifted the reins to one hand, so he could look at the paper the man had handed him. His load was to be forty curb stones, and they were bound for 115 Pine Street – the Techwood Homes project. He wondered about the limit of his wagon and how he was going to find Pine Street.

The wide, flat plain at the bottom of the quarry was like some strange, nightmarish military camp. Men with shotguns and rifles dotted the landscape overseeing other men in zebra-striped uniforms. He had seen prisoner of war camps in France that were not this well guarded. Some of the prisoners were breaking rocks into rubble with sledgehammers, while others worked stations loading blocks, slabs, and gravel onto waiting wagons and trucks. Buddy fell in line behind two vehicles at the curb stone station—a stone ledge that served as a loading dock.

As the truck pulled away with its granite cargo, Buddy observed the loading of the mule wagon in front of him. Two prisoners, under the watchful eye of a man with a shotgun in the crook of his arm and a coiled bullwhip over his shoulder, hoisted a slab that was about eighteen inches wide by four feet long and four inches thick, and slid it onto the wagon. Judging by the effort of the two loaders, Buddy estimated each stone to weigh about a hundred pounds. Forty of them would be pushing the limits of what Mike and Ike could pull.

Buddy was mesmerized by the scenes that were playing out around him, but he was also counting the blocks that were loaded onto the wagon in front of him. The driver appeared to pay no attention to the loading behind him as he had an animated conversation with the guard while the prisoners piled thirty-eight blocks onto his wagon. The driver pulled his wagon forward and made a wide U-turn which allowed Buddy to see it was marked Bennett's Feed and Livery. The driver gave Buddy a sly smile as he passed. Bennett's, he recalled, was Naomi's rival.

Buddy moved into position and showed the guard his ticket. The man said something to the loaders and moved away to watch the loading. He did not engage Buddy in friendly banter as he had with the Bennett's driver. The wagon shook and sagged a bit with every stone. Fortunately, the ground was rock, so the wheels could not sink into the soil.

They stacked the slabs on the wagon in four piles with ten slabs to a pile. But when he counted the last slab and prepared to pull away, the men kept loading. They placed two more slabs before Buddy stood from his seat.

"Hey!" he said to the loaders. "Hold on, there." Then to the guard, "What's going on here?"

"Thought you might like some extra money," the guard said with a smirk. "The more curbs you haul, the more you're paid."

"What if my mules can't haul that much?"

"Well," said the man as he reached for his bullwhip, "I'll be glad to give them some incentive."

"Like hell you will." Buddy sat back down and collected his thoughts. He was torn between challenging the man with the shotgun —clearly a bad idea—and begging the prisoners to lighten his load— an equally distasteful outcome.

So, he gave a loud "click, click" with his tongue and rattled the reins. "Get up!" he said to Mike and Ike.

***

95

"Where did you get off to this morning?" Max asked. "You were out before sunup."

"I drove a mule wagon out to some rock quarry for Naomi."

Max placed his plate and cup on the table and sat. He sipped his coffee, eyed Buddy over the rim of his cup, and waited for more.

"It was the ugliest thing I ever saw," Buddy began. "Negroes chained together like elephants, and white men standing over them with shotguns and bullwhips. And here I thought slavery ended seventy years ago."

"There's a rock quarry in this town?"

"Yep. It's a huge, deep pit, out west of town. They're blasting granite out of the ground. Making big blocks into little blocks and pounding them into gravel."

"You know there's work to be done around here, too," Max said. "Even though we're not doing shows, we need to work the animals and shovel shit."

"I know," said Buddy. "I'll get on it this afternoon." They ate in silence for a moment until Buddy asked, "You ever work with mules?"

"We had them on the farm," Max said. "Used 'em to pull a plow and drag stumps out of the ground."

"They loaded so many blocks on the wagon, I didn't think it would move." Buddy shook his head in amazement. "But those mules leaned into their harnesses and pulled us up that steep road out of the quarry like it was nothing. Naomi has 'em so well trained, I think they could have gone out there without me."

"You're getting mighty sweet on your colored, lady friend," he said, changing the subject.

"She's not colored. She's half Indian," Buddy said hotly, "like you."

"Come on, Buddy. That's not how it works. If she's got colored blood in her, she's colored."

"I don't give a shit." He gave a dramatic wave of his arm around the assembly and continued. "Since when do we care about stuff like that? We're all a bunch of freaks and misfits here."

Max placed a slab of ham on his bread and took a bite. "That's not what I meant," he said with his mouth full. "I just don't see it ending well. She lives in her world, and you're never going to be a part of it."

Buddy had no response to that, so he was relieved to let the subject drop when Detective Stokes entered the tent. Stokes helped himself to a cup of coffee and looked around. Smokey had not turned up yet, but the detective appeared to recognize Buddy and Max and made his way over to join them.

"Mind if I sit?" he asked.

Max nodded to the seat next to Buddy.

"What time does Mr. Walters usually turn up?" he asked.

"He doesn't usually eat lunch in the cook tent with us," said Max.

They sat in silence for a moment then Buddy asked, "Where's your sidekick?"

"He's out following a lead on the dead girl."

"Which one?" Max asked.

"The second one. The one from the trolley barn. The girl in the fire was burned so bad we don't have any leads on her."

"So, who was the girl in the trolley barn?" Buddy asked.

"That's what Rocker is trying to find out. All we know is that she's young, white, and well-dressed."

"How was she killed?" asked Buddy.

"That," said the detective, "I'm not prepared to say." Stokes sipped his coffee and looked sideways at Buddy. "You think of anything that might be helpful to our investigation? Anything you might have noticed when you were in the barn?" When Buddy didn't respond he continued, "What were you doing at the Trolly Barn with that colored girl anyway?"

"I already told you. She was helping me move the elephant."

"Yeah. So, you said." He pushed himself up from the table and dropped a business card between them. "If you think of anything, give me a call."

As they watched him walk away, Max said, "We need to do something about the elephant and the horses."

"I may have a lead on the zoo," said Buddy. "Last year, some rich guy donated a bunch of his animals to the zoo. Some of them were elephants."

"Elephants!" Max exclaimed. "Are you sure?"

"That's what I was told. He had his own zoo."

"So, if the zoo has his elephants, maybe they wouldn't mind having one more."

"That's what I was thinking," said Buddy.

"What about the horses?" asked Max. "Is your lady friend interested in them?"

"No, but I do have an idea. What if you and I go see this rich guy? If he likes animals, he might help us with the elephant *and* the horses."

"How do we find him?"

"That, I don't know," said Buddy. "I tried to find out last night from Naomi's preacher, but he was too busy to talk to me."

"We need someone who knows this city," said Max.

"What about Smokey's friend, Kasinski?"

"Good idea." Max stood and picked up his dishes. "Let's get the elephants cleaned and fed, so we can see if Kasinski is still around."

The layout of a circus depends on the size and configuration of the grounds in the various cities, but it revolves around the best spot for the main entrance to the big top. Once the big top is laid out, the menagerie tent and sideshow tents are set up next to it. All the rest of the circus elements are scattered around the circus grounds—except for the clowns. Clown alley is always located outside the back door of the big top. That's where Buddy and Max began their search for Wayne Kasinski.

"Have you seen Kasinski?" Max asked a young clown who was practicing his juggling.

The clown took his eyes off the balls and fumbled them. "Screw you," he growled at the interruption.

"Who wants to know?" asked another clown who was playing checkers behind them.

"Benny," Max said, "just tell us where he is."

"How should I know?

"This is clown alley." Max spread his arms and looked around. "He's a clown…"

"He's not a clown," said the juggler. "at least not one of us."

"Bugs is right," said Benny. "He doesn't stay over here. He stays with Smokey."

Max and Buddy exchanged a glance and changed course. They walked away from the big top and menagerie tent toward the backyard. They passed dressing rooms, the tailor's wagon and performer's rest areas; performing animal cages, the cook house, and the blacksmith shop; and dozens of performers, workers, and roustabouts scurryied around. Smokey's wagon overlooked it all.

"You in there, Smokey?" Max shouted with a knock and as much cheer as he could muster.

Smokey appeared at the door and said, "What do you two want?"

"We'd like a word with Mr. Kasinski, if he's here." Said Buddy.

"Let 'em in," said a voice from inside.

"I'm not letting them in here. They smell of elephant shit, and their boots are covered in mud."

Kaz appeared at the door and asked, "What can I do for you boys?"

"We've been told there's a rich man in town who donated a bunch of animals to the local zoo," Buddy began.

"Some of those animals were elephants," Max said.

"Maybe a man like that," Buddy continued, "could help us find a home for our animals. He would, at least, know who to contact at the zoo."

"Of course." Kaz slapped the door frame and stepped to the ground. "Why didn't I think of that. That would be Asa Candler, Junior. 'Buddie', they call him. Say," Kaz stopped and pointed at Buddy. "Isn't that?" he said without finishing the thought.

"Where can we find him?" Max asked.

"Buddie's old man," Kaz said, "bought the formula for the Coca-Cola recipe for a song and turned it into one of the world's largest companies. Buddie was his second son. He was known about town as an eccentric and alcoholic real estate developer. I've met the man, but he wouldn't know me." Kaz was walking around and waving his arms. "He dabbled in magic for a time, and we were introduced at one of his shows by a mutual friend."

"But what about his animals?" Smokey asked from the door of the wagon.

"Ah yes, I was just coming to that. He was like a bird drawn to shiny objects. When he took a fancy to fast cars, he built a racetrack south of town. When he took a fancy to exotic animals, he built his own zoo on the grounds of his estate up on Briarcliff Road. But animals escaped, his neighbors took him to court, and he finally closed it last year. Gave all the animals to the city zoo. Newspapers reported leopards, zebras, birds, a hyena, and a sea lion if I recall. There was a tiger named Jimmie Walker, and several elephants."

"Maybe I should go see him," said Smokey eagerly.

Kaz thought for a moment, and looked over his shoulder at Smokey, "Actually, it might be better if you send these men. Candler is not your typical rich guy who only associates with the upper class. He's a bit of a character if you know what I mean. Likes the common man."

Smokey looked down from his doorway for a moment, then wordlessly closed the door. Kaz sat on the steps and said, "Smokey likes to be the center of attention, but he'll come around. He's under a lot of pressure."

Buddy turned to leave but Max took a seat and asked Kaz, "How did you come to be friends with Smokey?"

"I had a magic act with the Rosco Williams Show years ago," he began. "Smokey's old man was the manager—Gus was his name, Gus Walters. Mean as a snake, he was. Used to abuse Smokey something awful." Kaz lowered his voice and looked from Max to Buddy. "Not physically, mind you. But up here," he pointed to his head. "I always felt sorry for the boy, and I stayed in touch."

"What do you do now?" Buddy asked.

"Oh, a little of this and a little of that," he said evasively. He looked at Buddy and changed the subject. "That woman who was here about the elephant yesterday morning, have you ever seen her before?"

"No," Buddy lied and glanced at Max, "Why?"

"No reason," Kaz replied. "Just thought I might have seen a look pass between you and her."

Max stood up to leave, but Kaz wasn't finished with Buddy. "Smokey tells me you aren't really a bull-man."

Buddy wasn't sure how to take that statement. While it was true that he hadn't been with elephants for long, he was proud of how much he had learned from Max. Saying he wasn't a *real* bull-man was something of an insult.

As if sensing Buddy's unease, Kaz stood and put his hands up. "I meant no offense. It's just that you handle that elephant very well for someone without years of experience."

"We'd better go," Max said. "Where can we find this Buddie Candler?"

13

THE BASEMENT OF the Candler Building at the corner of Peachtree and Houston was the most impressive indoor space Buddy had ever stepped into. Its low ceiling compressed the lower level, but the massive marble columns and gleaming floors exuded opulence. It would have been church-like and hushed but for the clinks and chatter of the adjacent restaurant.

Buddy and Max had slipped by the doorman when he was assisting a vagrant off the premises. They walked unnoticed down to the basement where Kaz told them Candler's office was located. Now, they had to figure out a way to get past the formidable woman who anchored the large wooden desk outside the man's office.

"I don't know when, or if, Mr. Candler will be in today," said the woman in reply to their inquiry. "He has a new office in the Briarcliff Apartment building up on Ponce. Besides, he doesn't take drop-ins. You'll need to make an appointment. May I ask what this is about?"

"It's about an elephant," Buddy said.

"Excuse me?"

"We're with the circus," Max explained. "We have an elephant we're trying to find a home for, and we thought he might be able to help."

"You need to talk to the people at the zoo," she said. "That's where all of Mr. Candler's animals are." She paused, then continued, "Look, his younger brother was killed in an automobile accident one month ago today. I'm sure he won't want to be bothered with this right now."

Buddy and Max looked at each other. To continue their quest seemed not only pointless, but insensitive. They walked out of the

102

office and started up the curved marble staircase when a voice behind them said, "Why do I smell elephants?"

They turned to see a man at the bottom of the stairs. He wore a rumpled suit, round Windsor glasses, and had a blunt, unlit cigar clenched in his teeth. Buddy felt like he had been discovered and was about to be thrown out of this ornate establishment. Max, however, was one step ahead.

"The only person who would recognize the odor of elephants is one who had spent considerable time with them," Max said with a smile. "You must be Mr. Candler."

They soon found themselves ushered past the stern-faced secretary and into Candler's office where they sat in front of his desk and told their story.

Candler lit his cigar and offered them cigarettes from a wooden box on his desk. Buddy took one and accepted a light from the man.

"Sorry to hear about your brother," Buddy said as he leaned back and exhaled smoke.

"How did you know about that?"

"Your secretary mentioned it," Max said. "She said he died one month ago today."

Candler looked surprised. "Was it that long ago?" He paused for a moment and continued. "Yes, I guess it was. He was in an automobile accident down near Valdosta. They say his car hit a cow and overturned. Broke his neck." He looked at his cigar. "There is something about losing a brother, especially a younger brother. Makes you wonder what's the point of life. Why am I here," he said quietly, "and he's gone?"

Buddy recognized something of himself in the man—a melancholy that he felt all too well.

"I wish I'd spent more time with him," Candler continued wistfully. "I got so involved with my real estate deals, some lawsuits, and that cemetery."

"Cemetery?" Buddy said.

"Yes," he said. "Cemetery. I had to take over Westview Cemetery. That's where we buried my brother, and that's where most of my problems lie. Kind of ironic when you think about it."

"So," Max said. "You even have dead people suing you?"

Candler looked at Max sharply but broke into a grin and shook his head before continuing the thought. "Dead people and zoo animals."

I had a whole zoo full of animals," he said, "at my property up on Briarcliff Road. Most of them came from circuses like yours that were going out of business and zoos that could no longer care for their animals. I felt good about what I was doing, rescuing these animals, and letting the children of Atlanta enjoy them." He puffed on his cigar and blew a thick cloud of smoke at the ceiling. "But one of my neighbors took exception," he continued with a note of bitterness, "and riled up the neighborhood. The next thing I know, they're suing me."

"Why didn't you just fight them in court?" Buddy asked.

Candler puffed on his cigar and looked at something on the wall behind Max and Buddy. Buddy worried that he had said something wrong.

"Sometimes, I wonder that myself," he said.

"Mr. Candler," his secretary said from the doorway. "Bill Davis is here."

She disappeared and Candler said with a rueful smile, "My lawyer. Somebody else is probably suing me."

"Look," he stood and continued. "A couple of years ago, I would have been all over this. But I'm out of the animal business." He pulled a piece of stationery out of a drawer and unscrewed his fountain pen. He bent over his desk and wrote as he talked. "I'll give you a contact at the zoo, but I wouldn't hold out much hope. They barely have enough room for the animals I gave them. I can't imagine them accepting another elephant. The horses might be a different story. I'm going to put you in touch with a friend who loves horses. She's got money and a large stable. Her husband's a bit of an ass, but he adores her. See if you can catch her at the stable, maybe early one morning when he's not around. Her name is Arabella Anderson. Here is her address."

***

Buddy stopped by the barn to tell Naomi about their meeting with Candler while Max went back to the circus grounds. But she was nowhere to be seen. Also gone was the freight wagon that had been parked by the road and the mules, Thelma and Bunch. He assumed she was out on a job.

Since there was no need to rush back to the circus, he decided to have a look around. He took a knee and rubbed each of the dogs, Inola and Yona. He had no idea which was which.

Eddie, the mean little horse, was happily munching hay until he spotted Buddy leaning on the door to his stall.

"Afternoon, Eddie."

The horse lowered his head and pinned back his ears but continued chewing as he eyed Buddy with suspicion. Buddy hated seeing this animal's distrust, so he went to the feed room in search of something to give him. He needed something to place in his hand, something the horse would perceive as a treat. He knew that, given time, he could coax the horse into submission.

Unfortunately, there was nothing but bags of feed and bales of hay and a telephone on the wall. But as he left the room, he did spy something of interest. Hanging on two nails above the door was one of the most beautiful rifles he had ever seen.

"Wow," he said to himself as he took it down and turned it over in his hands. "You're a beauty."

According to the tiny block letters on top of the bolt action lever it was a Model 1896 Springfield rifle. But the ornate engraving on the side of the breech indicated it had once been the property of the 9th Cavalry—the Buffalo Soldiers. This had been Naomi's father's gun.

He aimed it out the door and wondered about the stories it could tell, then placed it back above the door.

As he emerged back into the hall and passed Eddie's stall, he said, "Sorry, you little son of a bitch. I'll bring you something later."

"Well, Well," said a voice behind him. "What have we here?"

Buddy jumped. "Jesus!"

He turned to see Sergeant Rocker. Rocker was holstering his pistol and nodding down the hall where two other officers stood with rifles raised. The dogs eyed the men from the door of an empty stall.

"What's going on here?" asked Buddy.

"I could ask you the same thing," said Rocker.

"I'm waiting for somebody."

"Well," said the sergeant as he peered into the feed room Buddy had just emerged from. "I'm looking for somebody, too."

"She's not here," said Buddy.

"That's not who I'm looking for," Rocker said, confirming what Buddy suspected. Rocker motioned to the officers down the hall, and they split up, presumably to look around outside, while he gazed around the barn. He walked over to Thornell's room and asked over his shoulder, "Do you know where he is?"

"Who?"

The big sergeant walked back over to Buddy and said, "I think you know exactly who I'm looking for."

The other two officers appeared at each end of the hallway empty-handed.

Rocker came face to face with Buddy and said, "That boy was seen around the trolley barn, and my sources tell me he works here with your lady friend." Rocker's breath smelled of garlic and cigar smoke. "So, don't mess with me, circus boy."

With that, he punched Buddy in the stomach with a suddenness that caught him off guard and doubled him over. The dogs began to bark as Buddy went to his knees. Rocker spread him out on his back with a kick to the face.

As Buddy lay dazed with his nose bloodied and the ceiling going out of focus, Sergeant Rocker loomed over him and said, "Tell that bitch of yours I'll be back. I'll enjoy getting her to tell me what she knows."

***

"Buddy! Wake up!"

Naomi's hands were on his shoulders and her face pressed near him. He thought she was going to kiss him but the concern in her expression suggested otherwise.

"What happened?"

He pushed up on his elbows, and the dogs moved in to lick him on the face. He didn't know how long he had been out, but his stomach didn't hurt too badly and the blood on his nose had dried, so it must have been a while. He rolled onto his hands and knees and struggled to his feet. She helped him to a bench, retrieved a damp rag for his bloodied nose, and they sat together.

"Tell me what happened," she said again. "Who attacked you?"

He didn't want to tell her. He wanted to protect her. But she needed to know, so they could figure out what to do. He knew Sergeant Rocker would be true to his word—that he was looking forward to confronting Naomi. So, Buddy dabbed at his nose and explained their predicament while Naomi made a couple of telephone calls.

When Reverend King arrived, he looked out of place to Buddy in his dark suit, pressed white shirt, and shined black shoes. Yet, he seemed quite at home as he walked around the barn in the early evening shadows. He rubbed several of the horses that had their noses out the doors of the stalls and stooped to pet the dogs. He stopped at one of the mule stalls and leaned on the door. Buddy noticed that the mules didn't come forward to meet people like the horses did. They were more reserved—more judgmental. The "whatever you're selling, I'm not buying" members of the animal kingdom.

"What are their names?" he asked.

Naomi looked at Buddy with alarm. "Thelma," she said. "Thelma and Bunch."

He looked back at Naomi with his mouth open in surprise, probably at hearing his wife's pet name used outside the house. He peered back into the stall and said, "They must be two fine mules."

"They were Daddy's favorites," she said. "Hard working. Dependable."

"I'll bet they are." He unlatched the door and walked into the stall.

Buddy and Naomi walked over to join him, but they remained at the door as he rubbed the heads of the two mules. He allowed his hand to slide down Thelma's back and appeared to be talking to her. He leaned into Bunch's face and sniffed, then walked back into the hall and closed the door behind him.

"Hello!" said a voice from outside the barn.

"That'll be Detective Stockton," said Buddy.

He went out and escorted the detective inside.

"So," Stockton addressed the small assembly. "Why am I here?"

"I asked you to come alone," Buddy began, "Because I had a visit from your Sergeant Rocker this afternoon."

"The man's a vicious thug," said Naomi.

"He said you have a suspect in the murder of the woman in the trolley barn," Buddy cut her off.

"Did he do that to you?" Stockton asked, pointing to the dried blood on Buddy's nose.

"Yes."

The detective looked at Buddy closely. He looked at Naomi then at Reverend King. "And you are?"

"Martin Luther King," he said. "Mrs. Webster here is one of my parishioners at Ebenezer Baptist Church."

Stockton nodded. They found seats on the assortment of benches, stumps, and overturned buckets. The detective leaned back and looked at the ceiling.

"We do have a suspect," he said. "Or, I should say, *Sergeant Rocker* has a suspect." He hunched forward and placed his elbows on his knees. "I've only been in town a few months. I was brought in to help the chief clean up the department. But Rocker and his Klan buddies are going to be hard to root out. He is ruthless, and he has spies everywhere." He paused. "The young woman who was murdered, Sally Bingham, was white. Her body was discovered a few blocks from here. It's no surprise where this investigation is going to take us."

They sat in silence for a moment, an unlikely committee—male and female, colored and white, a policeman, a reverend, an elephant man, and a stable woman. It was the woman who broke the silence.

"If we can find the person you are looking for," she began, "What will happen to him?"

Buddy saw Naomi and Reverend King exchange a knowing glance. She must have already shared her concerns about Thornell.

"I'll have to put him in jail until he can be put on trial," Stockton replied.

"A Negro man accused of killing a white woman," said Reverend King. "How do you propose to keep him alive until his trial?"

Stockton had no answer for that.

14

Tuesday, November 3, 1936

"Are you Arabella Anderson?" Buddy asked.

"How did you get in here!?" She whirled and pointed her pitchfork in his direction.

Buddy backed up a step and raised his arms, palms forward. "Whoa," he said in the same tone he used with Tembo. "I just want to talk."

"Get the hell out of my barn!" She was shouting as she took a step forward and thrust with her weapon. "I mean it."

Buddy was shocked at her fierceness—and her language. He took another step back and raised his bullhook. "I'm with the circus," he said from outside the barn. "I just want to talk to you about some horses."

She eyed him closely, looked at the elephant hook he held up, and lowered her pitchfork.

He knew he'd better talk fast if he wanted a chance with this lady, so he explained the situation with the surplus circus Percherons and his referral by Asa Candler. He must have won her over because he soon found himself sitting across from her at a small table sipping coffee that had been served by a Negro maid. They were in an immaculate dining room that was incongruously attached to the barn. She had shed her coat and hat to reveal a mop of blond hair and a shapely figure, poorly hidden by a pair of men's pants and a flannel shirt.

She lit a cigarette and picked up the bullhook he had placed on the table. "Do you carry this with you everywhere?"

"Some men carry a cane or a walking stick," he said without finishing the thought and lit his own cigarette.

He crossed his legs and sipped his coffee, thankful to be inside. It had been a chilly, half-hour walk north from the circus grounds to an area known as Druid Hills. The Andersons were well known in the community and Kaz had told him where to find their estate. He suggested Buddy approach from the backside on Springdale Road. Buddy was here before dawn and located the stable in hopes that this woman would check on her beloved horses in the morning. He had not anticipated that she would be alone, or that he would frighten her half to death.

"Don't you have a stable boy to take care of this place for you?" he asked.

"He's upstairs in the loft," she said. "He has a room up there. He'll be down soon to do the cleaning." She placed the bullhook back on the table. "And he's not a boy. Fanny, here," she nodded at the woman who just appeared at the door, "is his wife."

She took a drag on her cigarette and blew the smoke at the ceiling. "I just come out here in the mornings to get out of the house and feed and water the horses."

"This is quite a place," Buddy said as he gazed at his surroundings. When she didn't reply, he continued, "So, are you interested in the horses Mrs. Anderson?"

"You can call me Bella." She stubbed out her cigarette and got up.

"I'm almost done here, Fanny," she said to her maid. "You can wake Sam and go back up to the house."

Fanny nodded, shot Buddy a suspicious look, and quietly left the room.

"I need to be careful," she said with a glance toward the door. "My husband indulges my fondness for horses, but his children do not. They think all of this," she waved her arm, "is folly."

Arabella Anderson was younger than Buddy had expected. She moved with the fluid grace of a dancer and spoke with the rough edge of someone who grew up on the streets, not in a mansion with servants. She was, Kaz had informed him, not Anderson's first wife. Their marriage had been quite a scandal.

"Surely, he can't put much stock in the opinions of children," Buddy said.

"He can when they're nearly my age." She laughed at Buddy's expression of surprise. "That's right. Thomas is twenty-seven and his sister LuAnn is twenty-four. They were teenagers when their mother died after being thrown from a horse in this very barn. Charles and I met and married a few years later. He's a wealthy real estate developer so, naturally, they assume I am after his money. Needless to say, they have no fondness for me or for this operation."

"Are you?"

"Am I what?"

"After his money." He smiled, hoping she would see that he was only joking.

She smiled back and moved towards the door. "Let me show you something."

She led him back into the hallway where they had met a short while ago and he had his first real look at his surroundings. High, vaulted ceilings soared over the long hallway. The space was well appointed without being ornate, and was remarkably well-kept, thanks, no doubt, to her man Sam. But something was missing. He didn't see any dogs.

He followed her to the far end of the barn where, in the last stall on the left, sat a new motor car. "This," she said from the doorway, "is my husband's pride and joy."

Buddy knew nothing about, nor cared for, motor cars, but even he was impressed with this one. He laid his hand on the fender, but Mrs. Anderson scolded him and wiped it with the tail of her shirt. It was, she informed him with some pride, a 1936 Cadillac. The long, sleek, silver-gray body was complemented by black fenders, white side-wall tires, and the chrome figure of a flying woman on the front of the engine compartment.

"But this is not what I want to show you," she said. She turned and led him out the back door. There, under a simple shed roof, sat an array of wagons, buggies, and old motor cars. She pulled the canvas cover off one vehicle to reveal a low-slung horse-drawn carriage. It was a beauty with its black lacquered finish, large wheels on the back, and slightly smaller wheels on the front.

"I just purchased this," she said. "I'm going to take it to our new plantation in South Georgia. I'd love to have a couple of horses to pull me around the property."

"You won't need two Percherons to pull this," he said.

"Of course not. I'd have them alternate on this, but we may have other uses for them, as well."

As he considered this, his eye was drawn to an odd-looking wagon near the end of the lineup of vehicles. It had red leather seats and brass fittings on a heavy wooden body. Wrapped around the backside were what appeared to be six cages.

"What in the world is this?" he asked, as he walked around it—this time keeping his hands in his pockets.

"My husband," she replied, "Is an avid hunter. The three-thousand acres he just purchased in South Georgia are for quail hunting and this is the wagon he'll use to carry his guests and dogs around the property."

"Why not use motorized vehicles?" Buddy asked. "The rest of the world is switching over."

"He says the people down there prefer horses and mule-drawn wagons." She paused, then added, "He wants a pair of mules to pull it. You're not selling any mules by any chance, are you?"

He thought of Naomi's mules but decided to keep quiet about them. "For right now," he said evasively, "It's just the horses."

"I'll talk to my husband."

***

The city was waking up as Buddy walked back to the circus grounds from Bella Anderson's barn. He tucked his bullhook under his arm and shoved his hands in his pockets as he paused at a busy intersection to let traffic pass. He scurried across and, as he walked on, he was saddened to realize something was missing. The roads were choked with motorized vehicles of all sizes—cars, trucks, omnibuses, and electric street cars. They moved passengers and cargo efficiently but left a haze of blue-gray smoke and the choking smell of gasoline and burned motor oil. And there was not a horse carriage, mule wagon, or pony cart to be seen. He missed the animals.

He pulled his coat tighter against the chill of the November morning and quickened his pace. He looked forward to being back on the circus grounds where he would be surrounded by elephants, horses, and performing animals, smelling fresh manure instead of motor exhaust fumes.

"Hey, circus boy!" a voice called.

A car slowed next to him, and Sergeant Rocker leaned out the passenger window. "You're a long way from home."

Buddy glanced at him but kept walking with his head down. The police car moved forward, keeping pace. He was, indeed, a long way from the circus grounds and, although he was doing nothing wrong, he didn't care to have the policeman know why he was wandering around this neighborhood of long curving driveways and hedge-lined properties.

Buddy saw Rocker motion to the driver out of the corner of his eye and the car sped up, but Buddy's relief was short lived. The policemen pulled into the empty parking lot of the Druid Hills Methodist Church and blocked the sidewalk. The driver remained in the car, but Sergeant Rocker emerged with his nightstick, folded his arms, and leaned on the car waiting for Buddy to catch up.

Buddy fought the urge to stop or change course. There were plenty of vehicles on the road, but nobody else on foot to give him some cover or comfort.

"What *are* you doing way up here, boy?" Rocker asked as Buddy came near.

"That's none of your business," Buddy replied.

The sergeant was half a head taller than Buddy and easily twenty pounds heavier. He eased up off the car and took a step to Buddy's left, lowering his nightstick to his side.

Buddy gripped his bullhook, ready for a fight. He glanced into the car to see if the other policeman was going to engage, but a Negro man was hunched down in the back seat, and Buddy hoped the policeman wouldn't want to leave the man unguarded.

"You're wrong about Thornell," Buddy said. "The man's harmless."

"Thornell?" Rocker said with a smile. "Well, at least I have a name to put to my murderer."

Rocker gripped his nightstick in his right hand and tapped it menacingly into his left as he drifted in a wide circle.

Buddy sensed that the big policeman was just toying with him. Unlike yesterday, when they were alone in the barn, now they were in public view, just feet from a busy road and in a church parking lot.

As Rocker completed his circuit and neared the police car, the driver leaned over and said, "We'd better go, Sarge."

Rocker glanced at the other policeman then looked at their prisoner in the backseat. But before Rocker could react, a car slid to a stop at the curb. It looked like the silver-gray Cadillac with the flying woman hood ornament that Arabella had shown him.

"Keeping the peace here, Sergeant Rocker?" the man said with a grin.

Rocker's demeanor changed in an instant. He dropped the nightstick to his side, straightened his posture, and walked to the passenger's side window of the car.

The car's driver appeared to be a few years younger than Buddy. He was hard looking with pock-marked skin, tousled brown hair, and crooked teeth. He looked out of place in the expensive car.

Rocker had leaned into the car, so Buddy could not hear their conversation, but the driver's mannerisms told a story. The driver spoke and pointed at the man in the back of the police car. Rocker nodded and shrugged his shoulders as if he was receiving a dressing down.

Buddy glanced at the hapless soul who continued to look at the floor of the police car, apparently uninterested in what was happening around him.

Rocker's back was turned, and he appeared to have lost interest in Buddy. Maybe it was time to get out of here. Buddy looked at the other policeman. Their eyes met, and the policemen gave a sharp toss of the head down the street. Buddy didn't need to be told twice.

***

"I think I found a buyer for a couple of the horses," Buddy said.

Max paused and leaned on his pitchfork. Buddy sat down, lit a cigarette, and described his visit to Arabella Anderson's barn, while the elephants looked on.

He didn't mention his two run-ins with Sergeant Rocker, so he was surprised when Max said, "Getting rid of a couple of Percherons would seem to be the least of your problems."

"What do you mean?"

"That little detective just left." Max replied. "He was looking for you."

Buddy just blew smoke toward the ground, so Max continued. "He said he had some follow-up questions for you." Max paused. "Follow-up questions about what, I wonder."

"It's complicated," Buddy said.

"Bullshit!"

Buddy looked up—startled. Max seldom got angry. That's one reason he was so good with the elephants.

"I didn't want you to get mixed up in my private affairs," Buddy said. He pointed at Tembo and continued, "You have enough going on here."

"That's not the way it works with me." Max was still agitated. "I've only known you for a few months, but I've seen how you handle him." Max nodded at Tembo. "Not many people would have risked what you did to keep him from harm. Maybe it's my turn to return the favor."

Buddy got up and began to pace. He told Max about his encounter with Sergeant Rocker in the barn and the meeting with the detective and Reverend King. By the time he was finished he was leaning against Tembo's side as the elephant munched hay.

Max didn't respond right away.

"You need to be careful," he said finally. "We're going to be back on the road in a few days. I know you're sweet on that lady."

"I'm not sweet on her," Buddy interrupted.

"What's wrong? Did she dump you?"

"No," he said.

Max paused, but when no further explanation came, he said, "Her family problems are not your affair. Besides, maybe this guy really did it."

"Maybe he did," Buddy said. "But maybe he didn't. He deserves a fair trial, just like the rest of us. He'll never make it to court around this town. Hell," Buddy continued, "he'll probably never even make it to jail."

They sat in silence as that sank in.

Buddy finally pushed himself to his feet. "I'm going to find Smokey and Amos to talk about the horses."

As he wandered among the tents and wagons, he thought about all the people who made this their home. He passed equestrians who spoke French, wire walkers who spoke German, and acrobats who spoke Chinese. There were Negro cooks and Mexican laborers. And the clowns—he hardly knew how to classify that bunch. But somehow, this motly collection of misfits living in tents, trailers, and train cars functioned as a community. They lived together in relative harmony.

He could not understand this hatred white people felt toward the Negro. It was worse here in the South, but it was bad in the North, as well.

And then, there were the Sergeant Rockers of the world. People like him just seemed to hate everybody.

Buddy wound his way across the circus grounds to Smokey's wagon, but he wasn't there. He then made his way back to see Amos and found both Amos and Smokey locked in a heated argument outside the horse tent.

"They don't need to be fattened up for the winter," Smokey said. "We're going to sell them."

"They still need to be fed properly!" Amos shouted, tossing the empty feed bag at Smokey's feet.

They paused as Buddy approached. "I may have a buyer for two of them," he said.

"Thank God!" Smokey said, throwing his arms wide. "How much are they willing to pay?"

"We didn't talk money. That's your department. Besides, I don't see people lining up to offer top dollar. I imagine you'll have to take whatever you can get."

"This is bullshit," Amos chimed in. "Getting rid of these horses is just crazy."

"When will you know something?" Smokey asked, ignoring Amos.

"It's a woman who fancies horses. She's got a nice barn and plenty of money, but she needs to ask her husband," Buddy replied.

Smokey paused and looked from Buddy to Amos then back to Buddy. "I'm going to see Max about that elephant."

But as Smokey turned to leave, Buddy saw Amos ball his fists and turn red in the face. He had to step quickly to get between Amos and Smokey, whose back was already turned. He gave Amos a look that told him to back off then caught up to Smokey and walked with him.

They found the elephants tethered to their picket line munching hay, but Max was nowhere to be seen.

"Tell Max I want to see him," Smokey said to Buddy. And he walked away.

Max emerged from the latrine as Smokey disappeared. "What did he want?"

"He wanted to talk to you about Tembo," Buddy replied.

"Then I'm glad I missed him."

"When are you going to the zoo?"

Max sat down heavily. "I don't know. I was hoping he'd change his mind."

"Doesn't look like that's going to happen."

Max looked at the elephants. "Why does he have to be such a pain in the ass?"

"Are you talking about Tembo or Smokey?"

Max laughed. "Both, I guess. You too, come to think of it."

Buddy wasn't smiling as he sat down and began to poke at the ground with his bullhook.

Unpleasant memories were intruding as he recalled another time when his life spiraled out of control. Nearly twenty years ago this month he was in a killing field a hundred miles north of Paris, France. It was his first taste of the ugliness of war.

15

CAMBRAI, FRANCE
NOVEMBER 1917

BUDDY WASN'T SURE what he'd expected war to look like, but it wasn't this. Cambrai was a small town in the north of France near the Belgian border. His unit had arrived after a two-day journey pulling wagons loaded with supplies, including tents, tack, and feed. The Americans weren't part of the battle. Buddy and his horses were used behind the lines, at first helping position some of the artillery and later to pull the ambulance wagons. With Joker and Ace off with the Brits, Buddy and Private Albert Elston worked their horses in teams. Elston handled Blackjack and Diamond on one ambulance, and Buddy was with Queenie and Raven on another. Elston was a soft-spoken Texan who was good with animals but appeared to have little use for people, including Buddy.

This was Buddy's first trip to the front, and he was stunned. The dead men reminded him of a man he had seen killed as a boy back home. But that man had died of misadventure and probably got what he deserved. These soldiers that littered the battlefield also had some knowledge of why they were here and what might befall them. The horses and mules, on the other hand, had no idea why they were in the fight.

Buddy's girls were wide eyed and skittish—probably frightened by the smell of death—and he wished he could shield them from the horror. He passed an injured horse that raised its head and gave a weak whinny. He wanted to stop and help, but the roadside and nearby fields were littered with animals. Stopping to give aid would be futile and he had no weapon with which to put them down. His heart ached for them, but he had to press on.

Buddy and his horses hauled people away from the front by the dozens—injured and dead—for more than a week before the battle at Cambrai was over.

"What do you think, Doc?" Buddy rubbed the forehead of the big, black draft horse. "Is she going to make it?"

"I don't know," said the man in the leather apron. "You've got your work cut out if she's going to pull through."

"Just tell me what to do."

Raven had come down with an ailment—a colic of some sort—on the way back to Paris. He had taken her and Queenie back to the veterinary field hospital and was being given instructions on how to care for her.

The veterinary field hospital was a collection of tents surrounding an old barn that served as an operating theater. Overall, it was a grim place with horses and mules in various stages of dying. Some were bandaged, some lay on their sides—apparently near death—and some were, in fact, already dead and awaiting burial.

Buddy had picked up plenty of veterinary information over the past couple of years, so little of what the vet told him was new. He knew about tube feeding mineral oil into one end of the horse and hosing warm water enemas out the other. Back in the States, he would have fed plenty of chopped vegetables and grass along with some molasses-soaked grain, but there was nothing like that available here. The war ravaged the countryside, leaving little vegetation of any kind.

By now, even the well-supplied U.S. Army was short of horses. With the increasing difficulty of replacing them, the loss of a horse was almost as much of a concern to the army as the loss of a human soldier. But with Buddy, it was personal. So, he took his instructions, grabbed Raven's lead rope mounted Queenie, and left.

His unit had left him behind so, as he rode back south toward Paris, his mind wandered. He thought about Gabrielle, wondered how she was doing. He wondered if she had suitors—and if not, why not?

They had been around each other off and on for months and she seemed to like being around him but, in truth, he barely knew her.

He looked around and was appalled. The dead soldiers had been removed from the area, but the land was pockmarked with shell craters, dead horses, and ruined equipment. He rode along the side of the road, passing vehicles, wagons, and soldiers for a mile or two before he realized the convoy he was following was not moving. He soon saw why. A truck had overturned in a shell hole and was blocking the road. He rode up on the scene just as a one-star general came running from the other direction red-faced and arms flapping.

"Get that god damned thing out of the road," he screamed at no one in particular. "Who's in charge here?"

"You are, sir," said a voice from the side of the road.

"Who said that?" He turned in the direction of the voice, but nobody stepped forward. "Don't screw with me."

Buddy watched as men began to scramble, turning one of the trucks around and attempting to push the downed truck up onto its wheels, to no avail. After a few minutes, he dismounted and stepped over to the general, saluted, and asked if he could be of assistance.

"What did you have in mind, son?"

"Sir, if someone can get me a harness and chain, my horse can have that truck on its wheels in no time."

The general looked closely at Buddy, then back to the big gray Percheron he had been riding. "You heard the man," he yelled. "Get a goddamn chain up here."

While he was waiting, Buddy walked over to a skinny corporal standing alone by the crater. "This your truck?"

The man took a drag on his cigarette and nodded.

"Will it run?"

The man nodded again. He had the shakes. It looked like shell shock. Buddy shifted his attention to a man sitting beside the road who was using his bayonet to cut a plug of tobacco.

"Is he okay?" Buddy nodded toward the corporal.

The man placed the plug in his mouth, sheathed his knife, and spat to the side.

"Jenkins is an idiot," he said. "He drove his truck into a fucking crater."

"Can you drive it out when I get my horse hitched up?"

The man chewed thoughtfully and spat again. He glared with scorn at Jenkins and finally said, "I guess so."

***

Pulling the truck upright had been more difficult than Buddy had anticipated—mostly because the men couldn't find a place to secure the chains. Buddy showed them how to wrap the end of the chain around the truck's front bumper and, once the job was done, the rest of the horseback ride to Gabrielle's barn was uneventful.

That evening, Buddy and Elston enlisted the help of a couple of soldiers to hold ropes attached to each side of Raven's halter. He had them keep steady pressure and hold the horse's head still. He attached another rope from her upper jaw to the rafter overhead. With this apparatus, he had Elston pull down her lower jaw while he passed a length of garden hose down her throat. He managed to get a half gallon of mineral oil into her. It was all he had. The other part of the job was to push his arm into her rectum as far as it would reach and pull out shit by the handful.

He spent the rest of the night waiting. Raven was restless, and he worried as she walked around her stall in obvious discomfort. They had been through a lot together—first in training in the States, then on the long voyage across the ocean, and now struggling through the horrors of war. He wondered what she thought of all this. She must have heard the dying horses and mules beside the roads. She must have smelled the decaying flesh of dead soldiers and heard the anguished cries of the living. God knows he sure had. But she was always happy to see him. She appeared to trust him, and he valued her presence in his life.

Shortly after midnight, he stepped outside for a smoke. It was a warm night—and quiet for a change. No shelling or sniper fire that he could hear. He returned to the barn and slept fitfully for a few hours, and by morning, Raven was squirting out the oil and seemed to be feeling better. It was a small victory amid all the death that surrounded them.

***

"Welcome back," said Gabrielle.

Buddy paused his sweeping and leaned on his broom. He had only been away for a few weeks, but he knew his appearance had changed. He could see it in the mirror when he shaved—his sunken, gaunt cheeks and the haunted look in his eyes. Being up most of the night with the horse hadn't improved his looks, but he did feel better after a shower and sleeping away most of the morning.

"It was bad?" she asked.

"Horrible," Buddy said, "especially for the horses."

"Let's walk," said Gabrielle. "I've something to show you."

Buddy turned the chores over to Elston and walked with Gabrielle —up a narrow dirt road, grown muddy from the use of men and horses, wagons, and motorized vehicles. She led him off the road and through a grove of trees thick with shrubs. They emerged into a weed-choked clearing with a small, ivy-covered stone building. After a furtive look around, Gabrielle pushed open the heavy oak door and ushered Buddy inside. She lit some candles and closed the door. Buddy was astonished. The room was much larger than he would have expected from the outside. It was elegantly furnished with tapestries lining the walls and ornate furnishings on top of oriental rugs. A bottle of wine with two glasses and a plate of cheese had been laid out.

"What is this place?" he asked.

"It is my *cachette*," she said taking off her hat and shaking out her hair. "My hide-away`."

124

He found new energy as he walked around the room. The only windows were high on the walls allowing light to penetrate but not prying eyes. A bed was tucked in one corner and an opening in the opposite wall revealed steps down to a dark tunnel.

"That leads to the house," she said as he peered into the darkness. She sat in one of the wingback chairs and poured two glasses of wine from a decanter. "Come join me."

Buddy sat and sipped his wine, trying to gauge what he was feeling—besides exhaustion and sadness.

"Since the British took over my estate," she continued, "I have been surrounded by men—important men. But they have either been single-minded warriors or single-minded womanizers. These men have patronized me, tried to seduce me, and one even tried to rape me. You are the first to treat me as an equal—simply as a person." She sipped her wine. "I just want to forget about the war for a little while and enjoy a glass of wine with my friend."

Buddy sat up at the revelation. "Did you report the assault?"

"Oh yes." She sipped her wine. "He was reassigned. I never saw him again."

"So, the bastard is still out there."

She didn't reply.

Buddy lost track of time—hypnotized by the wine, the seclusion, and the voice of an attractive woman. She talked of her country before the war and her husband before the war took him. He told her about his childhood and the death of his mother. He shared the irony of his running away from a life filled with zoo animals only to be redeemed from his failure at professional baseball by a barn full of horses.

She watched him closely as he spilled his heart and let a long pause hang in the air. Finally, she said quietly, "I haven't been with a man since my husband died."

Buddy was taken aback at her directness. He had been around her for so long, he barely thought of her as a woman. She was not old enough to be his mother, but he took comfort in her maturity and confidence. And seeing her with her hair down caused something to stir inside him. He leaned forward and touched his glass to hers.

They sipped in silence. When their glasses were empty, she stood, took his glass, and placed it on the table. She pulled him to his feet, leaned in, and kissed him. With nothing touching but fingers and lips, the sensation was electric. He tingled as the fragrance of her lavender soap seeped into his nostrils, creating the sensation of being enveloped in a cloud.

Of all the women he had been around, Buddy had never known such closeness. When they separated, the tenderness of the moment, the memory of long walks and intimate talks collided with his recent memories of the field of battle, tears came to his eyes. "I'd better get back," he said.

"No," she said. She clutched his hand, and he knocked over a wine glass as she led him to the bed. Her passion built with ferocity so suddenly that it caught Buddy off guard. He was grateful for the seclusion of their bedroom.

An hour later, they walked together through the woods but dropped hands as they returned to the clearing near the barn. Buddy pulled up short when he saw Major Miller. The major saw them, and Buddy knew the major well enough to realize he would be furious at Buddy for fraternizing with their hostess outside the stable. But in that moment, he didn't care. He let his hand brush against her and felt her push back against him. He was experiencing something special— something he desperately needed in the midst of the violence and bloodshed he'd witnessed.

16

PARIS, FRANCE
APRIL 1918

BUDDY STARED INTO the canopy of trees above him, smelling the wood smoke from a nearby fire and remembering the sound of Gabrielle breathing next to him in bed a few hours ago. They had been stealing away to their hideaway every few days, but she had become more distant as their quiet talks became less frequent but their time in bed more passionate—two lonely people desperate to escape the war. Now, but for the occasional cry of the wounded, the war seemed a long way off from where he lay on the seat of his ambulance wagon.

The British Army moved its headquarters out of the chateau through the back door as General Pershing's office staff moved in by the front. Major Miller had moved his office into the chateau as well and probably felt like he was part of General Pershing's command staff. He hadn't stopped watching Buddy, however.

"Rise and shine there, Sergeant."

Buddy pulled himself upright and looked down at the fat corporal who waddled down the lane with a fistful of papers. Buddy's wagon was now at the head of the line and would take the next casualty from the field hospital east of Paris near the village of Chelles to somewhere in Paris. He had been shuttling patients—mostly from the Battle of the Somme—for nearly a month in a grim procession that allowed him to spend his nights in the comfort of his base camp outside Gabrielle's chateau.

Behind the corporal, two orderlies escorted a man who looked at the ground as he walked but did not appear to be injured. They were followed by a small woman in a nurse's uniform.

As Buddy rattled the reins to move Queenie and Raven into position, he glanced at his passenger with curiosity. The orderlies each gripped an arm and, though he couldn't see the back of his wagon, he could both hear and feel the three men step inside. After a few minutes, the two orderlies stepped back out, closed the door, and banged on the wagon to signal that they were done. Because the patient was not physically injured, Buddy knew he would be secured in the back of the wagon like a prisoner. A mental patient, Buddy assumed, bound for the Saint Martin's Clinic. The nurse took the papers from the corporal and climbed up to the bench seat next to Buddy.

"Good luck with this one," the corporal muttered as he walked away.

Buddy rattled the reins and said to the horses, "Get up."

He glanced at the nurse as they pulled away and she met his eye.

"Shell shock," she said.

"Saint Martin's?" he asked in reply.

"No," she replied with a side-long look. "This one's going to the base hospital."

Buddy waited for more explanation, but none was offered. So, they rode in silence.

The Battle of Argonne Forest had been raging for nearly a month. The battlefield was a two-day wagon ride east of Paris—too far for his slow, horse-drawn wagon to be useful. The wounded were brought to the field hospital in motorized vehicles for sorting and minor treatment. They were then sent back to the front or on to other facilities, as needed. His ambulance was ideal for local transport.

"I haven't seen you before," he said to the nurse.

"Florence," she said. "Florence Walker."

He was going to ask her where she was from, but when he glanced at her, her eyes were closed and her head bobbing. He decided to let her rest and settled into his own thoughts as the horses pulled the wagon along familiar routes. She leaned against him, and he smiled as they bounced along the road until a pair of motorcycles rounded a corner ahead of him. They were followed by a convoy of trucks packed with soldiers. Buddy pulled the wagon to the side of the road and watched them pass.

"Cannon fodder," muttered Nurse Walker bitterly as she sat up.

Buddy glanced at her. She was glaring at the passing procession, so he decided to keep his mouth shut. They rode the remaining twenty minutes to the hospital in silence.

The courtyard of the base hospital was bustling, as usual. Buddy pulled his ambulance into the line with the other wagons, tied off the reins, and climbed down to help Nurse Walker. He opened the back door of the ambulance and stood aside for the nurse to enter. He watched her unbuckle the straps that restrained the man, anticipating that he would help them down and be on his way.

"All right, Private McMillan," she said as she unfastened his arms. "Let's get you out of here."

"No!" he shouted. "I'm not going back out there!"

He retreated to the front of the wagon and sat down on the floor, wrapping his arms around his knees and burying his head. He began to sob uncontrollably.

Nurse Walker placed her hands on her hips and looked down at the man, then backed away and climbed out of the wagon.

"I'd better get a doctor," she muttered.

"What am I supposed to do with him?" Buddy said as she walked away.

"He's not going anywhere," she replied without turning.

Buddy stood guard at the door watching the man and trying to understand how he felt. Buddy had heard the thunder of the big guns, but only from a distance. He knew what it was like to be shot at, but not as if he was charging forward into a hail of bullets.

A few minutes later, Nurse Walker returned with another nurse and a stooped elderly man in a white lab-coat. The man nodded at Buddy and wordlessly entered the back of the ambulance.

"Doctor LeFleur," Nurse Walker said by way of introduction.

Buddy and the two nurses watched as Dr. LeFleur sat next to Private McMillan and offered the man a cigarette. The private's hand was shaking so badly, he couldn't put the cigarette to his lips. The doctor placed the cigarette and lit it for the private. They sat and talked for what seemed an eternity until the doctor struggled to his feet and offered the man a hand up.

Buddy and Nurse Walker stood with Doctor LeFleur and watched Private McMillan as he was escorted away by the other nurse—head down and cigarette dangling from his lips.

"Is that what we call shell shock?" Buddy asked.

"I prefer to call it Da Costa's Syndrome," said the doctor. "*La fatigue,* the horror of the battlefield affects people differently," the old doctor continued in broken English. "Some people are terrorized on the spot, *comme cet homme*, and they exhibit symptoms that *neutralizer,* incapacitate them. For others, the symptoms are more subtle and may not show up until they are home and safe from the war. It is a concept that goes back to Roman times. When we get depressed or feel *melancolie*, it's as though a *chien noir*—a black dog—is following us," Doctor LeFleur said. "The dog is mostly off in the distance. We hardly know he's there. But sometimes he comes close, and you can't chase him away. When he does that," the doctor paused and watched Private McMillan walking toward the hospital, "it's the most helpless feeling in the world."

Buddy felt a sense of unease as the doctor spoke. He had felt that melancholy most of his life—when he ran away from home to play baseball, when he washed out of baseball and joined the army, and now seeing the death and destruction of a terrible war. Black dog, indeed.

When he got back to the barn at the end of his shift, he was happy to see Gabrielle walking across the garden as he pulled into the barnyard. She joined him as he unhitched the horses and led them into their stall.

"How do you like your new house guests?" he asked her.

"It's too early to say," she said, as she leaned against the door of the stall. "But they can't be any worse than the British."

He stopped and looked at her. "Were the British really that bad?"

When she didn't answer, he sensed there was more to it than just rude officers. He had been around enough French people to recognize their deep-seated hostility toward the British.

"Mrs. Saint-Simon," a man's voice called from the courtyard.

She turned and walked out of sight and Buddy heard her say, "General Armstrong. Please call me Gabrielle."

"Then, Gabrielle it is," said the general. "General Pershing is returning from the Front tomorrow and would like you to be his guest for dinner tomorrow evening."

Buddy eased over to the door of the stall and peered outside. Gabrielle's back was toward Buddy so he couldn't hear her reply, but she was nodding her head. General Armstrong was not what Buddy had expected. Most of the top brass he had been around were full of themselves—all bluster and strut—like the general who'd cleared the roadblock.

This man was different. He was polite and attentive—closer to Gabrielle's age, with sandy, blond hair and blue eyes. He stood with his hands behind his back and leaned into their conversation, his eyes boring into hers.

General Armstrong said, "General Pershing has assigned me to be your liaison. If there is anything you need, or anything we can do to make your life more comfortable, you're to let me know. *Je suis à votre service*," he said with a small bow.

"You speak French?" she said loud enough for Buddy to hear.

"*Un petit peu*," he replied with his finger and thumb pinched together. "Only a little."

As the general shook her hand, he leaned in and whispered something that made her laugh.

Buddy felt a stab of jealousy as he realized his dalliance with this aristocratic woman was coming to an end. She was far more likely to share her bed with a handsome general than a sergeant who drove a wagon. He turned back to the empty stall and jammed his pitchfork into manure and soiled straw at his feet. His horses watched him through the half-door to the outdoor paddock, so he wandered back to pet them.

He had known her for less than a year so he couldn't claim to love her. But her presence and comfort had brought him through some tough times. She had been a ray of light in his dark days. Tears filled his eyes as he wondered how he would get along without her, but Raven pushed him with her nose as if to remind him that he wasn't completely alone.

17

BUDDY BLEW SMOKE up toward the steel-gray sky and pushed back into the doorway of an empty storefront, hoping the scattering of policemen across the street wouldn't think him suspicious.

Kaz had given him directions to the local police station, and it wasn't hard to find once he knew where to look. The impressive brick and limestone building towered over Decatur Street, just a few blocks south of where he and Max had met with Asa Candler yesterday. Police cars and motorcycles were parked up and down both sides of the street while men and women—most of the men in police uniforms —streamed in and out of the building. He hoped to catch sight of Detective Stockton outside the station, and he especially wanted to do it without running into Sergeant Rocker.

"What are you doing out here, Mister?"

Buddy was startled out of his reverie by two policemen who appeared to be walking back to the station. He wondered how much to reveal, but decided he had nothing to hide.

"I was hoping to catch Detective Stockton," he said. "But I'm not sure I want to go inside there." He nodded at the building across the street.

The men looked at each other. One man shrugged his shoulders and said, "Never heard of him, but you can't loiter out here. Either go inside and ask at the desk or move on."

Buddy nodded in compliance and stepped out to cross the street. He could feel their eyes on his back, so he was forced to keep moving as he scanned the scene for signs of the detective or of Sergeant

Rocker. An odd sense of unease settled over him. His stomach knotted and his palms began to sweat. He wanted to run away but he felt trapped in a bad dream with men in uniform bringing back the smell of death and the memories of war.

But as he looked up to the top of the broad granite steps he stopped. Detective Stockton came down and headed toward him.

"How did you know I was here?" Buddy asked, as they walked away.

"I just happened to be looking out the window when those two cops sent you packing."

"I heard you were looking for me but, when I got here, I couldn't find the guts to go inside."

"Sergeant Rocker?" asked Stockton.

"I suppose," Buddy replied. "But all those uniforms brought back unpleasant memories. I was a wagon driver in the war," Buddy looked at Stockton and asked, "Did you serve?"

"I was with the fourth Marines," he said. "We fought at the Belleau Wood in June of '18."

"Jesus," Buddy said. "I was there, too. But my job was to pick up the casualties."

Stockton looked sharply at Buddy and a hint of pain flashed in his eyes. They were on a side street and out of sight of the station. Stockton lit a cigarette, and Buddy viewed him through a new lens. A Marine who lived through the Belleau Wood was not a man to be trifled with.

"Look," Stockton began as he blew out smoke and glanced nervously around. "The department has its sights set on your guy, and there's not much I can do about it."

"I thought you were supposed to be cleaning things up."

"I am. But there's only so much I can do. The whole department is run by the Klan—up and down the ranks. New recruits are initiated as part of their becoming policemen. Sergeant Rocker is one of the leaders, but he's just the tip of the iceberg."

Stockton smoked his cigarette and paced slowly, deep in thought. Buddy tried to imagine the detective as a fighting soldier. He decided that, despite his small stature, the man did exhibit a confidence and strength that Buddy had overlooked. He was a little ashamed. He should have known better.

"So, what do you suggest?" Buddy asked, finally.

"He needs to keep his head down until I can figure something out."

"How long will that take?"

"I wish I knew." Stockton dropped his cigarette and squashed it under his shoe like he was killing a bug. He began to walk away.

"I had another run in with your sergeant this morning," Buddy said to his back.

"He's not my sergeant," Stockton turned and said testily.

"He was ready to have another go at me when a man in a fancy car pulled up. I thought Rocker was going to bow down and kiss his ring."

"Probably one of his Klan buddies—maybe even one of his bosses. They have their own hierarchy. It's like a military organization that has spread through our society down here. That's why I was brought in from Boston. We have our own criminal enterprises up there, but it's nothing like the Klan."

Buddy watched the policeman walk away with a mixture of anxiety and dread. He worked with some of the largest, most dangerous animals on earth, but he would rather take his chances with a bull elephant than work inside the snake pit that was the Atlanta Police Department.

***

The sun came out during the walk from the police station, and the heat began to build. Fortunately, he found a cool spot in the loft of Naomi's barn. He had arrived to find a flatbed truck backed up to the barn unloading hay, and he joined the line of men in the loft passing sixty-pound bales to be stacked. After they finished and the workmen had scattered, Naomi climbed down to pay the driver. Buddy sat in the loft opening with his feet dangling above the barn door below, refreshed by the breeze.

"Fifteen dollars for some of the worst hay I've ever seen," Naomi grumbled as she plopped down beside him.

They watched from above as the truck driver stopped at the cab of his truck, scribbled something on a slip of paper, and placed the paper and the money Naomi had given him into a small, zippered pouch.

"We've seen that at the circus, too," Buddy agreed as the truck rumbled away. "Good hay seems hard to come by here in the South."

They sat in comfortable silence for a moment.

"Would you ever be interested in selling some of your mules?" Buddy asked.

She looked at him sharply. "No. Why would you ask that?"

He told her about his visit to Arabella's stable and her interest in horses and mules. "I just thought I'd ask," he said.

"I could part with some of the horses," she said quietly. "But not the mules."

Buddy waited, sensing she had more to say. When she didn't speak, he asked, "How old are those mules?"

She cast him a puzzled glance. "Daddy bought the four of them when I was about eight years old. They were young but looked fully grown. They must be twenty-five or thirty, now."

Buddy some calculations and said, "So, Herman worked with these mules."

"Daddy taught him to drive with Thelma and Bunch." She chuckled and continued, "They gave him fits."

Buddy smiled at the thought of finding the mule with Herman Dixon. Saving that animal was probably the only positive thing that could have come out of the French battlefield called Belleau Wood.

"You remind me of your brother in a way I can't quite describe," he said.

"I'm surprised you remember him that well," she replied. "How long has it been?"

He thought for a moment. "Must be nearly twenty years, now. But some things about that time are as clear as yesterday."

He turned his slightly, so she wouldn't see his eyes watering and continued. "He and I saw a lot of death and suffering over there, but seeing you and reliving my memories of Herman made me realize something. Death was never real to me until I saw them pull the sheet over Herman's head. Before that, it was something that happened to someone else."

He sniffed and saw her look at him.

"It's not your fault he died," she said.

"Oh, I know that." He said, quietly, "This is the first time I've talked about it with anyone." After a few moments, he fished a rag out of his pocket to wipe his face.

"Have you ever heard of the Trail of Tears?" she asked. When he shook his head, she continued. "About a hundred years ago, my grandmother and her family were rounded up from somewhere here in the south and marched out to Oklahoma. They were promised their own land and a new life. All they got was tears and poverty. By the time my mother was born, things had only gotten worse. So, when the Buffalo Soldiers arrived, they were not particularly welcome. When she fell in love with my father—well, you can imagine how well that went over with her people."

She paused, "Anyway, after my parents moved back here, they married and started this business. But, for her, something was always off. I think she might have had her own demons. The people here seemed to love her, but she told me she never felt fully at home. She could never accept the Christian religion, and that's the glue that holds us together around here. So, she left after my father died. I wonder, sometimes, if she's any happier out there."

"What about you?" Buddy asked. "Do you have any demons that haunt you?"

"Oh no," she replied with a chuckle. "God has blessed me. I have Jesus watching over me."

Buddy wondered how Jesus fit into the racism, violence, and lynchings that Naomi lived with, but decided to keep his mouth shut.

"Would you care to join us for our Wednesday night dinner tomorrow evening?" she asked.

"No," he said. "I'd better spend some time doing my job over at the circus. We have animals to train—equipment to clean."

He was startled to feel a dog push its head between Naomi and him and lay down. He looked at Naomi as she laughed and said, "Yona has learned how to climb the ladder to the loft."

Placing his hand on Yona's head sent a feeling of calm rushing through him. He rubbed the dog's head and scratched it behind the ears and, when Naomi bumped him with her shoulder and said, "Surely they can do without you for a few hours."

18

Wednesday, November 4, 1936

The morning air was crisp and cooler than yesterday. The sun was just cresting the horizon—a time of day that people who work with animals were accustomed to. Buddy had helped Max feed and water the elephants and promised to be back before lunchtime.

As he approached Arabella Anderson's barn, he asked, "Mind if I join you?"

She was sitting on a bench next to the open barn door smoking a cigarette. She had watched him approach across the field to her left, and Buddy had waited for some acknowledgment—a wave of the hand or a nod of the head—but she only puffed and watched. He wondered if she would tell him to get lost, but she nodded to the empty spot beside her. They sat in comfortable silence for a few moments.

"Any word from your husband?" he asked, finally. "I need to know about the horses."

"He's out hunting," she replied. "They expect him back at the house this evening. You can check back tomorrow if you like."

Birds flitted about the property and an owl gave its final hoot of the morning. Buddy looked over the grounds, which were not as well-kept as some he passed on his way back to the circus yesterday.

The back of the big house, about a hundred yards in front of him, faced a busy highway. But he had never seen the front door because he had been directed to approach the property from the backside off Springdale. The white, two-story wooden structure had wide porches all around, but it gave off an air of neglect. He could see the edge of a wide circular driveway in front and suspected that side of the property was the only view the owners attended. Between the barn and house, a fenced garden had gone to seed and the path was barely discernable.

"What's that building over there?" Buddy asked, nodding toward a small, vine-covered cottage with a rusted, metal roof.

Bella glanced in the direction Buddy was looking and said, "That's the old servant's house. We just use it for storage now."

"Where's that elephant stick you said you always carry?" she asked, changing the subject.

"Didn't think I'd need it."

She got up suddenly and said, "Sam and Fanny are off getting supplies this morning. I don't suppose you could help me in here for a bit."

He had been around enough horse barns to know what was required so, in about an hour, they were finished feeding and watering the animals and they sat sipping coffee. She had an easy confidence about her that Buddy found attractive. It was a quality that all horsewomen shared. Gabrielle had it and Naomi had it—that firm hand with a gentle touch, that saucy swagger with a smooth glide. A woman like Bella could walk into a stall with a half-ton, frightened horse and calm it with a gentle touch and a quiet voice. As she crossed the room to retrieve the coffee, her mood was changed by the sound of a car outside.

Buddy glanced toward the sound outside the door then looked back at her face. He couldn't decide if she appeared to be frightened or angry. The car crunched up the gravel driveway behind the barn and the motor stopped. Buddy expected to hear footsteps approaching, but instead another motor started, and a different car sped off.

Bella moved back to her chair and sat down heavily. Seeing Buddy's questioning look, she said, "That was Thomas, my stepson. He likes to drive his father's Cadillac when Charles is out of town. The flashy car makes him feel like a big man." This last phrase left little doubt about how she felt about her stepson.

Buddy thought about the man who had stopped to speak with Sergeant Rocker yesterday and asked, "Does Thomas have crooked teeth and pockmarked skin?"

"You know him?" she asked with alarm.

"No," he replied. "I saw him talking to a policeman who likes to give me a hard time."

"That'll be one of his Klan buddies," she said with contempt.

Buddy let that sink in for a moment then rose. "I guess I'd better be getting back. I have an elephant to find a home for."

"An elephant?" She stood as well and followed him into the hallway of the barn.

"It's a long story," he said as he walked away.

"Buddy," she said to his back. "My stepson is not a nice person. You should steer clear of him."

***

The zoo was nestled in the southwest corner of Grant Park, a ten-minute motorcar ride south of the circus grounds. As he and Max circled the lake and wandered its rows of cages, being in a zoo evoked some sad but familiar memories for Buddy. He wondered how it would compare to his father's zoo, the last zoo he had been in, nearly twenty-five years ago.

The mid-day sun warmed them as they wandered past shaded hoofed animal pens containing deer, water buffalo, and zebras, and along rows of cages overcrowded with animals—dozens of monkeys in one, eleven lions in another. They saw bears, leopards, hyenas, and a tiger with a hand-painted label that read, "Jimmy Walker." They walked mostly in silence until they reached the far end of the zoo where they found what they were looking for. Six elephants—two in a small pen constructed of iron pipes and railroad rails, and four chained to trees.

"Not what I had hoped for Tembo," Buddy muttered.

Max didn't bother to reply.

As they turned to leave, they were halted by an elderly bearded man in shabby clothes holding a wooden cane. He didn't hold the cane by its handle but clutched it in the middle and used it to point toward the elephants. He was using it, Buddy thought, like a hookless bullhook.

"Quite a sight, aren't they?" the man said.

Buddy and Max exchanged a look, and Max asked, "Do you work here?"

"I am the keeper of the elephants," the man proclaimed. He spoke loud enough that a small crowd began to gather. A woman with two children in tow and pushing a baby carriage, and an elderly couple, joined Buddy and Max.

"This is the largest herd of elephants in the southeastern United States," the man told his audience.

"Can you make them do some tricks?" one of the children asked.

"Not right now," the man said. "They're resting."

"What are their names?" asked the elderly woman.

"Uh, we don't like to name our animals here," the man said evasively. "Some people claim the lion is the king of beasts," he continued. "But in the jungle, the elephant is king. Nothing can hurt an elephant."

Buddy glanced at Max. His eyeroll indicated he had the same thought. This man was no elephant keeper. He was just some old man who liked to be the center of attention.

"Why are they chained to trees?" Buddy asked the man.

"These elephants just arrived a few months ago from a wealthy donor. We are building them a bigger barn down by Lake Abana," the man said. "Workmen are down there right now."

Suddenly, one of the children bolted from his mother's side and ran toward the elephants. The mother shouted, "Adam!" but remained with her stroller and the other child. "Adam, come back here this instant!" the mother exclaimed.

As Adam toddled toward an adult, tuskless elephant that Buddy assumed to be a cow, a nearby tusker took interest and moved toward the child. The self-proclaimed elephant keeper remained rooted to his spot.

Buddy and Max exchanged another look and took action. Buddy snatched the zookeeper's cane and Max asked to borrow the elderly lady's parasol.

"I'll take the tusker," Max said.

As Max intercepted his elephant, he held up the cane and said, "Whoa."

Buddy moved toward the elephant nearest the child, hoping these elephants had received some training. "Whoa," he said. "Steady."

The elephant was sniffing Adam's shoes, and the boy reached out his hand to touch its trunk. Buddy moved to the elephant's left side and touched her flank with the crook of his cane as if it were a bullhook. He looked at Max who was in a similar position next to the tusker, and they grinned at each other.

"What the hell is going on here?" said a man rushing up the sidewalk wearing a uniform and carrying a bullhook. Buddy's grin faded as he realized the real zookeeper just arrived. "You two get away from those elephants."

Buddy grabbed Adam's hand and led him back to his mother, as Max returned the parasol.

"It's all right," said the mother. "These men saved my child. You should have a fence around these beasts."

"We're building a new pen for them down by the lake," the zookeeper said. "Hiram here is supposed to be keeping people away from the animals, not regaling them with stories."

The zookeeper turned his attention to Max and Buddy. "You two looked pretty comfortable over there."

"We're with the circus," Max said.

"I know," said the zookeeper.

"You do?" they said in unison.

"I'm Mike Steele." He extended a hand. "I came to the zoo with these animals from the Candler Zoo here in town but before that I was with the Spinelli Circus. When elephants come to Atlanta, I make sure

I go and see them. That big tusker of yours looks to be quite a handful."

"Tembo's his name," Max said. "Can we see what you're building here? We might be looking for a home for Tembo."

"Ha," Steele laughed. He gazed at the elephants and said, "We've got our hands full with this bunch. In fact, we're looking for homes for some of them. There's no way we can take on any more animals." He shrugged his shoulders in apology and continued, "I would like to have you take a look at what we're building, though. Maybe you have some ideas for me."

As they walked away, they heard Hiram addressing a new crowd. "Some people claim the lion is the king of beasts, but in the jungle, the elephant is king."

As they walked past rows of cages toward the lake they passed on their way in, Buddy tried to process his thoughts on having Tembo end up here—even though they clearly could not take him. He had only been with the elephant for about six months, but he felt a connection. And the animal's life on the road seemed much more interesting than being chained to a tree in some park. He wasn't sure Tembo would survive very long in this environment. He had a streak of independence that Buddy had experienced first-hand.

19

WEDNESDAY NIGHT DINNER at the Ebenezer Baptist Church appeared to be more of a social event than the dinner he had attended on Sunday. As Buddy sat on the park bench with his back to the setting sun, he watched people across the street pour into the back door of the church—no fancy hats, frilly dresses or starched white shirts and ties. Just people in everyday clothes carrying dishes of food and wearing smiles.

The first time he had entered the church just a few days ago, he had been apprehensive about the unknown. Now he was apprehensive about something he couldn't explain. The people would be welcoming, and the food would be good. It would be like a family reunion, but he wouldn't be part of the family—not really. He was reluctant to go inside and face the crowd.

As Buddy scanned the area, watching people arrive, his eye was drawn to a man sitting in a car parked about half a block behind him. A white man in a colored neighborhood. He was smoking a cigarette as the evening darkness closed in, making no pretense of doing anything but watching the people enter the church.

"Buddy!"

He turned to see Naomi across the street in front of the church waving to him and beginning to move his way.

As she stepped into the street, a car came around the corner. Buddy watched helplessly as she fell back, and the car screeched to a halt.

Buddy ran toward it and people emerged from the church to surround the scene. He rounded the car and pushed his way through the crowd and was relieved to see her seated on the curb with Aunt

Thelma and Mrs. King attending to her. She appeared to be unhurt. Reverend King was speaking to the tall, middle-aged Negro who had been driving the car. Buddy wanted to punch the man, but he held back and moved in near enough to hear them speaking.

"She stepped right in front of me," the man said. "I couldn't stop. Is she alright?"

The man was clearly upset, and Buddy began to feel sorry for him. As he replayed the scene in his mind, Naomi had been looking at him and not where she was heading—which was into traffic. It wasn't the man's fault.

"She's fine," said Reverend King. "She just fell down as she backed away from your car."

"Do you live around here?" Reverend King asked as he watched his wife escort Naomi inside.

"No," the man replied watching Naomi closely. "I live west of town, over near University Homes."

"What's your name?" Reverend King began making conversation, probably trying to calm the man down.

"Glover," the man said. "I'm Elton Glover."

"Well, Elton Glover," Reverend King said. "Why don't you park your car here in our lot and come inside."

The man looked uneasy as he surveyed the crowd. He had almost run over one of their own and now he was being invited inside. Buddy would have run away as fast as he could.

Reverend King must have had the same thought because he placed his arm around Elton Glover and whispered something to a heavyset man standing man next to him. King gently escorted Glover inside as the heavyset man parked Elton Glover's car behind the church.

"Naomi is asking after you." Aunt Thelma stood in the doorway with her hand outstretched. Now, he not only felt welcome, but he also felt like a schoolboy who was being summoned to the office.

As he left the gloom of a November evening with its smell of gasoline and engine exhaust, he walked down the stairs and entered a well-lit room that smelled of baked ham and floor polish. The rumble of human chatter was punctuated with laughter, and he not only felt welcome, he felt he belonged.

Thelma pointed out Naomi, Reverend King, and Elton Glover standing near a table to his left.

"I feel such a fool," Naomi said, grabbing Buddy's arm.

Glover's eyes grew wide in surprise at Buddy's arrival as Reverend King did the introduction.

"Buddy Griffith is a friend of ours—an elephant man with the circus and a part-time muleskinner."

Glover quickly regained his composure and greeted Buddy with a faint smile and a firm handshake. Buddy sized him up as a man of substance. He was a little older than Buddy, well dressed, and—judging by his car outside—well-to-do.

"I need to circulate," said Reverend King.

"And I'm expected in the kitchen," said Naomi.

"Well," said Buddy as they walked away. "It looks like it's you and me."

Glover laughed, and asked, "So, how do you fit into all of this?"

Buddy gave him a quick rundown and asked, "How about you? Do you have a family to get home to?"

"No," he replied as he looked at the floor. "My wife died last year. Cancer. We never had children." After an awkward silence, he continued. "I own a bank down the street. I was just checking on a building we're financing."

As Glover spoke, Buddy's eyes scanned the room. He was shocked when his gaze landed at the bottom of the stairs.

"Oh no," he said under his breath. "What's he doing here."

Thornell had just entered and was making his way across the room toward Reverend King. Buddy grabbed Glover by the arm and, without looking at him said, "Excuse me."

But he stopped after half a step. Sergeant Rocker stood in the doorway at the top of the stairs.

"Might have known I'd find you here," Rocker sneered as he descended, and Buddy approached.

"What's wrong with you?" Buddy said. "This is a church meeting. These people haven't done anything wrong."

Buddy surveyed the room as he spoke and saw police officers with batons spilling through the doorway while church members armed themselves with knives, rolling pins, and other weapons. He was relieved when Reverend King approached with a frightened looking Thornell in tow.

"What's the trouble, officer?" King asked.

"You know why I'm here. This man," he looked at Thornell, "is under arrest."

As Rocker spoke, two officers took Thornell by his arms. Naomi stood next to Thornell looking defiant.

"On what charge?" King asked.

"Murder."

A low rumble skittered through the crowd as Rocker addressed Thornell. "Thornell Dixon, I'm arresting you for the murder of Miss Sally Bingham on the night of Saturday, October 31st at the Edgewood Avenue Trolley Barn." He nodded at the men on Thornell's arms and continued, "Take him away."

"No!" shouted Naomi.

The crowd grumbled and closed in, causing the policemen, including Rocker, to shift their nightsticks and reach for their guns.

Reverend King held up his arms and the room quieted. "Where are you taking him?"

"That's none of your business."

The room grumbled again, and the crowd moved in. Rocker was outnumbered, but if he was intimidated, he didn't show it.

"Mind if I send a few of my parishioners along to make sure there's no trouble on the way to the station?"

"Yes, I mind," said Rocker. "I don't need no nigger escort," he said loud enough for all to hear.

As soon as the policemen had cleared the doorway, Reverend King summoned two men. "Follow them," he said. "Stay out of sight but make sure Thornell gets to the station."

As the men left on their mission, King addressed the crowd. "Y'all try to enjoy your dinner. We'll deal with this Tomorrow. Is Marcus here?"

A man at the door of the kitchen raised his hand and King beckoned him to join him. He then turned to Thelma, Naomi, and his wife and motioned for them to follow him. Buddy decided to invite himself, as well.

Reverend King's office was a small room off the main sanctuary. The three women occupied the only chairs in the room. The three men stood.

"Marcus," Reverend King began, "Can you get over to the jail first thing in the morning and see if we can bond him out?"

"I'll try, Martin," said Marcus, who Buddy suspected was a lawyer. "But you know that's not going to happen with a murder charge."

"I know. But it'll give you a chance to see him. Make sure he's okay."

"I'd like to help."

Buddy turned from his spot along the back wall to the doorway where Elton Glover stood. He had apparently recovered from the shock of almost running over Naomi. He strode into the room and took control—a move Buddy found at once comforting and strangely familiar.

"I'd like to repay you all for your kindness." He nodded at Naomi, who smiled for the first time.

"We appreciate your offer," said Reverend King, "but Marcus here…"

"I don't mean to take business from your attorney," Glover said. "But I have resources that might complement his work."

"What kind of resources?" Mrs. King asked.

"Legitimate resources, I assure you," said Glover. "You know that building that is going up down Auburn Avenue?"

"The Masonic Lodge?" said Marcus.

"Yes. I'm financing it."

"So, you're a Freemason," said Reverend King.

"No," Glover replied. "But I admire their principles and have worked with them for years."

"Sorry," Buddy said. "But what's a Freemason?"

"It's a men's fraternity," Glover said.

"Secret society, more like," Marcus muttered looking at Reverend King for confirmation.

King continued to look at him, so Glover continued. "They prefer to think of themselves as a charitable organization with secret rituals. They are not Christian, per se, but they do require their members to profess a belief in God." Glover looked pointedly at Reverend King. "They raise money for the poor, they support widows and orphans, and they promote citizenship, moral values, and brotherly love—among all the races."

"So, why aren't you one of them?" Marcus asked.

"I have my reasons."

"What do you propose to do for us?" asked Reverend King.

Glover raised his hands with palms up, "I'm not sure, but the Masons have a wide network of men, probably a few in the room out there. Their members include important and wealthy men. They might even," he paused, "have a man or two sharing a cell with your friend right now. They can get information that you won't be able to find."

Shuffling feet behind him caused Glover to move from the doorway. One of the men King had sent to follow the police entered. He was breathing heavily and dripping wet. Buddy could hear the rain pounding on the roof.

"They didn't go to the police station," the man said.

Naomi stood; Thelma's hand went to her mouth.

"What!" said Reverend King. "Where did they take him?"

"The car holding Thornell turned off from the rest of them before the station," the man panted. "Bobby's following it. I ran back here to tell you. I got a bad feeling about this."

20

THE STREETS WERE wet as Buddy trudged down Auburn Avenue in the cool, pre-dawn darkness. The Masonic Lodge should be just past the church on his right, about two blocks ahead. He had put hay down for the elephants and slipped off the circus grounds before anybody was awake. Glover had suggested they meet before sun-up, and he would try to have some information about where Thornell had been taken. As he approached the building, a small knot of men emerged from the awning over the door.

"What do you want?" a voice said from the darkness.

"I'm here to meet someone."

"Not here you're not," said another voice.

Ten or twelve men fanned out on either side of Buddy. Some were carrying baseball bats. All looked determined to stop him. At first, he regretted not bringing his bullhook, but as he watched the men surround him, he realized that if he was armed, they would probably beat him to death and take the bullhook as a prize.

"What's going on here?" someone said from behind him.

"This bum is trying to talk his way inside," said one of the men.

Buddy turned and was relieved to see Elton Glover. "You told us to meet here this morning." When Glover didn't respond, Buddy continued, "At the church last night."

A light of recognition flickered, but Glover said, "I didn't mean you."

Buddy didn't know whether to be embarrassed or angry, but he trusted Glover for some reason and simply said, "I want to help."

"We don't need your help," someone said.

Glover just looked at Buddy. Finally, he nodded toward the door and Buddy was allowed inside. They stood in a small alcove. The building looked finished from the outside, but inside it was a mess, with debris on the floor and walls with no plaster.

"Still under construction," said Glover by way of apology. "We'll meet in the library."

Another man came inside, and Glover asked, "You got something for me, Jolly?"

"Yes suh. We followed the car west of town. He's in a small brick shed. Looks like some kind-a little jail."

Glover nodded and said, "That preacher from down the street should be here soon. Let him and his men in when they get here."

Jolly went back into the rain and Glover invited Buddy to sit at a large, oblong table.

"So," Glover leveled his gaze at Buddy, "What's your connection to all this?"

"The man the police took last night, Thornell Dixon, works at Dixon's Livery. His cousin Naomi runs it. She's the one you nearly ran over last evening. Well," Buddy paused, "I just found out a couple of days ago that I served with her brother in the war."

"You were in the war?"

"I was."

"If her brother was colored, you didn't serve with him."

"I drove a wagon," Buddy said. "I got assigned to his unit."

"Dixon you say?" Glover looked at the ceiling. He paused for a long moment until recognition flickered in his eyes. He leaned forward and studied Buddy's face.

"I remember you."

Buddy gasped. He suddenly knew why the man had seemed familiar. He was older and had put on weight. And the war was a long time ago. But Dixon had told him his whole unit had been recruited from Georgia.

"Major Glover," he croaked. "I've still got that pistol you gave me."

"I tended to Corporal Dixon's burial," Glover said to Buddy. "He died of the Spanish flu."

"I know," Buddy replied. "I was there when he passed."

The moment broke when Reverend King and the two men who had followed the car walked in, followed by Glover's man, Jolly.

Glover hesitated and regained his composure. He rose, pointed to some empty chairs, and got down to business.

"I've got some people watching the building where they took your man," he told Reverend King. "My guess is that they will be back after dark tonight to light some crosses and string him up."

"Then, we need to get to him before they do that," said Rev. King. "How many guards did they post?"

Glover turned to Jolly, who said, "A couple of guys in a car. It's an old storage building down a dirt road. Ain't nobody around to hear him if he hollers, and it's locked up tight."

Glover stood and addressed his man. "Gather up some of the brothers and get over there. Maybe we can get him out before they come back."

"Let me call the police station first," Reverend King said. "Maybe we can resolve this without resorting to violence."

"Who are you going to call over there?" asked Glover.

Buddy spoke up, "I talked to Detective Stockton yesterday. He told me he was brought in to help root out the Klan, but he's not having much luck. It might be useful to call him, but I doubt he's going to ride to the rescue."

Glover hadn't stopped pacing the room. He was clearly agitated, and Buddy was seeing Major Glover, Buffalo Soldier, ready to stir his troops for battle. But this wasn't the trenches of France, and his men weren't rifle-carrying soldiers. They were shopkeepers and laborers with pitchforks and clubs.

"Then we're going out there," Glover said. "Jolly…"

"Wait," Buddy said. "I have an idea."

***

An hour later, Buddy was heading west on a rain-slick DeKalb Avenue. The big, powerful mules Mike and Ike pulled the wagon he had used at the quarry, with Naomi in the driver's seat and Jolly kneeling behind them, giving directions. Maybe, Buddy hoped, an innocent looking couple hauling a load of hay with their workman in the back could get close enough to the building where Thornell was being held.

About a mile west of town, Jolly pointed to a dirt road that crossed the railroad track to their right and disappeared into the trees. "This is it."

Naomi pulled the wagon off the road. She and Buddy looked at each other. Across the tracks, the road dipped, and last night's brief rain had turned it into a quagmire of mud with water ponding in places. The road was impassable. As Buddy pondered the bad break, he realized this could also be good.

"Jolly?" a voice from behind them said. "What you doin' up there?"

"Artie," Jolly said to the man who had emerged from the woods and now stood on the railroad tracks. "He still back there?"

"Yep" said Artie. "And there's nobody watchin' him. They left early this morning before the road got bad. I recon they went out to get some breakfast but when they came back, they couldn't get through. They should be back any time now."

Cars and trucks whizzed by them on the busy avenue as they sat on the wagon.

"Pull up behind that building," Buddy said, pointing to an abandoned garage about fifty yards up the road.

Naomi looked at the building, glanced at Buddy, then shook the reins.

When they were off the road and out of sight, Buddy jumped down and began unhitching one of the mules.

"What are you doing?" asked Naomi.

"We don't need the wagon back there," Buddy said as he clipped a lead-rope to Mike's halter, unhitched him and threw the chain traces that were hitched to the wagon over his back.

Naomi watched Buddy in confusion then smiled in recognition and climbed to the ground. She turned to Jolly and said, "Can you stay with the wagon and hold the mule?"

He slid down from the wagon and clipped a lead rope to Ike's halter. Naomi pulled a long piece of chain off the wagon and draped it around her neck. She looked at Buddy, then nodded at Artie to lead them through the woods.

As they emerged from the trees, they faced a small compound of weather-beaten buildings. Judging by their location near the tracks, Buddy figured they had once been used by the railroad. They followed Artie to a windowless shed—not much larger than an outhouse—but constructed of bricks and with iron bars for a door.

Naomi ran to the door and reached in to grab Thornell's hand through the bars. "Are you okay?"

"I'm sure glad to see you," he said. "How did you find me?"

"We had some friends watching. Are you hurt?"

"They beat me up trying to get me to confess. When I heard you coming, I figured they were coming back to finish the job. I don't mind saying, I thought I was done for."

"They's back!" said Jolly as he emerged from the woods. "The car is coming up the road."

"Who's watching the wagon?" exclaimed Naomi. As Jolly scrambled back through the woods, Naomi turned to Artie. "Keep a lookout," she said, pointing to the path toward the road.

Buddy positioned the mule and fastened the loose chain to one of Mike's traces. He looped the other end of the chain around the bars of the door, and eased Mike forward until the chains were taut. Naomi told Thornell to stand back. She picked up a long, flexible branch from the ground and moved up behind the animal. She made eye contact with Buddy who held tight to the mule's lead rope.

"Haa!" Naomi shouted as she whacked the mule on the rump.

Mike lurched forward in surprise snatching the iron grate out of the wall and dragging it a few feet before Buddy got him to stop.

Naomi and Artie helped Thornell from his prison. He moved slowly.

"They's coming!" Artie said in a loud whisper.

Buddy quickly unhooked the chains and draped them across the mule's back. He grabbed the mule's halter and turned the big animal back through the woods toward the wagon with Naomi and Artie helping Thornell. A few minutes later, they were on the wagon with Naomi driving back toward town. Thornell lay hidden in the bed of the wagon between Jolly and Artie. As they passed the car, the men were nowhere to be seen, but their car soon passed the wagon, hurrying back toward town.

"How're you feeling?" Buddy asked him when the car had passed.

"Not too bad," Thornell replied. "When it got dark, most of them left. There was just one car here all night, but they left this morning before it rained."

"Thank you," Naomi said to Buddy. "For helping us."

"What are you going to do with him?" Buddy asked. "You know they're not going to let this go."

"Can you hide out back in Cabbagetown for a while?" she asked Thornell.

"Just drop me off at the Krog Street underpass," he replied. "I got a lady I can stay with."

She cast a sad look at Buddy and said, "We've been dealing with this our whole lives." She glanced at the three men on the wagon bed behind her. "We just want to live our lives. We want decent work; we want to raise our families. But there's a few people who feed on hate. Runnin' others down makes them feel big. Then, there are people like Sergeant Rocker and his Klan buddies. I think they're cowards. They're afraid of anyone who doesn't look like them."

"Uh oh," Buddy said.

Naomi pulled back on the reins. "Whoa," she said to the mules. Traffic had come to a stop. They had been trundling along, hugging the right shoulder of the road, allowing cars and trucks to pass. But that traffic had come to a stop.

"Why have we stopped?" Thornell asked.

"Police roadblock," Naomi replied. "Looks like a truck is broken down."

Lanes of traffic were being allowed to pass in alternate directions, and the wagon was inching forward when Buddy suddenly leaped over the seat into the back.

"What's going on?" Naomi shouted back at Buddy. But when she turned her attention back to the road, she saw the reason for his alarm. A car had just cleared the roadblock and was headed in their direction. In the passenger seat of the flashy Cadillac—out of uniform but unmistakable—sat Sergeant Rocker alongside Bella Anderson's stepson, Thomas.

She turned her head, hoping to avoid Rocker's gaze and let them pass. "They must have already been on their way out there. And they're not going to be happy in a few minutes," she said.

"How far to where we drop Thornell off?" Buddy asked.

"A couple of blocks ahead," Naomi replied.

Buddy looked at Jolly and Artie. The three men slipped from the wagon and walked down the railroad tracks on their left, disappearing in the traffic ahead.

"We need to get these mules put away and make ourselves scarce, too," Buddy said to Naomi. "We've stirred the hornet's nest, now."

21

It was late morning by the time Buddy made his way to Springdale Road. His walk from Naomi's barn had taken less than an hour, but he felt as though he was in a different city altogether. He passed stately mansions with gated driveways and name plaques on stone columns. On Auburn Avenue the homes were tidy, wooden structures that were alive with people in the streets. The only life he saw around these homes were the Negro gardeners laboring in their front yards.

Down a long, gravel driveway he approached the back side of Bella Anderson's barn. He knew she was not likely to be in at that time of day, but he hoped Sam, her stable man, would be.

"Morning," Buddy said.

Sam continued washing the car behind the barn and said without looking up, "Got nothing here for a handout."

Buddy held up his hands. "Not looking for a handout," he said. Sam paused and looked at him. "I want to speak to Mrs. Anderson. My name is…"

"I know who you are. Fanny told me."

"Is this Thomas's car?" Buddy asked, nodding to the car Sam was washing. He hoped to break the ice. The 1936 Cadillac was moved from where he had seen it parked on his first visit, confirming what he already knew. He also noted that the tires on the car were caked with mud.

"She ain't here," Sam said, ignoring the question about the car. He leaned the scrub brush against the car and turned off the hose. "Miss Bella went to town with Fanny. They should be back soon." He nodded toward the barn and Buddy followed him inside.

"I'll put you on some coffee," he said over his shoulder, "if you wanna wait.".

"When do you expect Thomas back?" Buddy said to Sam's back as he led the way into the dining room where Buddy had first met Bella. Buddy thought Sam was ignoring him as he set about preparing the electric percolator.

"Hard to say," Sam said. "Most likely not till this evening." He turned, leaned against the counter, and folded his arms across his chest. "Fanny tells me you're trying to sell Miss Bella some horses from the circus."

Buddy recounted his earlier visit and asked, "How long have you worked here?"

"I've been with Mr. Charles nearly twenty years now," he said. "Fanny's been here longer than that. She got me this job."

"Think they'll buy my horses?"

"Hard to say." The percolator stopped gurgling, so Sam poured Buddy a cup of coffee and headed for the door.

"Can't you join me?"

Sam stopped and looked at Buddy from the doorway. He looked nervously into the hallway of the barn.

"I'd better get that car washed," Sam said finally. "If it ain't done when he gets back, there'll be hell to pay."

Buddy took his coffee out to the bench in front of the barn and sat in the late morning sun. He felt a little awkward about being here for the third day in a row. She had told him to check back, but he wondered if he would come across as desperate. Maybe he wanted an alibi for when Sergeant Rocker came calling about the disappearance of Thornell Dixon. Or maybe he just wanted to be around the beautiful woman in her horse barn.

***

"How long have you been here?" she asked as she picked up his feet and placed them on the ground.

159

He peeked out from under his cap and pushed himself upright. He glanced at the sun and said, "I'm not sure. Maybe half an hour." He yawned, stretched, and took out his cigarettes.

They sat and smoked in silence for a few minutes. He glanced at her and noted her yellow hair seemed to glow in the sunshine.

"My husband has finalized the purchase of our new property in South Georgia," she said. "He's on his way back to Atlanta."

Buddy didn't respond.

"He wants to have a look at your horses," she continued. "And he's going to look for some mules to pull his hunting wagon."

"That's good news," Buddy said. "When do you expect him back?"

"His train gets into town this evening. We'll head back down to Bella Plantation on Sunday with the livestock and wagons."

"Sunday?" Buddy asked. "But that's only…"

"Three days from now," she continued the thought. "I know. We're to spend the winter down there. That's what many of his rich friends do."

"Bella Plantation?" Buddy asked.

"I know." She smiled warmly. "He named it after me."

***

"Want to come have a look around?" asked Buddy as he got out of the car. "I can show you the horses."

"No," she said. "I don't want Charles to think I've already been here without him." She looked at Buddy and tilted her head. "This needs to be his decision."

He nodded. "See you tomorrow, then."

He watched her drive away, then trudged back toward the elephant area.

He passed the hay car on the railroad siding and was halted by the shouting inside the car.

"Well, you'd better find some!" Amos emerged from the railroad car and jumped down.

"It's not a matter of finding it," said the feed manager from the door of the car. "It's a matter of paying for it!"

"What's going on?" Buddy asked.

"We're out of hay," Amos said as he pushed his wheelbarrow.

Buddy walked with him. "When's the next load to come in?"

"It's not."

"What do you mean?"

"I mean," Amos stopped and looked at Buddy, "We're out of money and can't afford to buy anymore hay."

Buddy was speechless. Hay was one of the most basic commodities of any circus. It was cheap, plentiful, and essential for elephants, baggage stock, and show horses. He rushed back to the elephant area, trying to remember how many days' worth of hay they had left when he fed the animals this morning.

He found Max sitting in his canvas chair with his feet up on a box reading a tattered paperback book. He sat down on a bale of hay and leaned back against a tent pole. "Did you know we're almost out of hay?"

"Yep," he said without looking up.

"How much do we have?"

"We're good for a day or two." He put his book down and continued. "But hay may be the least of our problems." Buddy looked up sharply. "Smokey's gone."

"What do you mean, *gone*?"

"I mean gone. He and Kaz cleared out overnight."

"Well," Buddy sputtered, "Who's running the show?"

"Benny thinks he is," Max said.

"Benny the clown? He's nuts. He can't run this show," Buddy said. He got up and began to pace.

Max thumbed his book and said, "He's the one going around and telling everyone that Smokey is gone, and he's taking over."

"Jesus," Buddy said. "What a mess." He sat back down and continued. "What do you suppose happens now?"

"I don't know," Max said with a sigh. "Circuses run on tight margins at the best of times. When we got stuck here and the money stopped coming in, I figure the owners either got tired of pumping money in or they ran out of money. Either way, they need to find a buyer, or we'll all be out of work."

"What about them?" Buddy was looking at the elephants.

"They'll be okay for a few days. We'll ration the hay and cut some leafy shrubs and branches from the area."

"Want me to talk to Amos?" Buddy asked. "Maybe we can rally some of the performers and see if we can deal with Benny and his crew."

"Get out of here!" a woman screamed.

Buddy and Max started in her direction when a policeman walked between the tents and passed around the corner. They exchanged a look.

Suddenly policemen were everywhere, looking in tents, opening boxes, and pulling open the doors to trailers. Buddy and Max rose and grabbed their bullhooks.

"Where is he?" Sergeant Rocker growled as he approached from behind their tent.

"Who?" Buddy asked.

"You know who. He's not at that mule barn and neither is your lady-friend. You'd better not be hiding him around here." He opened the flap of their tent and looked inside.

Rocker turned his back and looked out over the circus grounds as, one by one, policemen approached shaking their heads. Rocker gave one final look around, scowled at Buddy, and stalked off.

"Care to tell me what that was all about?" Max asked.

"The police arrested Naomi's cousin, Thornell, last night for the murder in the Trolley barn." Buddy said. "He escaped earlier today."

"Why in the world would they think he was hiding here?"

When Buddy hung his head, Max continued. "Unless you had something to do with it," Max continued. "Jesus Buddy!"

After he explained the situation to Max, Buddy set out to warn Naomi. But he didn't get far.

As he pushed out the back of the tent, he halted and backed inside. Peering through the opening, he watched Thomas Anderson sitting in the Cadillac across the railroad tracks with Sergeant Rocker standing next to the car. Rocker placed his arms in an empty-handed, palms-up gesture, then pointed at the circus grounds. He appeared to be explaining to his superior that they had not found what—or who—they were looking for.

Buddy wondered about the relationship between the gruff policeman and the refined dandy in the flashy car. What united them? Was it their Klan boys club? Or was it as simple as a joint hatred of Negroes, Jews, and anyone who didn't look like them?

Rocker finally clambered out of the car and got into the passenger seat of a police cruiser. As both cars sped off in opposite directions, Buddy stepped out into the late afternoon sunshine. He had one last look around and spied a car parked near the railroad tracks half a block down the street. The car—and the man inside it—were familiar. The police were watching in hopes, he assumed, that he would lead them to Thornell or Naomi.

He ducked back into the tent, moved through it, and plopped down next to Max outside.

"What's wrong?" Max asked.

"The police are watching us."

"You mean the Klan is watching us."

"Same thing."

"Well," Max said. "Since you're stuck here, how about helping me figure out how we survive without a manager."

"That's easy," Buddy said as he lit a cigarette. "You take over."

Max looked up and said, "Bullshit. I'm an elephant man. I don't know anything about running a circus."

"You can't be any worse than Smokey."

"Very funny," Max said

"You know what I mean." Buddy got up and began to pace. "Benny's an incompetent asshole. He'll run us into the ground. We need someone level-headed. Someone who can figure out how to make enough money to keep us going. We don't have enough food for ourselves, much less the livestock."

"And what makes you think I know how to do that?"

Buddy sat down heavily. He had no answer to that. "Let's go see if there is anything to eat at the cook tent," he said, finally. But before they could move, Detective Stockton arrived.

He sat on a box without invitation, leaned forward placing his elbows on his knees, and asked Buddy, "Any idea where Thornell Dixon might be?"

"No," Buddy replied truthfully.

"Figured as much," he said, "But I had to ask. You realize that if we had a suspect in custody, you would be free to pack up and move on?"

"He's not around here," Max said.

Stockton grunted and looked around. "This would be a good place for him to hide—in plain sight, as it were."

Buddy looked at the people moving around the circus grounds and realized that the detective had a point. So many shapes, sizes, and colors were represented, it wouldn't be difficult to disguise a person in this assortment of humanity.

The three men sat in silence for a moment, then Stockton said, "Sergeant Rocker and his Klan buddies are pretty upset that they lost their man."

"Their man was supposed to be arrested and taken to jail," Buddy said to Stockton. "Did he ever make it there?"

"I think you know the answer to that."

"How can you stand by and watch that happen?" Max asked. "They want to lynch him."

"Rocker was just here looking for him," Buddy continued.

"Look," Stockton said as he sat up straight. "If you know where he is, let me bring him in. I'll see he gets a fair trial."

"And how do you plan to do that?" Buddy asked.

"I'll take him out to the county work farm." Stockton stood and said, "They don't like being bested. They're going to tear that neighborhood apart. Nobody's going to be safe." He looked at Buddy and continued, "Even you."

"Then what?"

"I think they're covering for someone," Stockton said. "I think they know who did it. I've seen evidence of other, similar murders in other parts of town, but we've been careful not to put two and two together."

"Can't you take it to your superiors?" Max asked.

"I'm not sure who to trust," Stockton said. "The chief brought me in to clean things up, but that may have been for show. Not everyone is tied up with the Klan but stepping out of line is risky. I'm told some officers have gone missing or turned up dead."

Stockton stood and began to pace.

"We've got problems of our own," said Max.

"Problems?" Stockton snickered. "What kind of problems?"

"Smokey disappeared," Buddy replied.

Stockton stopped pacing and faced the men. "What do you mean *disappeared*?"

"He's gone," Max replied. "Left the show overnight."

"Hmm," Stockton said as he stared into the distance, apparently lost in thought. He glanced at Buddy and Max, turned on his heels, and left.

***

Benny Charles wasn't your typical clown. He wasn't particularly jovial or funny. He didn't stumble when he walked or stutter when he talked. He was just good at putting on makeup and playing the sad sack. Without make-up, he was a hard boiled, fifty-something man

165

with a chip on his shoulder and an opinion about everything. The only people who appeared to like him were the Randolph brothers, a couple of roustabouts with more muscles than brains. They were lurking in the evening shadows of the flickering campfire while Benny occupied the seat Detective Stockton vacated a few hours ago.

"You do what you gotta do, Benny," Max said. "But Mrs. Santorini will decide who runs the show. This isn't a democracy where we all get a vote."

"I know that," said Benny, "but a word from you might help her see what we need. It would be better to have one of our own running things instead of bringing someone in from the outside. That's what happened with Smokey."

"Any idea what happened to Smokey?" Max asked.

"No," said Benny. "But he was never the same after that old clown showed up. I never trusted that guy. He was just a little too nice for my liking."

Buddy didn't know Benny very well, but he knew Max didn't want to see Benny in charge and he wondered how Max would respond.

"So," Benny said.

"I'll think about it," Max said.

Buddy saw a movement just outside the edge of the firelight, behind Benny's bodyguards. He peered carefully, worried that it might be some of Rocker's thugs but not wanting to alert Benny.

It was Naomi. They made eye contact, then she was gone.

Buddy rose and casually adjusted his trousers. Since he wasn't a part of the conversation, he walked out to find her behind the tent. Together, they strolled into the night.

"What are you doing here?" he whispered.

"I just wanted to see if you're okay."

"The police are watching us."

"I figured they would be," she said. "I came in through the woods."

"How's your cousin?"

"How do you think?" she said testily. "He was about to be lynched."

They skirted the edge of the circus grounds, taking care to remain out of view from the street, and sat under a tree.

She was silent for a moment, then said, "Sorry about that. I've had a bad day."

"I know," Buddy said. "I was there, remember. Mine hasn't been so great, either."

"There's something else," she said quietly. "I may need to sell my livestock."

"What!" He looked at her sharply. "Why?" he whispered.

"When I got back to the barn this afternoon, I found a foreclosure notice pinned to the door."

"What if I take the wagon out to the quarry in the morning? We could have some money to the bank by the end of the day."

"That wouldn't be nearly enough," she said quietly. "My father worked so hard to build that business. Those animals were like his children. When Herman died in France, he was forced to take me on. But I could tell he didn't think I could handle it—being a woman and all."

"It's the times," Buddy said. "It's not your fault. People want motor cars and trucks. Horses and mules are too slow, too expensive, and too old fashioned."

"I should have sold the livestock years ago and bought trucks," she said. "But those animals depend on me."

"I may have someone who'll take them," he said.

"All of them?" She looked at him. "Good homes?"

"The mules for sure. And yes, a good home."

He told her about Bella and her fancy barn up on Springdale Road. He speculated about the hunting plantation in South Georgia and the quality of care the animals were likely to receive there.

She picked up a stick and poked at the ground. "I'll have to think about that," she said finally. "But it sounds like the sensible thing to do."

"Maybe you should come with us," Buddy said quietly. "Join the circus."

She laughed and looked at him.

"I'm serious," he said. "We could use someone who's good with animals." His enthusiasm faded as he remembered the current situation. He wasn't sure there would be a circus for her to join in a few days, so he let the matter drop.

They sat in silence for a moment before she stirred and stood. "I'd better get back to the barn."

"Now?" Buddy said as he stood. "It's dark."

"I need to check the animals."

"The police are probably watching it. They're watching us, here."

"I'll slip in the back way, put down some hay, and slip out. They won't even know I'm there."

She hugged him and, as she faded into the night, he thought about having her join them on the road. Maybe she could help Max run the show since she already knew how to run a business. It wasn't such a bad life, once you got used to it. Joining the circus had probably saved his life all those years ago.

22

PERU, INDIANA
MARCH 31,1919

BUDDY GRIFFITH HAD been home from France for two months and whatever relief he had gained from being home had been erased by his current assignment. Now that the war was over, the Army had no use for all the horses, mules, and donkeys it had stockpiled. Buddy had been travelling the mid-west with train loads of animals destined for farms, animal dealers, and glue factories. This trip was all horses and Peru, Indiana was his last stop.

When he and his horses had been picked up at the train station by a skinny kid in overalls named Arnold, he had wanted to get paid as quickly as possible, so he could be on his way. Arnold talked non-stop on their four-mile drive out of town to the circus grounds where, he was told, Mason & Barnes rented space from Hagenbeck-Wallace Circus for their winter quarters. The drive had been something of an agony, until they began to pass house after house that appeared to be occupied by circus performers with circus wagons, highwire apparatus, and brightly painted signs. Then, as they crossed a small bridge and turned a corner, he saw circus tents and an elephant barn. He was fascinated.

They stopped at the horse barn and were met by circus manager, Orla Pendleton—a loud, large character wearing a top hat and sporting mutton-chop whiskers. But Buddy's attention was quickly drawn to what was happening in the horse ring.

He had never seen a person ride a horse like that. The young woman made it look easy standing on its back with her bare feet on a blanket as the horse cantered in circles. Her brother Ernst held the twenty-foot lunge rope that was attached to the horse's bridle, turning with the horse as it moved around the corral. The woman's father, Jacob Driesbach, leaned on the fence next to Buddy watching the horse carefully. Five other horses were tied to the fence awaiting their turn under the woman.

"What did the Army have these horses doing?" Driesbach asked.

Buddy was mesmerized by the girl and did not respond.

Jacob looked at him, so Buddy said, "Most likely pulling cannons or wagons. In France, my horses pulled an ambulance."

"You were in the war?"

"Yes." When Driesbach didn't respond, Buddy changed the subject. "These aren't the best horses the army has. Those are still with the cavalry. But they have some good years in them. I left Fort Riley, Kansas with twenty-one surplus horses and was told to drop them at the slaughterhouse in Omaha but save six of the best ones for the Mason and Barnes circus. So here I am."

Driesbach grunted his response and climbed the fence. As the horse came around, he jumped into the paddock in its path. The horse shied and stopped but did not throw its rider. The man patted the horse on the neck and woman hopped to the ground.

As Driesbach climbed back over the fence and took up his station next to Buddy, Ernst led the horse out and brought another into the corral for the woman to mount and continue the show.

"What exactly are you looking for?" Buddy asked.

"I need two of your horses for my act," the man said. "Horses generally have one of four personalities. Three of them, I can't use. The nervous ones can be set off by the least distraction—even their own shadow. The stubborn ones don't want to work or be told what to do. They're like mules. And the treacherous ones are too mean to be around. The army probably wouldn't have any of those."

"I had a few, but I left them at the slaughterhouse. So, what's the fourth kind—the kind you're looking for?"

"The best horses for our act are the smart ones—the horses who are quiet and curious. They are aware of their surroundings and respond to things going on around them, but will tolerate almost anything, from a fluttering flag to a clown car. That horse we just tested saw me when he came around. He knew what I was going to do, and he took action but didn't over-react."

Buddy was fascinated by the Driesbach operation.

"Are any of these going to work?" Orla Pendleton asked as he joined the men at the fence.

"I found one," Driesbach replied.

The three men watched in silence as the woman hopped on the second horse and began her ride around the pen.

"What will you use the other horses for?" Buddy asked Orla.

"Baggage stock," the man replied. "Pulling wagons and props for the show." The watched in silence for a moment, then Orla continued, "You're not by any chance looking for a job, are you?"

Buddy looked at him to see if he was kidding. "Doing what?"

"Helping with the horses."

"These horses?"

"No," Orla said with a laugh. "I doubt Jacob would let you near his horses."

Buddy glanced at Driesbach in embarrassment, but the man appeared not to have heard. He was climbing the fence, ready to spook another horse.

"The army owns me for another few months," Buddy said. "My hitch isn't up until August, and I might decide to re-enlist."

Orla pushed away from the fence and said, "Let me know if you change your mind. We open here in Peru at the end of next month. Then we'll head east to Fort Wayne, Toledo, Cleveland, Akron, then south. By August we'll be in Kansas."

As Buddy watched the man walk away, he heard a commotion in the horse ring. He turned to see the riderless horse cantering around the corral and the woman flat on her back in the dirt. This horse, he guessed, failed its test.

***

It was well past midnight when Buddy stumbled out of the car and watched it speed off into the night. He had been provided a bed in the loft of the horse barn, but he was so drunk he wasn't sure he could climb the ladder without falling off. He touched the wad of cash in his pocket to remind himself that the poker game with Arnold and the other roustabouts had been real and stepped out of the moonlight and into the barn. As he waited for his eyes to adjust to the gloom, he began to sober up. Fear will do that. Someone was there.

A person was silhouetted by the moonlight coming from the other end of the hallway. He was next to the ladder to the loft, seated on a haybale with legs stretched out and head resting against the wall.

Buddy resisted the urge to run and took a step forward and pushed his head forward, trying to focus his eyes. "Hello," he said.

The figure lurched upright and asked, "Who's there?"

Buddy relaxed at the sound of a woman's voice and moved forward to find the woman who had been riding the horses—Jacob Driesbach's daughter.

"Oh," she said as he drew near, "You're the wrangler from the army."

Buddy stood dumbly and tried to clear his head. He didn't want this beautiful young woman to know how drunk he was.

"You'd better sit down," she said, "before you fall down." It was the kind of line that would have been delivered with a smirk if Buddy could have seen her face more clearly. "I'm Mae," she said. "Mae Driesbach."

"Buddy Griffith," he replied.

They sat in silence for a while, then he asked the obvious question, "What're you doing out here, Mae Driesbach?"

"You wouldn't understand. Family business."

"Looks more like family argument, to me."

She hesitated, and said, "My father expects me to go into the family business, but I don't want to."

"Actually," Buddy said, "I know exactly how you feel." After a moment, he asked, "If you don't want to be a bareback rider in the circus, what do you want to do?"

She glanced at him and replied, "You'll laugh."

"I doubt that. I ran away from home at about your age to play professional baseball."

She chuckled quietly. "I want to be a dancer."

They talked into the night. Mae, Buddy learned, lived with her parents, Jacob and Edith, and her brothers Ernst, Hans, and Paul. They had been the feature in the center ring of the Mason and Barnes circus since their arrival from Switzerland. The Driesbach family act consisted of athletic riding performances on the back of horses, such as one rider standing on the shoulders of another, riding on two horses with one foot on each horse and culminating with the entire family involved at one time—three riders standing astride four horses, supporting two more family members on their shoulders. Mae riding standing up, as he saw during the day, must have been the least of her talents.

Buddy told her about his recent returned to Ft. Riley, Kansas from France and his unsavory assignments hauling surplus horses around the country.

"Pa said that Orla offered you a job."

"That he did."

"Are you going to take it?"

"I don't know," he said. "What do you think? Is this a good place to work?"

"This life's not for everyone. We're constantly on the road. The only friends or family we have are right here. For me," she paused, "it's like living on the edge of the world. We see a lot of things, but we're not really part of it. We're just peeking through the curtain."

"What about you," he asked. "If I did come to work here, would you still be here?"

"Most likely," she said with a sigh. "I don't imagine I'll be going anywhere."

The first rays of the morning sun were filtering into the barn. Buddy turned his gaze to Mae as she leaned back with her eyes closed and wondered about the possibilities. She was a few years younger, but still a grown woman—beautiful, graceful, and full of hopes and dreams. Her description of life with the circus was attractive to him. In the weeks since he had returned from France, he had been having nightmares. Sleep was fitful, if it came at all. Perhaps a life on the road—or a life on the run—was just what he needed.

23

LOUISVILLE, KENTUCKY
SUNDAY, MAY 3, 1936

"I'M NOT SURE what you ever saw in him," said Hans Driesbach.

"Sometimes I wonder that myself," his sister Mae replied. "Just help me get him up."

"I can walk," mumbled Buddy as he pushed them both off and struggled to his feet. "What're you two doing in my wagon, anyway?"

"You need to wake up and get your wagon and horses loaded," said Mae. "We're pulling out, and Arnold is on the warpath."

Buddy first met Arnold Pendleton when he joined the Mason and Barnes circus after the war. Seventeen years ago, Arnold was a skinny teenager whose only redeeming quality was that he was the circus manager's son. Now, since his father died, he was running the show and Buddy wasn't sure how much longer he could put up with him.

"Mae," Hans said from the door, "we need to go."

She moved to the door as her brother disappeared and turned to Buddy.

"Don't give me that look," Buddy said as he pushed a hand through his tousled hair.

"What look?"

"That 'you're such a jerk' look," he said. "That 'why did I ever marry you?' look."

"I know why I married you," she folded her arms and leaned against the counter. "You weren't such a shithead back then."

"Well," he sat back on the bed. "You were smart to get rid of me."

"I don't like seeing you like this."

"Like what?"

"Drunk. Hung over," she waved an arm in his direction. "Whatever this is." She paused and said quietly, "Why don't you go home, Buddy. Go see your family. Get yourself together."

He glanced at his ex-wife. She was looking at the floor with tears in her eyes. Something stirred inside him, recalling when they met; the nights of passion in the loft of the winter quarters horse barn; the stolen moments when they were on the road. But those gorgeous, blue eyes could only break the spell of his demons for so long.

"I loved you, Mae," he said. "Still do."

"Well," she replied. "You sure have a lousy way of showing it."

"Griffith!" shouted a voice from outside. "Why aren't you loaded?"

Mae raised her eyebrows at him as Buddy struggled to his feet and stumbled to the door. It wouldn't take him long to get loaded. They hadn't done a full show here. They stopped so the owner could show off for some of his rich friends at the Kentucky Derby.

"Jesus," Arnold said. "Look at you."

"I'll be loaded in twenty-minutes," Buddy said from the door.

"Don't bother," replied his boss. "You're through."

Buddy watched him walk away and thought about how it would feel to place his boot in that fat ass.

***

The black dog of depression had been Buddy's off-and-on companion since he had come home from the war. But watching the Mason and Barnes circus pull out of town without him yesterday hit him especially hard. He spent much of last night fingering his old army pistol but just hadn't worked up the courage. Now, as he sat with his feet dangling over the edge of the Highway 31 bridge over the Ohio River with the setting sun in his face. He looked down at the barge passing under him and wondered if it would be better to land in the water or try to aim for a pile of coal.

He couldn't describe the empty, lost feeling. His brain told him he should go home, catch up with his father and sister, and get a job. He knew a good life awaited him there. But another voice told a different story. It whispered dark thoughts and seduced him with the idea that the world would be a better place without him. Buddy had no chance of finding a job. In a world of trucks, tractors, and motor cars, wagon drivers weren't in much demand.

Buddy pulled himself to his feet and took one more look at the river. "Damn it," he muttered to himself. "I can't even screw up the guts make this decision." He staggered down the sidewalk back toward the train yard where he found a comfortable spot sitting against the brick wall of a bourbon distillery and fell asleep.

When he woke, the morning sun was shining in his face as he watched the Santorini Brothers Circus train unloading. It was a familiar scene—men dragging rolls of canvas out of boxcars and teams of horses pulling wagons off the railroad flatcars. Their horse teams were his favorite animals, Percherons. If the circus boss didn't ask too many questions, he might be able to get on with them. He bundled his bedroll and stood. But before he could take a step, he was startled and pushed back against the wall by an elephant sprinting past him.

The animal was strangely silent as it ran, and a few yards after it passed, it wheeled around and faced back from where it had come.

Buddy had been around elephants ever since he joined the circus, but he had never handled one. He knew what a bullhook was, and he knew some of the commands. But he also knew a frightened animal when he saw one. He hesitated, expecting to see a trainer come running after him, but nobody appeared.

Buddy rubbed his eyes then scratched his head. He had spent yesterday thinking about killing himself. Now, he was a few feet away from an animal that could do the job for him. He had seen an elephant kill a man and, although it wasn't pretty, it was an effective way to go. All he had to do was provoke it.

Buddy approached the elephant, but its gaze remained on whoever was chasing it. He was a big, Asian elephant with short, thick tusks. As Buddy drew near, the animal shifted its attention, lowered its head, and fanned its ears. Buddy was no elephant man, but he figured the animal was letting him know that was close enough. As they stood there eyeing one another, men come up behind Buddy. When the elephant saw them, he backed up a step, Buddy took a couple of steps forward.

"You need to get away from that elephant, Mister," someone said.

Buddy paused but kept his eyes on the elephant. "Whoa," he crooned as he held out both hands. When he was near enough to place both hands on the elephant's trunk and move in to hug the beast, all thoughts of ending his life melted away. This animal needed him—and he needed it.

Someone walked up from behind and Buddy stepped away as the man gently took command. "Tembo, move up," The handler said. And off they went.

Buddy watched them walk away, then asked the man who remained behind, "That your elephant?"

"Just bought him. Looks like he could use some work." The man turned his attention from the elephant and eyed Buddy. "How long you worked with elephants?"

"About five minutes," Buddy said with a chuckle.

"Jesus," the man said. He continued to look at Buddy, perhaps to see if he was being serious. When Buddy said no more, the man continued. "I'm Smokey Walters. I run the Santorini Brothers Circus. Max could use some help with the elephants, especially that one."

"I've never worked with elephants," Buddy said. "I'm a horse man."

Minutes before, Buddy was feeling a powerful connection to the elephant. Perhaps the animal could save his life. Now, he was pushing that feeling away. That had been the story of his life since the war. He was suspicious of anything that might be good for him. Happiness was an illusion. Contentment meant danger was lurking.

Smokey hesitated for a moment. When Buddy failed to reply, Smokey said, "We'll be here a couple of days." He nodded over his shoulder at the train cars.

Buddy's mood darkened as he watched the man walk away. He returned to the spot where he had spent the night and sat back down against the wall. The sun was climbing into a cloudless sky. A flock of geese honked overhead as they flew north in V-formation. And he had just been offered a job. His stomach grumbled its displeasure at his poor decision making. He didn't even have a cigarette to lift his spirits.

"Mind if I sit?" The man who had led the elephant away returned. He looked like a bear with his long hair and bushy beard. Even his deep, booming voice sounded bear-like. "I'm Max Winston," he said.

"Buddy Griffith."

"Smokey tells me he offered you a job."

"I don't know anything about elephants."

"What *do* you know about?"

"Horses," Buddy said. "I ran the baggage stock for another circus."

"Do you know what this is?" Max stopped poking the ground and raised his bullhook.

Buddy looked at it. He turned his gaze to Max and said, "Of course, I know what it is."

"I could use someone to help with the elephants. My last guy left a couple of weeks ago, and I'm stuck with one of the clowns."

"Nah," said Buddy. "I'd probably not be much better than your clown."

"You can't be any worse," Max said. "And that elephant might respond to you."

Max leaned back and faced the sun. They sat in silence for a moment. Finally, Max pushed himself to his feet. "Let me know if you change your mind," he said.

Buddy cracked his eyes open and watched the man walk away. But something was off, so he opened his eyes wider and took a long look. Max wasn't carrying his bullhook. Buddy glanced to his right. The bullhook leaned against the wall.

24

ATLANTA
FRIDAY, NOVEMBER 6, 1936

BUDDY KNEW THE police were still looking for Thornell and he assumed they were also watching his every move. So, he took his time eating breakfast and walking over to Dixon's Livery. He didn't much care about the police because he had nothing to hide.

When he entered the barn, he paused to allow his eyes to adjust. The dogs rushed him with tails wagging.

"Naomi," he called.

It was quiet, and he assumed she had slept in, so he opened the doors, let the horses and mules out to their paddocks, and set about cleaning stalls and feeding the animals. His cleaning of the stalls was quick and cursory. He picked up clumps of manure with the pitchfork and hauled it out back, looking over his shoulder the whole time, expecting the arrival of Naomi—or the police. He fluffed up soiled straw bedding and put down fresh hay. It was mindless work that relaxed him and gave him time to think. He rolled yesterday's events around in his head.

Discovering that Elton Glover had been Dixon's major in France had seemed an odd coincidence until he remembered that some wartime units were comprised of enlistees from the same city. He wondered why Smokey had disappeared with Kaz. Circus people just didn't do that. Sure, the circus was in trouble, but circuses were always in trouble. Sometimes they went broke and had to be sold or auctioned off. Sometimes workers had to find a new show. But what would a guy like Smokey do other than work in a circus?

Footsteps in the hallway broke his chain of thought. His pulse quickened. He raised the pitchfork he had been fluffing hay with and faced the door of the stall but relaxed when Detective Stockton peered in. He was wearing rough clothes and had a flat cap pulled low.

"I didn't expect to find you here," Stockton said.

"I could say the same to you."

"Where's Mrs. Webster?"

"Good question," Buddy said. He walked into the hallway to join the detective. The dogs sniffed the new arrival, but Stockton appeared not to notice them. He made no move to pet them and even recoiled at their approach. Buddy called them off, and the men sat to talk.

"There's been a new development," said Stockton. "Another body's been found."

Buddy looked up sharply. "I suppose Thornell is the prime suspect."

"Actually he's not—for me, at least."

Buddy waited for him to continue.

"This one looks like the murder of the girl in the Trolley Barn, but it occurred while your guy was supposedly in police custody. We'll have a hard time pinning it on him." The detective paused. "So, it got me thinking. Are there any others out there? I started looking through some older reports and found three others dating back to earlier this year. I have a feeling that, if we had the resources, there would be a lot more—and they're all over town."

"Then," Buddy began hopefully, "Thornell is in the clear."

"Not that simple," Stockton said. "If this gets out, there'll be a panic. This town has a history of lynchings and riots over stuff like this. They'll pin this on a Negro in a heartbeat. I came here to warn Mrs. Webster to make sure they don't find him."

"What do you think they'll do next?" Buddy asked.

Stockton shrugged his shoulders and shook his head. "There is a rally outside of town this evening at a place they call Stone Mountain."

"Jesus," Buddy said.

"I'm told there'll be chants, and pledges, and they'll burn a giant cross. They'd love to get their hands on your boy. Maybe have themselves a lynching as part of the ceremony."

"What time is it?" Buddy asked.

Stockton pulled a watch from his pocket. "Nine-thirty."

"Naomi should be here by now." Buddy stood. "I'm going to go by the church and see if Reverend King has any idea where she might be."

Stockton left and Buddy went into the feed room to fill the dog bowls. It was a mess. He quickly realized that there must have been a scuffle. He picked up overturned chairs, replaced lids on trash cans, and retrieved a note that sat on the table under a saltshaker.

Return the murderer, the note read. *Bring him to Stone Mountain by 8:00 tonight or we'll hang her instead.*

***

Buddy felt helpless, alone, and desperate but it still seemed strange to find himself standing outside the door to a church. It wasn't God he sought inside, though. He had hoped Reverend King might have some suggestions about where to begin his search. But the secretary told him the reverend was visiting one of his parishioners at the hospital. As he stood on the church steps, pondering his next move, his eye was drawn to workmen scurrying around the building a couple of blocks down the street at the Masonic Lodge.

He walked down there, knowing from yesterday's reaction, he would not likely be welcomed—especially with the enhanced police presence in the community. The search for Thornell Dixon had everyone on edge. But he mounted the steps to the lodge and pushed his way inside with nothing more than a few dirty looks. He was relieved to find Elton Glover in an office next to the library and his door was open.

Glover was on the phone but caught Buddy's eye and raised his hand. He ended the call, waved Buddy in, and pointed to a chair. The desk was little more than an old door propped on two sawhorses and covered with papers stacked in neat piles. Construction drawings lined the unfinished walls.

"Sergeant Griffith," he said, "what brings you here?"

Buddy was taken aback at the reference to his old military rank.

"It's Naomi Webster," Buddy began, "I went to see her at her barn this morning. She wasn't there, but I found this." He handed Glover the note.

"Damn," Glover muttered as he threw the note onto his desk. He stared out the door for a moment then jumped up. Buddy turned in his seat to watch Glover rush to the doorway and looked up and down the hall. "Jolly!"

Buddy couldn't hear what was said, but Glover did all the talking and much of it was done with a red face and a finger pressed against Jolly's chest. After the man ran off, Glover returned to his seat.

"We'll find her," he said, "and someone's going to pay for this."

They sat in concerned silence for a moment, until a man behind Buddy burst in.

"Jolly said you wanted to see us, boss?"

Buddy turned to see three men standing in the doorway. They weren't workmen, and he doubted they were Masonic brothers. They were nicely dressed and looked like men he wouldn't want to tangle with. Buddy knew gangsters when he saw them.

Glover glanced at Buddy then waved them in and explained the situation. "Get out there and ask around," he told them. "See if anyone saw anything."

Glover took a cigar out of a box on his desk. He offered one to Buddy, but he declined, producing his own pack of cigarettes.

They smoked in silence as the minutes ticked by. Buddy kept glancing at the small clock on Glover's desk. It had been just after ten o'clock when they sat down together. Shortly after that, Glover had turned his men loose. Buddy felt helpless just sitting there, but he knew there was little else he could do. He was relieved when one of the men finally returned.

"We may have something," he said from the doorway. Glover waved him into the office, and he continued. "Someone saw a flashy Cadillac speeding down Dekalb Avenue heading toward Moreland just after sun-up. It caught his eye because it was being followed by a police car without lights or sirens. They were moving pretty fast but just seemed to be traveling together."

"Of course," Buddy said. Glover looked at him, so he continued. "The man who drives the Cadillac is somehow connected to Sergeant Rocker."

"We know all about Sergeant Rocker," said Glover. He and his man exchanged a glance. "Who's the other guy?"

Buddy told him about Thomas Anderson and quickly explained what he knew about the murder, about the Klan's involvement, and about Detective Stockton's investigation. He then said, "I don't know your streets here. But, judging by the directions, where might they have taken her?"

"Anywhere between here and Stone Mountain," Glover's man replied.

"What direction is Stone Mountain?"

"East," said Glover.

"Same direction we found Thornell," said Buddy as he stood up.

"Get some of the boys," Glover said to his man as he stood, as well.

"No," said Buddy. "I need to do this alone. Can Jolly give me a ride?"

"Boss?" the man asked, questioning Buddy's authority.

"Look," Buddy said to the room full of Negros, "if she's where I think the is, and anybody is around, you all won't be able to get near the place."

Glover looked hesitant, but nodded his approval and said to Buddy, "I hope you know what you're doing."

As they walked out of Glover's office, Buddy said to Jolly, "I need to stop by the circus grounds and pick something up."

***

After he retrieved his pistol, Buddy had Jolly drive him out to where Thornell had been held. There were other buildings near the one they had pulled the bars off of.

The mudhole at the train tracks had dried up since yesterday, but Buddy had Jolly wait in the car near the spot where he had parked the wagon, so he could slip through the woods unseen. But it was no use. The buildings were vacant.

"Nothing?" asked Jolly when Buddy flopped down on the seat next to him.

"Nothing."

"Who was the guy in the flashy car we saw yesterday?" Jolly asked.

"Thomas Anderson," Buddy replied. "I think he's pulling the strings on this."

"So, he probably knows where she is."

Buddy looked at Jolly as he processed what the man was saying. He slapped his thigh and exclaimed, "Of course he does! Do you know how to get to Springdale Road from here?"

"You're not just going to ask him, are you?"

"If I'm right, I won't need to."

Ten minutes later, Buddy slipped into Bella Anderson's barn, being careful not to be seen from the house. As he had hoped, Sam was still cleaning stalls just before lunchtime.

"Could you get Mrs. Anderson for me?" Buddy asked.

"Gone to the station to pick up Mr. Charles," said Sam.

Sam put down the bale of hay he was carrying and said, "You'd best be on your way." He avoided looking Buddy in the eye, and he rubbed his coveralls with his hands. "She won't be back for a while."

As Sam was talking, Buddy eased over to the front door of the barn and peered at the old servant's house tucked in under some live oak trees between the barn and the big house. The man sitting in the car reading the newspaper confirmed Buddy's suspicions. If Thomas

Anderson was calling the shots, he would probably want to keep Naomi close—someplace he would assume no one knows about.

"Mind if I wait for her?" Buddy asked as he moved back down the hall and sat on a bench.

They looked at each other for a long moment and an understanding passed between them.

Sam leaned back against the wall and looked at the ceiling. "I can't get involved in that boy's business. Me and Fanny need our jobs."

"I don't need your help," Buddy said. He slipped the pistol from his waist band and held it down between his knees. "He's holding a woman I care about in there."

Buddy glanced at Sam and fingered the pistol. The only person he had ever thought about using it on was himself. It hadn't been fired since the war. He wondered if it would even work. A movement outside the barn toward the big house caught his eye. He tucked his pistol away and got up. Fanny was walking their way carrying a tray of food. "Looks like your wife is bringing your lunch."

"That ain't my lunch," Sam said joining Buddy at the edge of the door. "She's takin' it to the man in the car."

They watched Fanny walk back to the house with her empty tray as the man tucked into his food.

"Is there another way in there?" Buddy asked.

Buddy made his way back out to Springdale Road and down to where Jolly was parked. He woke him up and explained the situation. They could see the house where Naomi was being held through the trees. If Buddy walked a few yards onto the neighboring property, he could approach the house without being seen while the man in the car was busy eating.

"Let's go," Jolly said as he pulled the handle to the car door.

"Wait," Buddy said. "You might draw some attention we don't want."

Jolly flashed a look of defiance but soon settled.

"Do you have something I can pry a window open with?"

Jolly reached behind the seat and pulled out a bent iron bar that was flattened at one end. He handed it to Buddy. "It's a tire iron," he said. "But I keep it handy for other purposes."

Buddy fingered the iron bar, nodded at Jolly, and got out of the car. Springdale Road wasn't heavily traveled, but cars did occasionally pass. So, Buddy tried to walk casually, making a wide circle back down Springdale, onto the neighboring property, and toward the old servant's quarters on the Anderson property. He could feel Jolly's eyes on him and hoped Naomi's guard was still eating, as Sam had predicted. He felt the weight of the pistol under his belt and hoped he wouldn't need to use it.

He flattened himself against the wall and listened for any sounds inside the house. It was strangely quiet. He slipped the tire iron under the window and pried it up. He was surprised that the window was not locked. He slid it open carefully and peered inside between the curtains. Naomi was tied to a chair in the middle of the room, gagged and blindfolded. She appeared to be alone, but people could be in the other rooms.

He crept through the window and across the room.

As she heard him approach, she began to struggle against her bindings, and she shouted into her gag. If anyone was in the adjacent room, they would have heard the commotion. He pulled off her blindfold and pressed his finger to his lips.

She responded with tears.

He untied her hands, and while he untied her feet, she took off the gag. He pulled her to her feet and whispered, "Are you okay?"

She just nodded and clung to him.

"Can you walk?" he whispered.

"Yes."

As he pulled her toward the window, one of the cords that had bound her feet caught the chair leg, and it toppled with a crash. They froze and watched the door but when nobody rushed in, they clambered out the window.

"Well, lookee here," The man from the car was waiting for them with a shotgun pointed at them. "We ain't done with you, Missy."

"Look," Buddy said with his hands up. "We don't want any trouble."

"Oh, you got trouble alright."

The man raised his shotgun, and Buddy's hand edged closer to his pistol, but they were both interrupted by a loud clang as the flat end of a shovel hit the man on the back of his head. He dropped like a sack of flour.

Sam emerged from the corner of the house holding the shovel and said, "Y'all better get on out of here."

***

"Head for the church," Buddy shouted as he and Naomi piled into the back seat of Jolly's car.

She leaned her head back against the seat and closed her eyes.

"You okay, lady?" Jolly asked over his shoulder. "They hurt you?"

"No," she replied. "I'm okay. Just scared—and mad."

Buddy's heart was racing as he looked out the back window of the car. His fear and anger melted with every block they traveled without anyone following them.

"I don't want to go to the church," Naomi said. "I want to go to Elton."

"No," Buddy said more forcefully than he meant to. "You'll be safer at the church with Reverend King."

She leaned forward and touched Jolly on the shoulder and said, "You can drop Buddy at the circus." She then turned to Buddy, placed her hand on his, and said, "Look, I appreciate what you did, but I need to thank Elton for his part, too." She leaned in and kissed him on the cheek and sat back.

He could see there would be no changing her mind, so he just leaned back in his seat. His impulse to resist that idea was nothing but jealousy. He knew she would be safer surrounded by Glover and his men—at least for now—so he let Jolly drop him at the circus grounds and sent them on their way.

25

As he watched the car drive off, his loneliness began to overwhelm him. He wanted to be with her but couldn't. The circus was where he belonged, but he didn't want to be here either. He wandered back to the elephant area and saw that the elephants were out of hay. He leaned into Tembo with his forehead, thinking about his visit to the zoo.

"This is not what we signed up for, is it boy?" he said.

As the presence of the animals helped him relax, he realized he hadn't seen a soul on the grounds. It was too late for lunch and too early for dinner. He looked around and noticed that even Max was among the missing. As he paused, a distant commotion caught his ear. Something was going on inside the big top.

His curiosity rose as he approached the tent and found that someone was using the loudspeakers to address the audience which, he observed as he entered the tent, was the entire circus—performers, trainers, roustabouts, and cooks. He found Max and sat next to him.

Buddy picked up the narrative in mid-sentence as the man said, "And because of this attachment for bankruptcy, I have been appointed as the Receiver. I will need to place at least two notices in the *Atlanta Constitution*, our daily newspaper, and an auction will be scheduled for one week from today."

The man began stacking his papers to leave when someone shouted, "What about us? What about our jobs?"

The man glanced at the people seated on each side of him and said with some reluctance, "I'm sorry, but the only thing we can do is see that you receive back wages from the proceeds of the auction."

"What about the animals?" someone else asked. "My horses are my property."

"If you can prove they're your property, you can keep them, and be on your way. If they're owned by the circus, they'll be auctioned off with the rest of the physical assets."

As the meeting devolved into shouting and chaos, Max stood and said, "Let's get out of here."

They walked back to the elephant area in silence through the deserted grounds.

"Who was that guy?" Buddy asked as they began shoveling manure into a wheelbarrow.

"T. Raymond Brown," Max replied. "I guess he's an attorney."

"Who's going to buy these elephants?"

"I hope some other circus," said Max.

"But what about us?"

Max leaned on his shovel. "Well, that's a good question, isn't it. Maybe they'll take us along with the elephants, and maybe they already have all the elephant men they need."

Buddy had seen some of the acts beginning the process of moving on. Those who could were packing up. Willie Tilson was lining up his dog crates and the Renoir Family were boxing their high wire and trapeze equipment. He imagined that phone calls were being made and telegrams sent as people tried to line up their next gigs.

As for Buddy, he wasn't sure what to think. He wondered what it would be like to stay in Atlanta and drive a wagon for Naomi. Maybe Thornell could maintain the wagons and care for the livestock, Buddy would drive the wagons as the white face of the company, and Naomi could do whatever it is that owners do. Count their money, he supposed.

But if he left the circus, what would become of the elephants? Where would Max find another assistant—especially one who would take the time to care for Tembo?

"Wait a second," said Buddy. He stopped shoveling and looked at Max. "I thought these were your elephants."

"What made you think that?"

"Well," he pointed to white lettering on one of the leather head dress harnesses that proclaimed *Max Barnes' Elephants*. "What about that?"

"That doesn't mean I own the elephants."

"But Alice and Tony Morgan own their horses, don't they? And Willie Tilson owns his 'Flying Dogs'."

"That's different. My name's on the act just for show purposes. These elephants are way more important to the show than some dogs that jump through hoops. If something happens to me, they'll probably just change the name on those harnesses to *Buddy Griffith's Elephants*."

"Hey, Buddy," Amos Driesbach interrupted. He was standing at the edge of the tent pointing toward the road. "Somebody's out here looking for you."

Amos stood back as Bella emerged.

"There you are," she said.

Buddy looked over her shoulder and emerging from the car across the tracks near the street was a mature man in khaki pants and jacket, a tweed cap, and well-worn leather boots. He was helping a dark-haired, young woman from the back seat.

Buddy recognized the silver-gray Cadillac with the black fenders and was relieved that Thomas Anderson was not in the driver's seat. He wondered who the bastard was terrorizing today.

***

Charles Anderson looked older than Buddy expected, but his pale blue eyes were sharp and his handshake firm. He had walked from his car with the fluid grace of a man used to the outdoors. His voice carried the confidence of a man who could sell an ice box to an Eskimo.

Bella clung to his arm and watched Buddy closely as she introduced him to her husband.

193

"This is my daughter, LuAnn," Anderson said with the sweep of an arm. "She is a confirmed animal lover and circus enthusiast. She insisted on joining us."

"And this," Buddy said, turning to his side, "Is Max Barnes, our head elephant trainer."

After Max and Anderson had shaken hands, Buddy continued, "I understand you're interested in some horses."

"Mules are what I'm really after," he said. "The horses are for my wife."

Buddy stepped discreetly aside and turned to Max, hoping he would take charge in Smokey's absence and escort them to see Amos and his horses. He was shocked when Max said, "I'm afraid we can't sell you any horses."

Charles Anderson looked sharply at Bella, who was raising her eyebrows at Buddy, who could only shrug his shoulders in his own surprise.

"But Max," Buddy began.

Max held up his hands in apology and faced Charles Anderson, "We just found out we are under receivership. An attorney is going to oversee an auction of our assets next week, and the horses will be part of the sale."

He went on to explain about the murders, being stranded in Atlanta, and the already tight margins they operated on.

Anderson looked around and took it all in then asked, "What about the mules? I understand you have some mules."

Max looked at Buddy, who said, "The mules are not ours. I have a friend who runs a struggling freight business. I've been trying to persuade her to sell her mules."

"Her?" Anderson questioned.

"She inherited the business from her father."

"Are they good animals?"

"She has two pairs," Buddy said. "I've driven one pair and can vouch for them. But she'll need some persuasion to part with them."

"There are mules in South Georgia," Anderson said firmly. "I won't be taken advantage of."

"It's not about the money," Buddy said. "They're like family to her. The persuasion will be some assurance of a good home."

"We treat our animals well," Anderson said. He glanced at Bella and LuAnn and continued, "Some might say too well."

"Can we see the rest of the circus?" LuAnn asked. Buddy had to avert his eyes from her to keep from staring. He had a habit of comparing women he met to Gabrielle Saint-Simon, but this woman —except for the blue eyes—was a younger version of Gabrielle in her khaki slacks and riding boots.

"Of course," Max said. "Let's start with the elephants."

"I'd like to see the horses," said Bella. She turned to Buddy and asked, "Can you show me?"

Buddy kept his hands clasped behind his back as he and Bella walked to the horse tent.

"I'm sorry to hear of the trouble with the circus," she said. "What will you do?"

"I'm not sure. We've only just heard the news. If the elephants are picked up by another show, I might be able to go with them. If not, I'll see if I can find work with another circus. Or I might just stay here."

"Why don't you come with us to South Georgia? Charles is looking for someone to drive his hunting wagon."

Buddy laughed, but when he glanced at her he saw she wasn't kidding.

"When are you moving down there?" he asked.

"The day after tomorrow."

"What," Buddy stopped walking. "How can you move that quickly?"

"This has been in the works for months. We'll spend the winters down there and come back here for the summer. LuAnn will keep the house here."

"What about the boy—Thomas?"

"Thomas does his own thing. He gets an allowance, but he and his father don't see eye to eye on certain things."

"What kind of things?" Buddy pushed the issue.

"That's a family matter," she said tartly.

"Would it have anything to do with his Klan activities?"

She stopped and faced him. "What do you know of that?"

He told her.

"God." She started walking again. "Charles is not like that. If he was, I wouldn't have married him. He can be ruthless when it comes to business—that's how he got so rich—but he won't stand for the way some of his friends treat the Negroes."

"What if I told him the mules are owned by a Negro woman who owns a livery stable over on Howell and Edgewood?"

"It wouldn't make a bit of difference."

He stopped walking again and asked, "Were you serious about me coming to South Georgia?"

"Yes," she said.

Buddy's loyalties were confused, and he ran through the possibilities in his mind. He had risked his life to protect the elephant from harm and leaving Tembo felt like breaking a promise. But nobody was threatening the elephant. He was just facing new ownership under Max's hand. Besides, Buddy really had no say in the matter.

On the other hand, it might be nice to be back on the seat of a wagon, and the mules reminded him of the horses he was forced to leave in France. He was no stranger to upheaval in his life. It might be nice to make a move on his own terms for a change—running toward something instead of running away.

26

SATURDAY, NOVEMBER 7, 1936

BUDDY WAS SICK of johnny cakes and oatmeal for breakfast, but complaining wasn't going to get him any sausage or eggs. So, he and Max ate in silence. In fact, the entire mess tent was like a scene from a funeral. Instead of the clanking of utensils and the excited chatter in anticipation of a Saturday matinee, people just mumbled and grumbled. They had been in Atlanta for a little over a week, and they faced the end of the road, here. There would be no Saturday matinee. So, perhaps it *was* a funeral.

Buddy was so engrossed in the pile of crumbs on his empty plate, that he didn't know he had company until the man sat down next to him with a cup of coffee.

"Mind if I join you boys?" said Detective Stockton. He wore a tan trench coat and a matching fedora, both of which he kept on.

"I'd offer you some breakfast," said Max, "But we've barely enough to feed ourselves."

"That's alright," Stockton said sipping his coffee. "I've eaten."

"I still don't know where he is," Buddy said without looking up.

"We've found another body," Stockton said without ceremony.

"Jesus," Buddy said. "What next?"

"Well," said Stockton. "Here's what's next." He paused until both men were looking at him. "We're pretty sure it's Jackson Walters, the man you call Smokey. He's been murdered."

Max and Buddy exchanged a look of shocked surprise and Max said, "What do you mean 'pretty sure'? You know what he looks like."

"I'm sure, but I can't make the formal identification. We need a family member."

"He doesn't have any family," Max said. "At least none that we know of."

"Then we'll need two or three reliable friends or acquaintances. We could use one of you two but not both. We need to be sure you're not suspects or in collusion."

"Suspects?" Buddy questioned.

Stockton removed his hat and sat it on the table. He rubbed his thinning hair and took a sip of coffee as he weighed his words. "You're suspects until you provide an alibi."

"What about Thornell Dixon?" Buddy asked. "Is he off the hook?"

"I'm not so sure." When neither of his companions spoke, he continued. "I'm not a big fan of pinning the murder of every white woman on a Negro man. White guys kill people too. But, it is at least plausible that this Dixon fellow killed the girl in the trolley barn. It's less plausible that he's been doing it all over town for months or even years."

"Why would a Negro man who presumably wants to rape white women kill a middle-aged circus manager?" Max asked.

"Why, indeed?" said Stockton.

"So, Thornell must be in the clear," said Buddy.

"Not to some people."

"Why not?" asked Buddy. "Can't you just tell them?"

Stockton looked around the mess tent, leaned onto the table, and lowered his voice. When they leaned in and nodded, he continued. "Smokey wasn't strangled like the girls, he was stabbed. So, you'd think there is no connection to the previous murders. But the curious thing is that his body was found inside the back door to the trolley barn in the same location as the body of Sally Bingham. That can't be a coincidence."

Buddy and Max also leaned back and looked at each other as they processed this information.

Stockton took a small notebook and pencil out of his coat pocket and laid the notebook on the table. "What can you tell me about his movements?"

"Not much," said Max. "His wagon is over by clown alley, so we don't know the details, but we're told he was gone yesterday morning. Apparently, he cleared out overnight. Left the circus broke, and all of us unpaid."

"What do you know about the guy that was always with him? Do you think there was anything," he paused, "Um, between them?"

Buddy and Max exchanged a look.

"Who knows," Buddy said. "Wayne Kasinski was his name. Kaz joined us when we got to Atlanta. Said he was an old friend of Smokey's."

"What was he like?"

"Nice guy," said Buddy.

"Maybe too nice," Max added.

"What does that mean?" asked the detective.

"I don't know," Max said. "Just a little too quick with a compliment. A little too eager to avoid conflict."

Stockton wrote all this down, closed his notebook, and stood. He took a final sip of his coffee and donned his hat. "Don't discuss this with anyone," he said. "Can one of you show me to his wagon?"

"Maybe Benny can help you identify the body," Buddy said to Max.

"I'm not letting that son of a bitch help me with anything," Max replied.

Buddy watched the two men walk away and turned things over in his mind. Smokey and Kaz disappear together, and Smokey turns up dead. The implication seemed obvious. Either Kaz killed Smokey or Kaz was dead, too. But why wouldn't their bodies be found together? And if Kaz killed Smokey, why did he kill him at the trolley barn? Maybe Kaz killed Sally Bingham, and Smokey found out. That would mean Thornell was in the clear. But the Klan faction of the police department wouldn't like that outcome. What a mess.

Buddy got up and piled their plates and cups for the kitchen crew. He wanted to tell Naomi the news.

***

"She's not here," Elton Glover said. "She's at her barn."

"I thought Jolly was bringing her here for safe keeping," Buddy said.

"She's safe," Glover said. "Jolly and a couple of the boys went with her. Come on in and have a seat."

Glover rose and went to a side table. He poured himself a cup of coffee and raised an empty cup in Buddy's direction. Buddy nodded and he poured another. They were at the oval table in the library where they met the first time Buddy was at the Lodge.

"I came to give her some good news," Buddy said. "It looks like her cousin, Thornell, might be in the clear." He went on to tell Glover about the news from Detective Stockton.

"Well," Glover said as he looked over Buddy's shoulder and processed this information. "He might be in the clear legally, but that won't satisfy the Klan. That group is like a dog with a bone. They won't turn loose of their man without a fight. Thornell might need to go away for a while—maybe for good."

The two men sat in silence for a while and sipped their coffee. Buddy told Glover about the troubles at the circus—the receivership, the pending auction, and the lack of food for people and animals.

When Jolly stuck his head into the room, Glover stood and said, "What are you doing here? Where is Naomi?"

"She sent us away, Boss. Said she had to run some errands and didn't want us hovering around watching her work."

Buddy and Glover jumped up and ran to the car. Glover was at the wheel, but he had to drive slowly to avoid the attention of the two police patrol cars and six beat cops they passed. The six-block trip seemed an eternity and Buddy's heart stopped when he saw Thomas' car and a patrol car parked outside the barn.

Buddy placed his left hand toward Glover and said, "Pull over. Let's wait here for a minute."

The police officer leaning on his patrol car stood up as Thomas Anderson and Sergeant Rocker emerged from the barn. They were empty-handed. They engaged in animated conversation before getting in their cars. The policemen sped off, but Thomas Anderson made a U-turn and headed back toward Glover's car. Buddy and Glover ducked down as he passed.

As they pulled forward to check Naomi's barn, Glover said, "Sergeant Rocker is pretty well known in this neighborhood, but who is the other man?"

"He's the man who was holding Naomi. It was his house Jolly took me to." Buddy glanced at Glover. The man's countenance darkened, and Buddy sensed a hardness he had not seen before.

They looked around the barn, but Naomi was not there.

"You want a ride somewhere?" Glover asked.

"No," Buddy said. "I think I'll stay here and clean the place up a bit."

Glover paused at the door of the barn. He turned back to Buddy and asked, "Are you and Miss Webster…?"

Buddy leaned on his pitchfork and chuckled. "No. When we first met, I had intentions. I like to think she did too. But somewhere along the way, we shifted into something like brother and sister."

Glover looked at Buddy for a long moment. Buddy expected him to turn and leave, but the man walked back inside and sat down on a hay bale. He stroked one of the dogs and said, "After I met you at the Lodge and realized who you were, I began to remember some of our time in France. I had blocked most of it out. Bad memories. But that white sergeant who showed up at our unit made an impression on me and my men. You saved Dixon's life when he was shot. It didn't seem to matter that he was colored. Now, here you are all these years later taking care of his sister. The only white face in the crowd, just like in France."

Buddy was uncomfortable being the center of attention and didn't know what to say. He walked over to an empty stall and began to pick through the straw.

Glover stood and walked back to the door. "How about bringing her back to the Lodge when she gets back. I'll be there the rest of the day."

After Glover left, Buddy cleaned one stall and put down fresh hay. The rest of the barn had already been done. He filled the dogs' water bowl and while they lapped noisily, he placed a small scoop of food in each of their bowls.

A chill wind blew through the open barn, so he retreated into the feed room and closed the door. He sat down in one of the chairs, put his feet up on an overturned bucket, and pulled his hat over his eyes. It wasn't long before his breathing became regular, and his hands relaxed on his chest. He was sound asleep when raised voices woke him. It took him a moment to recall where he was and another moment for him to jerk upright fully awake at what he was hearing.

The raised voices belonged to Naomi and Wayne Kasinski.

***

"Stop fighting!" Kasinski shouted.

"Why are you doing this?" Naomi sounded frightened. "I don't even know you."

Buddy slipped out of his chair. He crept to the door and listened.

"I've seen you around the circus with that elephant man," Kasinski said. "I've had my eye on you for days."

Buddy heard a loud smack.

"Help!" she shouted.

The dogs began to bark as Buddy reached for his absent pistol then grabbed the rifle that hung above his head. He opened the door and worked the bolt on the rifle. The loud click caught Kasinski's attention, and he dropped his raised fist.

Naomi was tied to a post in the center of the room. Her blouse had been ripped open, exposing her breasts. Blood dripped from her nose and the side of her face was beginning to redden from where Kasinski had just smacked her. The dogs barked furiously in the stall behind him.

"Untie her, you son of a bitch."

Kasinski just sneered.

Buddy reached back and released the dogs. Kasinski used that moment to lunge toward Naomi, but the dogs were too quick for him. With primal, deep-throated growls, they raced toward the man in a blur. Buddy was shocked at how these mild-mannered, tail-wagging barn dogs had turned into raging beasts. They jumped on the man, bringing him to the ground.

Buddy moved quickly to untie Naomi.

She pulled her blouse closed and sagged into him, as she composed herself.

She walked over the screaming man and shouted to the dogs, "Inola. Yona." She grabbed each by the collar, and gave Kasinski a kick before she pulled them off.

"Better lock them up and go call the police," Buddy said.

She took the dogs to the stall and closed the door on them. They barked in protest as she walked back to Buddy and placed her hand on the gun. "You go call the police," she said.

He looked at the man on the ground. He was bleeding and whimpering. Buddy handed Naomi the gun and walked back to the feed room. But as he picked up the phone, he heard the distinct click of Naomi pulling the trigger on an empty chamber.

***

Detective Stockton was first to arrive, probably because that's who Buddy had called. But he was soon joined by an army of uniformed officers along with an ambulance crew. Buddy insisted they look at

Naomi, but Kasinski was bleeding, and she just appeared to be bruised and upset from her ordeal.

Buddy took her to the feed room, sat across the table from her, and held both of her hands. She was shaking and refused to look at him. Detective Stockton joined them and took their statements. The three of them watched through the door as Kasinski was carted out on a stretcher.

Sergeant. Rocker appeared at the door and said, "Looks like I missed all the fun." He turned to Naomi and continued, "We still need to have a word with your cousin."

"That won't be necessary, sergeant," said Stockton. "Our killer is in that ambulance out there."

"That may be," said Rocker, "But her cousin is a fugitive, and I mean to have him back in custody."

Stockton opened his mouth to set the sergeant straight, but he had already turned to walk out.

"Son of a bitch," Stockton muttered as he, too, walked out.

"How are you feeling?" Buddy asked.

"My head hurts, but otherwise, I guess I'm okay." Her hand shook as she clutched at her blouse and continued. "Can you help me get these animals fed? It'll be dark soon, and I need to go home and take a long, hot bath."

"I'll bring the mules in," he said.

He put on his coat, grabbed a bucket, and dipped it in the bin of molasses and oats.

As he walked out, she pushed up from the table and said, "Don't give 'em too much of that."

"I won't. This is just to get them to come to me."

Buddy climbed the ladder to the loft, threw down three bales of hay, and divided one bale between the two mule stalls. He left the rest for Naomi and her horses. When he walked through the stall and out to the mule pasture, the sun was setting over the bell towers of Ebenezer Baptist Church a few blocks to the west.

He sat the bucket down and paused to settle his thoughts. Mike and Ike came trotting over to see if he had a treat for them. He shoved his hands in his pockets and leaned against the doorframe. Thelma and Bunch were not so easily led. They would wander over in their own time. Mike stuck his nose in the feed bucket.

"Hey," Buddy said with gentle shove. "Get out of there."

Ike rested his chin on Buddy's shoulder.

"Looks like you've made some friends," Naomi said from the fence of the adjacent corral.

Buddy scratched Ike behind his ears. The big mule stepped on the edge of his boot causing Buddy to wince and pull away. He picked up the bucket at his feet and gave it a shake. The mules heard the grain swish against the metal pail and jumped to attention. They ran to their separate stalls and waited for Buddy to deposit a few cups of the delicious mixture into their concrete troughs. He touched each of them before he walked to the hallway and latched their stalls.

When he returned the bucket to the feed room, Naomi was at the table with her coat on and ready to lock up for the night. She stood as he entered but bent forward, placed both hands on the table, and began to weep quietly.

Buddy hesitated, unsure of what to do.

Finally, she straightened up and said, "Thank you. For," she paused, "everything."

"I'm just glad I was here."

She thought for a moment and said, "Why were you here?"

"Glover and I came over here looking for you. I was going to tell you that it was Kasinski who killed those women. Thornell is in the clear—legally, at least."

"Why was Elton Glover here?" she asked.

"Good question," Buddy smiled. "I think he's sweet on you."

She looked at the door and smiled at the thought. But her smile faded as she clutched at her coat and tears came back to her eyes. "Will you walk me home?" she whispered.

***

After he said goodbye to Naomi and walked back to the circus grounds, the events of the day faded as he remembered he had five hungry elephants.

"Any idea where we're going to get hay after we run out tomorrow?" Buddy asked Max when he returned.

Max poked at the campfire with a long stick as Buddy and Amos looked on. "No," he said, "But I'll bet your friend Bella Anderson could come up with some hay if she was asked real nice." He looked at Buddy with a smile then resumed poking the fire and continued. "We can cut down a tree for the elephants if we have to. I'm more worried about food for us."

"I passed a cleared lot on my way back over here," Buddy said. "Looked like they are getting ready to build a house and cut down a bunch of trees."

"Well, let's go," Max said as he abruptly stood. "We can use the leaves to make our hay go further."

"It's 7:30 on a Saturday night," said Amos. "People will think we're up to no good."

"Everyone's up to no good if they're out on a Saturday night," Max said with a laugh.

Amos stood and said, "I'll get the machete. Come on Buddy. The walk'll do you good."

An hour later, they were hauling the last of the branches to the brush pile behind the tent and rekindling the fire that had gone out. The evening air wrapped the three men in its embrace as they leaned in, waiting for the flickering fire to roar back to life.

Amos said, "That young Anderson lady, LuAnn, was in love with those horses, especially Diablo. Maybe she'll buy them at the auction."

"LuAnn seemed like the smartest one of that bunch," said Max. When Buddy and Amos looked up sharply, he continued. "I know. You wouldn't expect someone that young and that good-looking to be smart, too. She wanted to meet every single act. She talked to Benny and the clowns, watched the Renoirs practice on the tightrope, and let Tembo get snot all over her clothes. She was especially taken with Alice and Tony Morgan and their horses."

"She reminds me of my Aunt Mae," Amos said.

Buddy glared at Amos

"Who's that?" asked Max.

Amos glanced briefly at Buddy and said, "She's part of the Driesbach Family Equestrian Act—my family. It's a bareback act my grandfather and his brother brought over from Switzerland way before I was born. Their wives and all their children are in it, but Aunt Mae was the star of the show." He didn't mention that Mae was Buddy's ex-wife, and he didn't need to explain what an equestrian act was to Max and Buddy.

"They've been the feature in the center ring of every show they've been with. She rides standing on the shoulders of other riders, rides on two horses with one foot on each horse, and even somersaults from one horse to another. But it was her looks that captivated audiences, her dark hair and blue eyes—like LuAnn Anderson. You don't see that very often."

27

THE LIGHT RUMBLE of one of the elephants woke Buddy. As he tried to orient himself and remember where he was, the other animals joined in. It sounded like a combined chorus of well-tuned motor cars. They were agitated, but not unduly alarmed, so he remained inside his bedroll. The gloom inside the big tent made the time of day difficult to judge, but he suspected it was later than he usually woke.

As the fog in his mind cleared, he recalled the sudden, late-season thunderstorm that prompted Max to get the elephants inside and out of the elements. The unused big top was the logical space to stake the animals with Max and Buddy in their bedrolls to keep them company.

Buddy's stomach grumbled, and he wondered if there would be any food for breakfast. He also wondered how long he could hold out in his cocoon before he had to empty his bladder.

"It's dark in here," a woman's voice said from somewhere inside the tent.

"Let's wait over there," another woman said. It was Bella Anderson. The other woman must be LuAnn.

The elephants sensed the presence of strangers, and their rumbles grew louder.

"Oh my God. It's the elephants."

"I thought they might be in here," said Bella.

"I'm going to pet one."

"No!" said Bella. "They might not like strangers."

Buddy lay still and listened as the two women stepped farther into the tent, and the wooden bleachers creaked as they sat down.

208

"What do you suppose daddy's going to do?"

"Hard to say," Bella replied. "Depends on what the lawyers tell him."

Tembo trumpeted for his morning feed, and LuAnn screamed. Buddy sprang from his bedroll, unable to contain himself any longer, and they screamed again.

"I'll be right back," he said as he rushed past Max pushing a wheelbarrow of hay into the tent.

When Buddy returned from the latrine, the elephants had been fed, and Max and the ladies were gone. He found them sipping coffee in the cook tent.

"Looks like we may have some good news about the horses," Max told Buddy, as he sat down at the table.

"Charles went to see his attorney when we left here yesterday," Bella said. "He thinks there is probably a way around this receivership. He went back to the attorney's office this morning."

"On Sunday?" Max interrupted.

"Daddy can be very persistent when it comes to business," LuAnn added.

"He'll meet us here when he's done," said Bella.

Do you suppose I could have another look around your circus?" asked Luann.

"It looks like we could get another rain shower," said Max. "The place is already muddy mess."

"I don't mind," she said. "I dressed for it." She stood and spread her arms, showing her long leather coat and her hair pushed up under a broadbrimmed safari hat. She lifted a leg to show her well-worn riding boots.

Max looked at Bella then at Buddy, neither of whom moved, so he stood. "What would you like to see?"

"Everything," LuAnn said as they walked away.

Buddy and Bella sat in awkward silence. Buddy pushed his porridge around in his bowl and sipped his coffee.

Finally, they spoke at the same time.

"Look, I…" he said.

"We should…" she also began.

They laughed.

"Go ahead," she said.

"I'm interested in what you said the other day—about me driving your husband's wagon."

"But what about the circus," she asked, "the elephants?"

"I'm not really an elephant man," Buddy replied. "I'm actually better with horses and mules. Besides," he continued after a pause, "I'm tired of being on the road. I need to settle down. Put down some roots. It doesn't look like this circus has much of a future. There's no telling where I'll end up or if the people who take the elephants will need me.

Buddy looked at her. She smiled and said, "Charles is as excited as a child on Christmas morning about this move. He was talking from the moment he got off the train about the beauty of the property, about the hunting dogs he had purchased, and about his need for some mules and a wagon driver. I suppose that last bit was still in my mind when we talked before." She paused and sipped her coffee. "After we left, I told him about the Negro woman and the mules at her livery stable on Howell and Edgewood. He was most interested in that."

"We should go find Max and LuAnn," Buddy said.

She stood and said, "Let's go see the horses first."

A gust of wind blew the tent flaps as the rain outside began to pound the roof of the mess tent. They paused and looked at each other. As they tried to decide whether to continue, Max and LuAnn burst into the tent, laughing and shaking the rainwater out of their hair. Their boots and pants were caked with mud and their coats were soaked. Neither seemed to mind.

Max helped LuAnn out of her coat, and the four of them moved to a spot near one of the large iron stoves that heated the space. They looked so comfortable together that Buddy shared a look with Bella. She could only shrug her shoulders.

As they chose a table, Max said, "I'll go see if we have anything ready for lunch."

But before he could move, Charles Anderson strode into the tent and shook the rain from his umbrella.

***

"I put in an offer," Charles said after they were seated, each with a cup of coffee.

They looked at him in puzzlement until LuAnn asked hopefully, "For the horses?"

He produced a cigar and lit it with a flourish. "For the *circus*."

Mouths dropped open and silence ensued.

"The circus?" repeated LuAnn.

"Yes, for Christ's sake. The circus—all of it, not just the horses."

He took a sip of his coffee and spit it on the ground. "Good God! This is awful." He gazed around the tent and watched as people walked in for lunch. He then motioned to his driver, who stood by the door.

"Sam," he said, handing him a five-dollar bill. "Remember that diner we stopped at yesterday down on Edgewood? Run over there and get us some coffee and a box of their biscuits. And Sam," he continued as the man walked away, "Get something for yourself."

Sam tipped his cap and left.

"I had Sal track down the owners of this place and call them," Charles said to Bella.

"Sal Eversole," Bella explained to Buddy and Max, "is Charles' attorney."

"It seems the old lady who owns it—a Mrs. Santorini—died last week," Charles continued. "Her children want nothing to do with it and they were happy to sell. That's why none of the bills were being paid."

Charles got up and began to pace, becoming more animated as he talked. "Sal is still negotiating the price, but this is an impressive operation. We've got the big top, this mess tent, the menagerie tent, and the sideshow. We've got smaller tents for horses, dressing rooms, the blacksmith, and the repair shop—just to name a few. We'll need to get rid of some of the wagons, like the cook wagons, and replace them with trucks and motor cars. We'll keep the band wagon, the calliope, and the animal cages."

"What about the people?" asked Max.

"We should be able to keep most everybody," Charles replied. "Except Benny the clown and some of the roustabouts. They're the ones who filed the lawsuit for back wages. Them and someone named Stanley Warner. He's also a party to the lawsuit."

"Never heard of him," said Max.

"He's your Advance Agent," said Charles. "The guy who goes from town to town putting out playbills and posters."

"What do you know about running a circus?" LuAnn asked her father as she blew on her coffee.

"Not a damn thing," Charles replied.

"Then how are you going to run it?"

"I'm not," he replied. "You are."

All eyes turned to LuAnn, who could only stare at her father in astonishment.

"I don't know anything about running a circus, either!" she sputtered.

"Then you'll have to find someone who does," Charles replied.

"How am I going to do that?"

"You might want to start by looking around this table."

All eyes turned to Max.

He put his hands up and said, "Whoa. Wait a minute. I…"

Charles cut him off. "While you were showing LuAnn around the other day, I had a look around on my own. The equipment is a bit run down but that can all be replaced. The animals and the people, on the other hand, aren't so easily replaced. That's where I was pleasantly surprised. I believe this circus has potential."

"But…" Max began.

"But nothing. Everyone I talked to out here said the same thing. They want a new manager, but not that clown. They want Max Winston." Charles paused and looked around the table. "We'll run this like one of my businesses. I'm the owner—rather, I should say Bella and I. LuAnn is the managing director. Max here will be the operations director. You two," he addressed Max and LuAnn, "just need to figure out who does what to keep this place running. Like you." He turned to Buddy. "What was your name?"

"Buddy Griffith."

"And what do you do around here?"

"I'm an elephant man. I assist Max with the elephants."

"Well," said Charles, "Max won't have time to manage the elephants anymore, so you'll need to step up."

"But I've only worked with elephants for a few months," Buddy sputtered. "It took Max years to get where he is."

"Max will still be here. He'll just be busy doing other things." Charles settled back as though the matter had been settled. "Find someone else to be your assistant."

Sam returned with a paper sack of biscuits and a pot of coffee and placed them on the table. Charles got up and served everybody like the host he now was.

Buddy could sense Max's unease and wondered how Charles Anderson was going to convince this reserved, private man to accept so public a job.

"I don't know about this," LuAnn said.

"Look," her father said in exasperation, "You've been working for that accounting firm for three years. It's time you stepped out on your own. Bella and I are going to be in South Georgia for the winter. You'll be here in Atlanta taking care of our property. Running the circus will be like managing the house and grounds—money in and money out. Put your accounting experience to use, lean on Max if you think he's being too free with our money, and help him figure out how to make enough money to keep us afloat. This'll never be a moneymaking proposition for us, but I don't want it to be a money pit either. It's my gift to you to do with as you please."

LuAnn got up, walked around the table, and hugged her father around his back. He patted her hand and buttered a biscuit. Everyone was smiling except Max and Buddy, who just looked at each other.

***

"Max," Buddy said. "There's something I need to talk to you about."

The Andersons had just left, and Max was still in shock. But, as Max and Buddy were about to sit, the dinner bell rang.

"Let's go see what's for lunch first," Max said.

"I'm surprised they have anything left to serve," said Buddy as he pushed himself up from the table.

As they grabbed their trays and jostled for a place in line, they heard the first man in line say, "What! Not this shit again."

Buddy and Max exchanged a look.

"This is what the new manager has to look forward to," Buddy said with a wry smile.

Max did not appear to be amused. They moved up in line and received their porridge and johnny cakes. They walked back to their table in silence. Buddy glanced at the door to the tent and noticed the rain had stopped, and the sun had come out. His spirits lifted slightly.

His spirits lifted even more when he noticed Naomi standing in the doorway peering into the tent.

"What are you doing here?" he asked, as he approached her.

"Nice to see you, too."

"I just meant I thought you'd be, uh, resting."

"I brought you something," she said. She stepped aside and cast an arm back to her heavy wagon pulled by Mike and Ike. It was piled high with hay and bags of animal feed.

Buddy looked at her in surprise, waiting for an explanation.

"Two women stopped by the barn early this morning," she began. "Said they knew you, and wanted to buy some feed for the animals at the circus."

"But what about your animals?"

"Believe me," she laughed. "With what they paid for this," she looked back at the wagon, "I can buy more."

"What's this all about, then?" Max said as he joined them outside the tent.

Buddy explained and said, "Looks like LuAnn Anderson was taking care of you before she knew it was her job."

Before Max could reply, a caravan of cars trundled up Highland Avenue and stopped in front of the tent.

"After they explained about your need for animal food," Naomi said with a nod toward the street. "I got to thinking. What about the people?"

Thelma Dixon and Mrs. King emerged from the lead car and picked their way through the mud as the folks from Ebenezer Baptist Church began unloading platters, pots, and covered dishes from their cars.

"I hope it's alright if we have our Sunday lunch over here," said Thelma. She peered into the tent and said, "I suppose this is where we'll serve."

Buddy and Max went with Naomi to unload the animal feed for elephants, work horses, and equestrians. By the time they returned to the mess tent, it was bustling with activity. The church ladies had pulled some tables off to the side and piled them with food—platters of ham and fried chicken, pots of mashed potatoes and green beans, a steaming pile of fresh bread and glass urns of an amber liquid Buddy knew would be their sweet tea.

The circus kitchen crew mingled with the church people and carried plates, utensils, and cups to the line that had formed at the head of the tables. Buddy and Max were soon seated near one of the stoves with their plates piled high.

"Ach!" Max said after his first sip of tea. "What is this?"

"It's iced tea." Buddy laughed. "They call it sweet tea."

"It must have a pound of sugar in it."

Buddy was tucked into his fried chicken and didn't respond. Amos joined them and the three men ate in silence.

Buddy looked around the tent as he ate. The people who were serving the food looked to be as happy as the people who were being fed. There was laughter and conversation across the serving table between people who were strangers to each other.

Naomi joined them at the table and Buddy asked her, "Aren't you going to eat?"

"I'll eat later," she said. "This food is for y'all."

"We sure do thank you," Max said.

"What will you do after this?" she asked. "We won't be able to feed you Tomorrow."

"Tomorrow, we'll be just fine," said Max. "Tomorrow we'll be under new ownership."

"What!" exclaimed Amos. "Since when?"

"Since this morning," Max replied. "LuAnn Anderson's father bought the circus for her."

Buddy leaned toward Naomi and said, "One of the ladies who bought the hay from you."

"How did they know about my stable?"

"I may have mentioned something to the other woman, LuAnn's stepmother, Arabella."

"They were also very interested in my mules," Naomi said.

"About that," Buddy said. He looked to see if Max was listening, but his attention had turned to the door of the tent. Elton Glover and Reverend King had arrived.

***

"I wondered where you got off to," Glover said from the edge of the elephant area.

Buddy stabbed his pitchfork into the ground and gave Tembo a pat before he joined Glover.

"I had to get out of there and feed the animals before I ate myself sick," Buddy said. "What can I do for you?"

"Mind if I sit?" Glover asked.

Buddy pointed to a chair next to the fire he built to ward off the afternoon chill. He shoved what was left of his lunch into a nearby garbage can and sat down, too.

Glover lit a cigar, offered his light to Buddy's cigarette, and said, "I just wanted to thank you for what you did for Naomi yesterday."

Buddy blew out his smoke. "Word gets around fast."

"She came to see me. You must have told her I was helping you look for her." Glover paused. "I'm thinking about calling on her."

"She's used to being on her own," Buddy said. "She told me she doesn't want some man telling her how to run her business. That probably extends to the rest of her life, too."

"I get that," Glover said. He stood and moved closer to the fire. "But she's not safe here—not on her own."

Buddy watched Max and LuAnn Anderson talking in the distance ankle-deep in mud. They kept glancing toward him and the elephants, probably discussing his future. He felt like walking over and telling them he had other ideas about his future.

"Why are you telling me all this, anyway?" Buddy said to Glover's back.

"She trusts you. She'll probably ask for your advice."

"And why would I advise her to hitch up with you."

"I can protect her."

"From what?" Buddy asked.

"From the likes of that rich son-if-a-bitch who kidnapped her."

"Bullshit," Buddy scoffed. "What can you do about him?"

"I've already taken care of him," Glover said. "He won't be bothering Naomi Webster or anyone else ever again."

Buddy was stunned. His concern for Naomi shifted from jealousy to her safety from the very man who sought to protect her. Buddy thought about asking what *taken care of* meant, but something in Glovers demeaner told him not to.

Glover returned to his seat. "You're not the only one with secrets. I'm part of a larger organization that seeks to protect Negro businesses and the people who run them."

"Like a protection racket?"

"No," Glover said. "Not a protection racket. We're not a bunch of gangsters running numbers and moonshine. We're just taking care of what's ours."

When Buddy didn't reply, Glover continued.

"Thirty years ago, a white mob tore through our neighborhoods not far from here assaulting hundreds of Negroes. They burned our businesses, pulled us off streetcars, and beat up men and women alike. My father drove me through the ruins and made me promise not to forget what I'd seen. I was fourteen years old. We got organized after that and formed the National Association for the Advancement of Colored People, but not much changed."

"What about the war?" Buddy asked. "You were an officer. That must have counted for something."

Glover laughed, "Oh yes, the war. During the war, when some of us joined the military service and went off to fight for our country, white people passed local laws that required all Negroes to work outside of their own households, so we could continue to serve them. And when those of us who did fight for our country came home, we were put right back in our place, getting lynched if we stepped out of line." He stood up and began to pace. "Now, we have Roosevelt's New Deal with jobs for all. Except we are still kept in our place with discriminatory practices and the occasional lynching—as you've seen."

A profound feeling of sadness crept over Buddy. He recalled a conversation with Herman on the grounds of a base hospital outside Paris. Dixon had enlisted to fight in France for freedom, so he might have democracy at home. A month later, he was dead, and nothing ever changed at home.

"I appreciate you telling me all this," Buddy said, finally. "But I've known Naomi for less than a week and won't presume to advise her on how to live her life." He looked at Glover and continued, "She deserves a good man to share her life with. Maybe you're it. But you'll have to trust her judgement on that."

***

A brisk wind had swept in a blast of cool air from the north. The late afternoon sun felt good on his face as Buddy walked to Naomi's stable. She had informed him that the two women who bought the hay also made an appointment to return at four o'clock with Mr. Anderson to look at the mules. Naomi hadn't yet decided if she wanted to part with them, but the ladies had been insistent. Since they were kindly purchasing hay for the animals at the circus, she didn't want to be rude to them.

Buddy had not been able to tell Max or Naomi of his plans to leave the circus. He would tell Naomi if she decided to sell her mules to the Andersons. It might help her decide to sell if she knew they would be in good hands. He would inform Max this evening.

As he turned South off Auburn Avenue onto Howell Street, he was surprised to see the Andersons standing outside the stable talking to Naomi. Charles and Bella Anderson were early, and Buddy should not have been surprised to see Elton Glover standing next to Naomi. As Buddy approached, they shook hands all around.

They all moved inside, and the dogs scampered around the people's feet looking for attention.

"So," said Charles ignoring the dogs and looking around the barn, "Where are those mules I've been hearing about?"

"Thornell," Naomi called out.

Thornell appeared from inside one of the stalls and stepped into the hallway. Buddy couldn't help but look over his shoulder. He was alarmed to see Thornell out in the open.

"You want to bring Mike and Ike out?" she said.

Thornell slipped back into the stall and brought out the reddish-brown mules one by one, clipping them to a post by their halters with short lead-ropes.

Charles walked over to them and rubbed their foreheads. He passed his hand along their backs, looked into their eyes, and checked their teeth. Charles was a good-sized man, but next to those enormous mules he looked small.

"What are their names?" he asked Thornell.

"This one's Mike," Thornell said, grabbing his halter. "That one's Ike."

Charles looked at them closely and asked, "How do you tell them apart? They look identical."

"Ike has a white spot on his right flank." Thornell pointed it out. "After you get used to them, you'll see Ike is a little lighter in color all over."

Charles looked over the two mules closely then turned to Naomi. "I understand you have two pairs."

"The females aren't for sale," she said.

He stared at her for a moment. He was, Buddy suspected, accustomed to getting his way.

"I need two pairs," he declared. "I may want to run two wagons, or I may need to alternate pairs if we're hunting a lot."

"I'm sorry," she said. "I can't part with the females. And, as for these," she continued, "I'd like to know more about how they will be used."

Charles walked back over to one of the mules and said over his shoulder, "They will pull my hunting wagon down in Quitman, Georgia. When we're not hunting, they'll live in a five-acre pasture with the horses."

"Who will care for them? Do you have a driver?"

"My man Sam will be coming down to help me find someone," he said.

Buddy exchanged a look with Bella. This was his moment but, before he could speak, Naomi said, "How about taking Thornell?"

All eyes turned to the man standing between the mules. Thornell appeared to be as surprised as Buddy was.

"I don't know," Charles said. "I was hoping to find someone from the area—someone who knows the property."

"Thornell needs to get out of Atlanta," Naomi said.

"Why?" Charles asked. "Is he in some kind of trouble?"

Thornell looked at Naomi, but she appeared unsure of how much to say. Perhaps she was still shaken from yesterday's encounter with Kasinski. Everyone was looking expectantly at her, so Buddy spoke up.

"The Klan is after him. He was accused of a crime, but the police have arrested someone else." Buddy glanced around the room. He knew that Charles Anderson's son was no longer a threat, but Sergeant Rocker and his buddies were, so he continued. "Everyone knows how the Klan operates. They'll not let him off that easily."

It was one of those moments that defined Buddy Griffith's life. Like when he ran away from home to play baseball, when he joined the army, and when he signed up with the circus. But this was not a moment to run away. When Charles Anderson purchased the Circus and suggested Buddy manage the elephants, his fate was sealed. Tembo and the other elephants needed him. For once in his life, he needed to stay put.

Charles and Bella turned to take another look at Thornell, but Thornell was now looking at Buddy. Buddy knew he was in trouble for mentioning the Klan, and Thornell's involvement, so he decided to go all-in.

"What if she throws in the other pair of mules?"

Charles raised his eyebrows in surprise and looked quickly at Naomi who glared at Buddy.

Charles walked over to Thornell and asked, "What do you think about all this?"

Thornell looked at the floor. He then looked at Buddy and Naomi before addressing Charles.

"A fresh start might be nice, especially if I get to stay with the mules. The fact is, I've worked in this stable since I was old enough to push a wheelbarrow. This," he said looking around the inside of the barn, "is all I know. Hell, this is where I slept until I had to hide from the Klan."

"Well?" Charles was looking at Naomi.

Naomi stared at Thornell for a long moment, apparently turning things over in her mind. Finally, she gave an almost imperceptible nod.

After everyone filed out of the barn, and Naomi sent Thornell back to Cabbagetown, she and Buddy retired to the feed room. They had both just made difficult decisions, so he sat quietly until she asked, "Did you know the gun was unloaded yesterday?"

"What?"

"You left me guarding that filthy man with an unloaded gun," she said with a touch of anger. "Did you know it?"

"I never checked," Buddy replied.

"What would you have done," she continued accusingly, "if the dogs hadn't intervened?"

"I would have pulled the trigger on an empty chamber," he paused and looked at her, "Same as you."

"Except it wouldn't have been the same as me," she said without meeting his eye. "He was down—defenseless—when I pulled the trigger. I guess I should thank you. I was almost a murderer."

"It's a terrible thing to pull the trigger and end somebody's life," Buddy said quietly.

"He would have deserved it," she said. When Buddy didn't reply she looked closely at him and asked, "Have you ever killed anybody?"

Buddy stiffened, then relaxed. He hadn't thought about the end of the war in years—at least not consciously. But those final days in France had stirred the black dog that stalked him and the nightmares that haunted him. Perhaps it was time to share his experience with someone.

28

IN THE WEEKS that followed Herman Dixon's death, Buddy thought a lot about Doctor LeFleur's *chien noir*. Herman had been so full of hope with so much to look forward to while Buddy was cast adrift in a sea of loneliness.

He had become close with a lonely French woman and was convinced Gabrielle had felt the same. But any thoughts of remaining in France evaporated when General Armstrong began to pull her away. He wasn't sure which was worse, feeling rejected or feeling stupid. Either way, he was sad and thankful for his horses and the comfort they provided.

When the Armistice finally came, Major Miller's mood began to shift, as well. By Christmas, he was almost pleasant as the stream of sick and injured men eased, and the unit settled into an easy routine of cleaning the barn and disposing of unwanted equipment, anticipating the journey back across the ocean.

Buddy, too, was looking forward to getting away from France and the unpleasant memories it held. But some things he would soon discover, you can't run away from.

"Morning, Sergeant."

Buddy quickly leaned his pitchfork against the wall and saluted Major Miller. "Morning, sir."

"Lieutenant Williams said you wanted to see me."

"Yes sir," Buddy said. "I didn't expect you to come out here. I would have gone to you."

Buddy followed as the major turned and walked out to courtyard away from horses and the flies. He sat on a stone bench and lit a cigarette.

"So," he said. "What's on your mind.?"

"Sir," Buddy began. "Now that the war is over, what's going to happen to these horses?"

The major puffed his cigarette and blew smoke toward the ground. "They'll be staying here," he said without looking up.

Buddy gasped.

Eventually, the major glanced at Buddy and continued with distaste in his voice, "I've been ordered to *dispose* of them."

"But sir," Buddy replied, "I was hoping I could buy them when we got home—Raven and Queenie. I'd like to go into business with them."

"Sorry Sergeant."

"But…"

"Look," the major cut him off, "I don't like this any better than you do. But those are the orders."

Buddy's heart was racing as he fought back tears. "When?"

"We ship out next week. The horses will help us load our equipment at Montparnasse train station where we're leaving from. Then, we'll deliver them to the stockyards that are being set up at the East train station about six kilometers up Sebastopol Boulevard."

"What will happen to them?" Buddy asked.

Major Miller didn't answer right away, then said softly, "The healthy ones will be auctioned off to French farmers. Others will need to be put down." The Major stood and stepped on his cigarette. "I'll have someone pick up the horses from Montparnasse when were done loading."

"No," Buddy said a little more forcefully than he meant to. The major turned and Buddy continued, "Sorry, sir. But I'd like to handle that myself. I owe it to them."

The major hesitated and looked at Buddy for a moment. Buddy knew the major was overwhelmed with logistical decisions and hoped he would let Buddy have his way. Finally, Major Miller nodded and walked away.

***

Buddy leaned against the door of the damaged barn and gazed up at the night sky. The crescent moon was framed by a million stars, and the landscape was hauntingly silent. He took a drag on his cigarette and watched the smoke dissipate in the frigid air. Since the hostilities ended nearly two months ago, he had been busy planning what to do with his horses.

"I'm not sure why he cared for you so much," he said with a glance back over his shoulder. "But he sure did. Maybe you reminded him of home—of happy times. God knows we could all use a little of that."

He took a final drag, flicked his cigarette into the darkness, and turned back into the stillness and warmth of the barn.

"I suppose that's why he named you after his Aunt Thelma." Buddy walked up to the mule and placed his forehead on hers. He hugged her huge head, and she did not push him away as she usually did.

As soon as they finished loading the train at Montparnasse train station, he saddled up Queenie, placed a lead-rope on Raven, and left with Hound following them. He headed up Sebastopol Boulevard toward the stockyards, as ordered. But as soon as he was out of sight, he turned west. He stopped by Dixon's old Unit at the 92nd Infantry and convinced the corporal in the stable that he was there to pick up a big, blonde mule named Thelma. He left the 92nd heading south. He had passed this old farm hundreds of times as he moved around the areas south and west of Paris. It was home to one of the barns he and Gabrielle had raided for hay over a year ago and a place he thought might provide some refuge.

The army was on the move eastward toward the coast. In fact, he needed to be back to Montparnasse at 0600 to join his unit. They were bound for Saint Nazaire to board a troop transport ship for New York. His first thoughts was to take his animals west and to disappear into the French countryside. But that wasn't a plan. It was a hopeless dream.

"Gabrielle will sure be surprised when she comes out to her barn this morning and finds you girls there," he said. He looked at the horses standing quietly in the dancing light of the small fire he had lit in an old oil drum. They appeared to be asleep on their feet.

"I asked her," he continued, "But she said she couldn't take you because she can't afford to feed you. I suspect her new boyfriend might be pulling the strings. But she loves animals. Well, the horses, at least. I'm not sure what she'll make of you, Thelma. And as for you, Hound. You just need to keep your head down and try to be a good barn dog."

The bolt action of a German Mauser rifle was unmistakable, even for someone who had never been in combat. That sound coupled with Hound's low, throaty growl raised the hair on Buddy's neck. Someone stood at the door of the barn just outside of the light of the fire. As the man moved slowly into the light, Hound started barking. Buddy stood up and raised his hands as he felt the weight of the pistol in his coat pocket.

"Do you speak English?" Buddy asked.

The dog lunged at the man but stopped when the man stepped forward and shouted, "*Bleib*!"

The guttural command and the tattered gray-green field jacket marked the man as a German—probably a deserter. He was young and appeared to be frightened but moved with the caution of a veteran. He kept the gun trained on Buddy as he moved around the barn. Buddy could see the wheels turning in the man's mind as he looked at the horses, saw the saddle on the rack outside the stall, and thought for a moment.

The man motioned with the rifle toward the saddle, then toward Queenie, while he looked Buddy in the eye. "Saddle up this horse for me," he implied.

Shit, Buddy thought. *There's no way he's taking my horse.* Buddy shook his head no and pointed toward the mule. He wouldn't mind sacrificing the mule for this man. In a way, he felt sorry for him. He wondered how he had survived these past few months since the war ended. How had nobody discovered him?

The man shifted the rifle slightly and pulled the trigger. As the bullet whizzed past Buddy's head, the man worked the bolt on the rifle and the dog charged at him. The man aimed his next shot at the dog's head, but Buddy had pulled his pistol from his coat and fired first. The bullet hit the man in the stomach, and he crumpled forward onto the ground with the dog standing over him.

Buddy pulled the rifle from the man's hands and threw it into an empty stall. He turned the man over. Without the rifle in his hands, he looked different. He was little more than a boy. He appeared frightened and in pain.

Buddy instinctively glanced at the door. The gunshots might bring the Military Police patrolling the nearby roads. He needed to get going.

***

The rocking of the train car lulled Buddy into a trance that should have put him to sleep. He was exhausted after his all-night vigil, and he had not had breakfast, so sleep should have come easily. He had made the Unit's 0600 train departure for the coast without arousing any apparent suspicion from Major Miller.

The train buzzed with conversation; everyone was elated to be going home. But Buddy's relief at having survived the war was laced with profound sadness.

"You don't look too happy to be going home."

Buddy yawned and turned to the man next to him. "Just tired I guess."

227

"That was a hell of an end for our unit, wasn't it? I mean, coming over here with all those horses, and then killing them instead of bringing them home?"

"I couldn't do it," Buddy replied.

"What do you mean?"

It must have been the exhaustion that loosened Buddy's tongue. He told his seatmate how he had successfully slipped in the backdoor of Gabrielle's barn in the pre-dawn darkness and placed the horses and the mule in their stalls with feed and water. How he had tied the dog to a post and left the way he had come. He also told the man that he was certain that Gabrielle would not be able to turn out Queenie and Raven. Thelma he wasn't so sure about, but if Gabrielle didn't keep her, she would likely find a home for her.

"Shit!" exclaimed the man. He then lowered his voice and looked around. "You could be in some serious trouble for disobeying orders."

Buddy looked out the window and said, "You going to report me?"

The man thought for a moment, then said, "Hell no. I just wish I could have done that for my boys."

Buddy watched the French countryside slide by. He didn't care what happened to him at this point.

He didn't tell the man about the German soldier. Didn't tell him that as the man lay bleeding to death, he asked Buddy not to leave him. How he used sign language pointing to Buddy's pistol and to his own head. How he convinced Buddy to do for him what Buddy could not do to his horses.

Buddy hoped to be left with the lasting image of Queenie, Raven, and Dixon's mule Thelma living happily ever after in the barn of a fourteenth-century castle. But he was left with the German boy's pleading eyes, the sound of a gunshot that would close those eyes forever, and the haunting dreams of all the animals he could not save.

29

"WHAT DO YOU suppose happened to your animals after the war?" Naomi asked.

"I wish I knew," Buddy replied. He glanced absently from his seat at the table out the feed room door. "The barn where I left them was like something out of a fairy tale, and Gabrielle was a good-hearted woman, so I like to think they lived happily ever after."

"What is it that haunts you most about the war?"

"I don't know. If I did, maybe I wouldn't be so messed up. I was never very stable to begin with. Hell, I snuck away from a good home to play baseball. Turned my back on those who loved me." He paused, "I think it was your brother's death that began to unravel me. I'd seen plenty of death, but when his spirit left his body that day, I felt a profound sense of loneliness. Then I faced the potential loss of my animals, followed by that German boy." He lit a cigarette and blew smoke at the ceiling. "I do sometimes wonder about that kid," Buddy said. "If it wasn't for me, he might've gone home to a girlfriend in some German village. He would have grandchildren, by now."

"You did what you had to do," Naomi said. She reached across the table and covered his hands with hers. "It was war. He was going to kill you."

"I hadn't thought about that boy for a long time." Buddy said wistfully as he pulled his hands away and stood to leave. "These last few days helped me realize a few things."

She just looked at him.

"The circus is where I belong. It's time I stuck with something and quit running away."

"What about your family?" she asked. "Why don't you go home to see them? Do they even know you're alive?"

"You're probably right, but the longer I stay away, the harder it is to go back. I should have gone home after the war, but when I began to push the past out of my mind, I pushed all of it out. It's just a habit, now." He paused again and changed the subject. "Now that you've sold your mules and taken care of your cousin, what will you do?"

"I don't know," she looked around the room. "Stay here, I guess."

"Maybe you should come with us tomorrow."

She studied her hands as if examining their slight tremor. Then she rose and joined him as they walked out into the barn.

"Come to the church dinner tonight," she said. "I can't process all that's just happened, so I want to talk to Aunt Thelma and Reverend King before I decide anything about my future."

***

As he walked back to the circus, he was awash in memories long suppressed. He forgot the detail of the warning shot that the German soldier had aimed at him, then the boy's being ready to pull the trigger on the dog. There was a moment when Buddy feared for the dog's life. That was why he had shot the boy. But as the memories swirled and faded, he was left with sadness and what might have been.

"You look like you just buried your best friend," Max said when Buddy returned.

"I feel like I did," Buddy said. "Are we packing up to leave?"

"Packing up," said Max, putting down his wheelbarrow of tent stakes and mopping his forehead, "with nowhere to go. We didn't show up for our date in Columbus this weekend and word got out that we were broke. When LuAnn and I called Birmingham this afternoon to see if they'd still have us, they weren't so sure. She's going to have her old man call someone he knows down there in the morning to vouch for us."

"So why are we packing if we've nowhere to go?"

"Gotta get out of the grounds here. It seems we've overstayed our welcome."

Buddy looked around at the activity. Most of the canvas was on the ground and being rolled up. The ramps and crossover plates were on the train cars, ready to roll the wagons onboard. And people were scurrying everywhere.

For days, Buddy had been thinking he'd left all of this behind. He was looking forward to sitting on Charles Anderson's hunting wagon in the South Georgia woods staring at Mike and Ike's muscular behinds. But being a muleskinner wasn't in the cards for him. He was bound to the circus and would continue to be an elephant man. He walked over to Tembo and leaned into his forehead. For the first time in his life, he wasn't running away. He was staying put.

"What about the animals?" Buddy asked Max.

"We won't load them until we know where we're going," said Max as he picked up the wheelbarrow. "How about helping me take down these tents?"

"Are we taking everything down?"

"Everything but the cook tent," Max said as he looked out over the grounds. "We'll all sleep in there tonight then stow it in the morning. For now, I need you to pack the harnesses, head dresses, and show costumes while I tend to the rest of this mess. By the way..." Max put down the wheelbarrow again. "...was there something you wanted to talk to me about?"

"No, not anymore."

Buddy had been through countless takedowns over the past dozen years, but this one was different. Takedowns were normally run with military precision after the eight o'clock, Saturday evening show ended, and the last person left the grounds. This one was different. It was less military and more Keystone Cops. Wagons were parked all over the grounds as people ran back and forth. Tents lay flat on the ground like deflated balloons with no people tending to them. Max waded into the fray wielding his bullhook like a club.

"Is it always like this?" Detective Stockton appeared at Buddy's side.

"God no," Buddy laughed. "What brings you out here?"

"Uniforms told me you were packing up," he said. "Can't say I'm sorry to see you go."

"Can't say I'm sorry to be leaving."

"What'll become of that Negro man you rescued?"

Buddy glanced at the detective, unsure of how much to say. "He's leaving town."

"That's good. Word around the station is that they're not done with him."

"What are you going to do about Sergeant Rocker and his buddies?"

"Not much I can do about them," Stockton replied. "But I am planning to arrest his accomplice—Thomas Anderson."

Good luck with that, Buddy thought. "His family's lawyers will have him out of there in no time."

Buddy looked across the field toward LuAnn Anderson, who was talking to Max and continued. "How's Kasinski?"

"He'll live."

"What'll happen to him?"

Stockton lit a cigarette. "He's not talking but we've got enough evidence to pin the Trolly Barn murder on him. And we've got him for the assault on Miss. Webster. There'll probably be more. He might talk when he realizes he's facing the electric chair."

"What about the body in the fire?" Buddy asked.

"That one we'll probably never know, unless he confesses to that, too."

Buddy watched LuAnn and Max finish their conversation. She made her way toward him.

"I'll be on my way, then," Stockton said. They shook hands and Buddy watched him walk away with a mixture of admiration and pity.

"Is that a policeman?" LuAnn asked as she approached and watched Stockton return to his car.

Buddy chuckled. "Yes."

LuAnn looked over the circus grounds and said, "I've just told Max you'll be leaving in the morning for winter quarters in Bradenton, Florida."

"Bradenton," Buddy said. "Why Bradenton?"

"It was Max's idea. He knows someone who has a farm down there. He says plenty of circus people winter in the area, so it'll be a good place to recruit new acts. He also said you can make a couple of stops on your way down there to make us a little money," she said. She walked away and said over her shoulder, "I'll see you in the morning."

***

The clattering of silverware and the scraping of empty plates told Buddy what he already knew. He was too late for the church dinner. He was a little bit relieved. He had changed into a clean shirt and washed his face but would still smell of elephants to anyone who came near. As he entered the Fellowship Hall this time, his arrival rated no more than a glance. He looked around the room and saw some familiar faces, but not Naomi.

He trudged back outside where the air was crisp as darkness began to settle over the community. A police car lurked in the shadows down the block. He lit a cigarette and was trying to decide where to go when Reverend King came around the corner from the direction of his home clutching some papers. He pulled up short when he saw Buddy.

"What are you doing out here?" he asked.

"Naomi asked me to stop by."

233

"Well, you'd better come in then," King said. "She wasn't here tonight. I was a little concerned after what happened to her yesterday."

But before they could move, a car glided to a stop at the curb. Elton Glover emerged from the passenger seat, and he opened the back door for Naomi. A look passed between them before Glover nodded a hello to Buddy and Reverend King.

As King led the three of them into the church and down the steps to the basement, he explained that he had gone home to fetch some flyers for tomorrow morning's voter registration meeting.

Buddy hoped Naomi invited him here to tell him she was joining the circus. Now, he wondered if Elton Glover had other ideas. King dropped off the flyers in the meeting room and ushered them into his office.

"Did you two vote last Tuesday?" King asked Naomi and Glover as they all found their seats.

When they didn't reply, he let out an exasperated sigh. "Those folks in the other room are trying to get our people to register to vote. It's the only way we'll ever get anything to change around here." They sat in uncomfortable silence for a moment before he continued. "So, why are we here?"

Buddy wasn't sure how to answer that. Sitting in a preacher's office was the last thing he expected, and he was so uncomfortable with the situation that he had to stand. "Look," he said. "I invited Naomi to come away with us when we leave town tomorrow. I thought it might do her good to get away from things here. I never expected to be in here talking about it with you two."

A knock at the door interrupted them.

"Reverend," a young woman at the door said. "I'm sorry to disturb you, but we have a question about the flyers you gave us."

After King left the room, Naomi said, "I'm sorry, Buddy. But I'm going to be staying here in Atlanta."

"With him?" Buddy nodded at Glover.

"That's none of your business," Glover said hotly.

"He's not the only reason."

"Did he tell you what he does for a living?" Buddy glanced at Glover.

"He's a banker," she said with a touch of hostility.

Buddy was going to tell her the rest of the story, but Reverend King reentered the room. He must have sensed that something transpired because he let silence settle over them.

Buddy sat back down and addressed Reverend King. "I want to thank you for welcoming me into your community."

King nodded a response and asked Naomi, "What have you decided?"

"I'm staying here."

"What about your business—your animals?" King asked.

"I'm selling most of the animals," she said. "Elton is going to help me buy a couple of trucks."

"What about you?" Reverend King asked Buddy. "What will you do?"

Before Buddy could answer, another knock came to the door.

"What now?" asked King.

"You'd better get out here," said the woman who interrupted them a few minutes before.

The urgency in her voice caused everyone to rise and troop out into the Fellowship Hall where Sergeant Rocker and one of his officers stood, with nightsticks in hand.

"What can I do for you, gentlemen?" asked Reverend King.

"We're looking for an escapee," Rocker replied. He looked at Naomi and continued, "and I think you know where he is."

Buddy saw Glover edge toward Naomi, pushing her gently behind him as his hand moved toward his pocket. At the same time, three of Glovers men appeared behind the policemen at the top of the stairs. They wore business suits and looked like they meant business.

Reverend King stepped in front of Glover and said, "You're welcome to look around, officers. You'll not find what you're looking for here."

King was firm and appeared unafraid. He was a solidly built man who could clearly hold his own in a fight, but Buddy couldn't imagine him taking a swing at anyone—even a man as deserving as Sergeant Rocker.

Rocker, on the other hand, was known for using his nightstick but, like most bullies, uncertainty flashed in his eyes when confronted with someone who would not back down. He stepped back, took a cursory look around, and turned to leave, but Glover's men had come down the stairs and stood between the policemen and the exit. Hands went to guns.

"This is God's house!" King thundered. "There'll be no violence here."

Buddy saw Glover nod at his men, and they stood aside. As Rocker went up the steps, the kitchen workers returned to their pots and pans, the voter registration volunteers went back to their flyers, and Reverend King led the way back to his office.

"Were those some of your *Masonic brothers*?" King asked Glover with a hint of irony when they were all seated.

"Something like that."

"Where were we?" King asked.

"I was just saying my goodbyes," Buddy replied from his place by the door. "I have some elephants to attend to."

Naomi stood and grabbed him in a fierce hug. Buddy was uncomfortable having Glover and Reverend King watching, and he was unsure of where to place his hands. So, he let them hang in the air behind her back.

Both men rose and King said, "You must be a good man, Muleskinner. The Good Book says that that good people care for their animals and have respect for God's creation. *A righteous man regardeth the life of his beast: but the tender mercies of the wicked are cruel* Proverbs 12:10."

Naomi continued the thought. "My daddy said there's something of the spirit of God in all of us because we are made in God's image," she hesitated, "but he liked to include animals in that, too."

"With all the meanness and misery in this world," Glover mumbled, "…especially *our* world, I'm not sure I agree with all this concern over animals."

Buddy turned to Reverend King and said, "When you met the mules in Naomi's barn last week you appeared to be moved by the experience."

Reverend King smiled and stared over their head for a moment.

"I grew up on a farm down in Stockbridge, about twenty miles south of here," he said quietly. "We had chickens, pigs, and an old mule that pulled my father's plow. In the winter, when Mrs. Low was teaching school, I had to take care of the animals before he would let me go to school. So, I woke up on those cold winter mornings when it was still dark outside and fed the animals, carried water, and brought in firewood. But I saved my favorite chore for last. I loved currying that mule. I don't think he had a name. The kids teased me when I got to school because I smelled like a mule. But I didn't care. I just felt safe and loved when I was with him—touching him. I don't have many happy memories of my childhood, but the smell of a mule surely is one of them." He paused and closed his eyes as if lost in prayer. "Isn't it odd how we can sometimes feel a greater closeness to these creatures than we can to our fellow human beings."

Buddy shook Reverend King's hand and moved toward the door, but was surprised when Glover rose, as well.

"I'd best be on my way, too," he said.

Buddy and Glover walked through the empty hall and up the stairs together. As they emerged into the night, Buddy was unsure how he felt about Glover. He had been jealous of Naomi's attraction to the man but seeing how protective Glover had been when faced with Rocker's threat, he knew this was where she belonged.

"You know," Glover said as he approached his waiting car. "All this talk of mules reminded me of something I hadn't thought about in years—something from the war." He leaned on his car and crossed his arms. "The morning we were supposed to ship out, one of our animals went missing. My men were pretty evasive. Said it must've been stolen by some French farmer. But we were in Paris. There were no farmers anywhere around. I let it go. It seemed like nothing at the time. One less thing to worry about. When Reverend King was talking about his mule, I remembered that mule in France had someone, too. Herman Dixon found that mule when he was out with you. So, now I wonder if you had anything to do with that mule disappearing. It probably would have been shot or turned into dog food if it hadn't disappeared."

A knowing look passed between them before Buddy stepped forward and shook Glover's hand.

"Take good care of her, major," he said before he turned and walked into the darkness.

30

THE ELEPHANTS WOULD be the last to load. They were chained up on a new picket line where Buddy could keep an eye on them while Max scurried around dealing with last minute issues.

Buddy sat on a roll of canvas with his collar turned up and his hat pulled low watching his frosty breath float in the humid, morning sunshine. Amos and two of his horses pulled wagons up the incline ramp to the last railroad car and across the plates that connected the run of a dozen flatcars. Buddy reflected on the events of the past week and the distant past he had been forced to confront. For the first time in recent memory, he was facing those memories clear-eyed, and neither drunk nor hungover.

"We're done," Amos said as he approached Buddy with his team. "Want to give me hand loading these guys?"

Buddy did not reply. He stood and helped unharness the horses. He took the lead rope of one of the Percherons and followed Amos up the side ramp into the stable car. The box car had been modified to contain the work horses in stalls much like a barn, with the animals kept in two-horse pairs. Buddy had seen similar set-ups in war-time army tents, cargo ship holds, and countless stables. A brief memory of Queenie and Raven flitted past him like a shadow as he leaned against the open door of the boxcar.

"You look like you're remembering an old girlfriend," Amos said as he closed the gate to the horse stall. When Buddy cocked his head in confusion, he continued. "You were smiling."

Buddy returned the smile. "Actually, it was a couple of old girlfriends." As they walked down the ramp he continued, "I'll go see if Max is ready to get those elephants loaded."

Buddy found Max and LuAnn standing at the head of the train. Buddy was surprised by the absence of a locomotive. He had expected they would be ready to go as soon as the elephants were loaded.

"Do you think you and Amos can handle loading the elephants?" Max asked as Buddy approached.

"I don't know," Buddy said. "Tembo's pretty wound up this morning. You know he doesn't like the train car."

"See what you can do to calm him down," Max said. "Our engineer was drunk when he showed up this morning. They're looking for a replacement." As Buddy turned to leave, Max said to his back, "Keep an eye on me. I'll let you know when the locomotive gets here."

Buddy walked back down the line to where Amos stood. He wasn't sure he was going to like this new arrangement. He would prefer to have Max drop what he was doing and take charge of the elephants. But that couldn't happen.

He thought about the first time he saw Naomi in her denim pants, cowboy boots, and red coat, and felt a profound sadness. He wished she was going with him. In her, he saw Gabrielle Saint-Simon and Arabella Anderson. He saw his friend Herman Dixon. All had touched his life, and all were no longer a part of it.

The sound of the locomotive chugging down the track was unmistakable. Buddy glanced that way and saw Max wave.

"Let's get these guys unchained," he said to Amos, "And bring 'em in line."

As the animals stood side by side, ready to walk up the ramp into their boxcar, the locomotive revved its engine and backed up to couple with the train. Buddy didn't know much about trains, but he recognized some familiar sounds, and he knew that the locomotive had been going too fast and had hit the cars too hard. The banging cascaded down the line of cars until it reached the elephant car, where the animals were preparing to load. The movement of the car nudged the loading ramp off of the boxcar, and it hit the railroad track with a thunderous clang. Tembo, who had been swaying and grumbling to begin with, broke out of line.

Amos jumped in front of the animal, but Tembo swatted the man with his trunk sending him flying. The elephant trotted away from the train trumpeting his displeasure. After a few steps, he stopped and wheeled around to face Buddy.

Buddy gave Amos a hand up. He appeared to be okay. Max came charging up followed by a half dozen roustabouts who set to work hoisting the massive elephant ramp back into place.

As he turned to face Tembo, Buddy heard Max behind him command the other elephants to "Come in line!"

Buddy took a step forward, but the elephant backed up and lowered his head. Work behind him stopped and a hush settled over the crew as Buddy and Tembo faced each other once again. Tembo's warning—a low rumble—reverberated like distant thunder.

"Whoa," Buddy crooned—his voice steady, his tone deep and smooth, hoping to calm both himself and the elephant. "Tembo, steady."

He stepped forward slowly but with confidence until he could lean-in and place his forehead on Tembo's. The elephant stood motionless as Buddy sensed his tension and the elephant's fear disappear.

Buddy backed up a step, wheeled around, and placed his bullhook behind the elephant's front leg.

"Move up," he said.

Author Notes

Although this story is entirely a product of my own imagination, the elephant interactions are drawn from my experience as a bullhook-carrying zookeeper in the 1970s. The Santorini Brothers Circus is fictional, but its parade route was one of several in use at the time. In October 1938, the Atlanta Constitution newspaper reported that the Rollins Brothers Circus had run its last parade because the roads had become too congested with automobile traffic.

The city of Atlanta is as authentic as I could make it. The Highland Avenue Circus Grounds once stood adjacent to the present-day Eastside Beltline near the Inman Park Village. The Bellwood Quarry and Stone Mountain have been converted into public parks, but their infamous histories (along with the history of the Ku Klux Klan) are well documented.

The Edgewood Avenue Trolly Barn is still standing, as is Fire Station Number 6 at the corner of Boulevard and Auburn Avenue. A stroll down Auburn Avenue toward downtown will take you past the Ebeneezer Baptist Church (1922) and the Prince Hall Masonic Lodge (construction began in 1937). A walk up Auburn Avenue in the other direction leads to a modest, two-story home at 501 Auburn Avenue, the birthplace of Martin Luther King, Jr. He would have been seven years old at the time of our story. His home is located about a mile from the old `circus grounds.

When I decided to include the King family in my narrative, I wanted to find a "hook", so I read Martin Luther King, Sr.'s autobiography, *Daddy King*. On page 30, I found what I was looking for. He and I share an affinity for mules. I drove a mule wagon for a quail hunting operation in South Georgia after I retired. Daddy King had fond boyhood memories of currying a mule before going to school on cold winter mornings. Martin Luther King, Jr. is one of my heroes. I hope he and his Daddy would be proud to be included in my story.

About the Author

J. D. (DOUG) PORTER developed his love of nature growing up in the piney woods and mangrove swamps of Florida's gulf coast. He nurtured that passion for over forty years as he managed parks, zoos, and museums, and studied wildlife in the Amazon rainforest, the Galapagos Islands, the African savanna, and the Arctic tundra. He is a zoologist and educator with a bachelor's degree in zoology and a master's in adult education. Doug combined his experience with animals and his love of historical fiction into his first novel, The Menagerie, A Zoo Story in 2012 and continued following one of his characters when he published The Dogcatcher and The Fox in 2020. The novels explore the history of the American zoo and the origins of America's animal welfare movement. When he retired at the end of 2015, he found himself driving a mule wagon for a South Georgia quail hunting operation—a job that allowed him plenty of time to pursue his interests as an author, newspaper columnist, and freelance writer who focuses on animals, nature, and the outdoors. Doug used his COVID isolation during the summer of 2020 to publish his memoir, Lessons from the Zoo: Ten Animals That Changed My Life. In 2024, he compiled his newspaper articles into his latest book, Roaming, Rambling, and Reminiscing: Musings from a South Georgia Mule Wagon. He now lives in Decatur, Georgia with his wife, Karen Liebert.

Follow the author at
www.jdporterbooks.com

www.historiumpress.com